Divisible by Six

By Andy Rane

http://samulraney.com

For all of my patient readers.

Chapter 1

"I said…hand me the goddamn crowbar! Jesus…maybe I *should* have put you out of my misery."

Rain poured off the man's newsboy cap, down the sleeves of his black leather jacket, and onto the car jack at his knees. The half of his face that still functioned properly was curled in anger at the diminutive, balding, bespectacled man at his side.

Dr. Fred Taylor rubbed his right ear. No sound penetrated it; only a reverberating high-pitched ring that he knew only he could hear. An exploratory finger came away with fresh blood. He sneered down at the man who knelt before him attempting to change the flat tire. What he really wanted to do with the crowbar was swiftly plant it in the back of the man's skull. But, he knew better. They both knew better. Instead, Taylor handed the tool to the man and stood by obediently, now straining to hear what the man was saying. He had actually welcomed the rain, hoping that it might wash some of his personal stench away. He hadn't bathed in at least three days and his own smell was beginning to offend him.

The man in black worked on the tire like he had worked in a NASCAR pit crew. Within minutes, he had finished and the spare tire was on. He handed the crowbar and jack back to Taylor and said something that Taylor once again didn't catch. Taylor placed the objects into the trunk then closed it. The man was on him in a flash.

"Why am I keeping you around? If you can't hear me…and follow basic fucking orders, why the hell do I have you around?" The man shouted into Taylor's face. Taylor turned his bad ear toward him.

"I don't know—," Taylor said.

"I really should have just left you in the Masterson boy's house. But, no…I had a little moment of weakness—"

"A first, I'm sure," Taylor muttered low enough that the man didn't hear, or didn't care.

"—and what has it gotten me? A bum ride, a knot on my head, and so far I haven't been able to do my goddamned job. And do you know what happens when I can't do my job? I get a little…bit…cranky," the man stood nose to forehead with the smaller Taylor. His crooked palsied face was made that much worse by the water covering it and the red glare from the tail lights. The rain ran down off the man's cap into Taylor's face.

"Are you done?" Taylor asked, tensing himself for the blow that he assumed would follow.

"Get in the goddamn car before I leave you here," the man said.

He turned and opened the trunk, heaving the flat tire into the back.

Taylor got into the car, happy to be out of the rain, but now miserable for the fact that he was absolutely soaked through. The man in black climbed in and pulled out his cell phone. He held down a single number and pressed the phone to

2

his ear. Taylor strained to listen with his good ear. The ringing still hadn't subsided from his right, but he could still hear a little with his left.

"It's me...no...no. Well, maybe if this wasn't such a clusterfuck, I would have finished it by now. I don't know. You tell me. Who's the old man? The one that's after the kids. What do you mean you don't know? Find out. I hate competition. Where are they headed? Ok," he said, and hung up the phone.

"So?" Taylor said.

"So what?" the man said.

"So, where are we going?" Taylor asked.

"C'mon, Doc. You know damn well where we are going," the man said.

"Then you can enlighten *me*—," Taylor flinched so violently that he pulled a muscle in his neck. Despite his lack of hearing, he had seen the barrel of the gun press against the back of the man's head and the ethereal voice resonate out of the rear seat. For a split second, the man in black looked surprised. Then he smiled his half-Cheshire cat grin.

"Dammit, Richy boy, you just never know when to back down. Do you?"

"Got nothing left now...thanks to you...so why back down?" Agent Richard Norris said.

The barrel of his snub-nose .38-caliber revolver was pressed firmly against the man's head, while in his other hand, he held a smaller caliber semi-automatic. Taylor craned his

3

neck slowly back. Not much bigger than Taylor, Norris had concealed himself on the floor of the back seat. It looked as if he had pulled an old blanket over himself until the time was right. Norris looked tired, but Taylor also thought he saw something else in the man. Something off color, sickly.

"C'mon, Rich. Just let me do my job and go home," the man said.

"Just do your job…right. Don't sit there and act like you're a fucking plumber," Norris said.

"I am a fucking plumber. Just another chump with a day job. If I don't do it, you know someone else will, Rich," the man said.

"Oh, I'm not going to prevent you from continuing. You're going to keep right on doing what you're doing…except you won't be killing anyone," Norris said.

"You have to sleep sometime, Rich."

"I stopped sleeping the day you killed Maggie," Norris said.

The man in black moved slowly and removed the sodden cap from his head. He placed it on the bench seat and ran a hand through his fading auburn hair. He looked back at Norris from the rear-view mirror.

"I didn't kill Maggie and you know it. She got in the way," he said.

"It was your bullet they pulled out of her," Norris said through gritted teeth.

"Bad luck. She could just as easily been killed by one of those DEA assholes," he said.

Taylor glanced back at Norris furtively.

"Oh, I'm sorry. We haven't been properly introduced? My name's Richard Norris, and you are?"

Taylor looked back at Norris.

"Fred...Fred Taylor," Taylor said.

"Oh, don't be so modest, Doc. Fred's a doctor, Rich. Maybe he could take a look at what's killing...err...what's ailing you," Dennis said.

"You son of a...," Norris blurted, but the rest was drowned out by the lung-wrenching barrage of coughs that followed.

Taylor turned and watched as Norris kept the gun pressed against the man's neck all the while trying to keep his eyes on him. He watched as the man in black stalked his prey in the rear-view, his eyes scanning, waiting for the right moment. When he did move, even Taylor didn't see it coming. In a flash, the man had grabbed Norris' arm and, for a split second, Taylor panicked as the gun barrel waved in his face. Then, Norris was reaching over and pulling the man into the back seat. They thrashed in unison once and it was suddenly over. Taylor shrank against the door and looked back at Norris who had produced a previously unseen blade and was pressing it against the man's neck.

"Give me one good reason why I shouldn't kill you," Norris sputtered, straining against the man and still apparently trying to hold back a cough. He was breathing heavily and there was a distinct rasp.

"Because this isn't the ending you want, Rich. Not like this," the man said.

"Fuck you," Norris spat.

"It's true…and you know it," he said, and Taylor was surprised to hear what appeared to be the slightest sense of resignation in his voice.

"You don't do things my way, I kill you. Got it?"

"Fine."

"Dr. Taylor, I'm not really sure where you fit in all this, but I'd appreciate your help at the moment. Please be a good fellow and remove the gun from his ankle holster. He won't be needing it," Norris said.

Taylor looked warily back. It was a bit of an odd sight. Norris had the man in a sort of half nelson and the blade had pierced his neck ever so slightly, letting out a trickle of blood that was about to reach the collar of his shirt. Norris' knuckles were white from the tension. The man in black looked back at Taylor with what could only be disgust.

"Left leg, if I'm not mistaken, Doctor," Norris said.

Taylor lifted the left pant leg, half expecting to receive a knee to the head or at least a shin perhaps. He slipped the gun out without so much as a flinch.

"Toss it in next to me, thanks. Any others?"

"Just his useless hand cannon that's full of blanks," the man said.

"Doctor, could you open up the glove compartment?"

Taylor turned and opened the glove compartment. It appeared to be relatively empty at first glance, the interior being completely black. An insurance card and registration were clearly there. Then, Taylor noticed that the cavity was much smaller than the compartment door suggested. He ran his hand along the top and his finger caught on a latch that blended in with the rest of the opening. He pulled on it and a small metal door opened. It was only two inches in height, but the false ceiling was packed with papers on one side and a small-caliber pistol on the other. Taylor pulled it out and held it up for Norris to see.

"Oops! How forgetful of me," the man said.

"Yeah…oops," Norris said.

8

Chapter 2

Senator George McCloud tried to push the small collar on his $700 winter coat closer to his neck, but it was to no avail. The primary concern of the designers had been form, not function. He'd once bragged that he could go out in a blizzard with nothing more than a scarf and a good pair of shoes as the rest of his body seemed to care little about the weather. Now, though he wasn't in the mindset to challenge his own boast, he was certainly having a strong desire for that scarf. It was with this thought in mind that the secret service agent nearest him interrupted.

"Sir, no offense, but are you sure this is where your meeting is planned?"

The agent, a young man named Tom, who had only just recently been assigned to him, looked as if he was ready for a half-dozen scarfs.

"I planned this meeting. He'll show. Punctuality isn't his thing, but he's never missed a meeting yet," the Senator said.

He looked up the street and back down. Though this area of the park was near playing fields, the recent snow and successive days of rain had made it a swamp. The days of freezing temperatures had then turned the mud to something just slightly softer than stone. They were the only two people within sight. That is, until he looked back to the south. The first words that popped into his mind were "bum" and "hobo." This was followed by "derelict" and "homeless," before finally settling on what he'd been trained by years of politicking to say.

"Transient," he said.

Tom followed the Senator's gaze and appeared to stand a little taller. The faint sound of a squeaky wheel on the shopping cart came into range. It had a rhythmic cadence to it—tic-tic-squee tic-tic-squee! They watched as he moved into and out of the cones of light cast down from the street lamps. The Senator noticed a distinct limp to the figure. Whether it was a man or woman was indistinguishable at less than ten meters. For a brief moment, the Senator envied him or her, for the apparent number of layers *it* had on was numerous and he doubted the person even felt a lick of wind but for the small patch of nose and forehead that was left exposed. Then it dawned on him.

"He's fucking brilliant," the Senator said.

"Sir?"

The walking coatrack moved steadily closer down the sidewalk toward the park bench on which the senator sat. Tom rocked on his toes, his instinct kicking in to the presence of another human being, despite his or her appearance. If it hadn't been a natural instinct, the agency had certainly done everything in its power to drill it into his essence. Now, as the tic-tic-squee pulled within 10 yards of their position, the agent began to move forward.

"Stand down, Tom, before you get yourself killed," the Senator said, dryly.

The agent ignored the Senator's statement and positioned himself at an equal distance between the only two people in a two-mile radius. The cart, which the Senator now realized was overflowing with every type of carpet and towel known to man came to a stop, but the man stepped around it and headed toward the Senator as if he'd been pushing nothing all along. The facial hair that almost blended in with the hat and scarf identified it as a man. Tom moved his feet into a defensive stance and the Senator repeated his order.

"Sir?"

The transient stopped and rocked on his feet.

"You waiting for something?" Tom said to the man.

"Just waitin' for you to be a good little dog and do as your master says," the man said, any hint of emotion hidden beneath layers of wool and hair.

"What?" Tom said, his hand moving toward his holster.

"Oh, now you shouldn't have done that," the man said.

He crossed the five steps between them before Tom's hand had even touched the handle of the gun. The man had him down and kissing pavement before the Senator could even utter Tom's name.

"Tom...stand down! God dammit!"

Tom continued to struggle, much to the glee of his attacker. The lump of clothes was nearly smothering Tom, but the man seemed as nimble as if he had on a tracksuit.

"Jesus...Christ...get off me!"

"You gonna play nice?"

11

"Get the fuck off me," Tom shouted.

"Senator, he don't wanna play nice," the man said.

"Jesus, Bruce. Just let him go," the Senator said.

Bruce stood up and proceeded to brush the filthy clothes off as if it were a fine tuxedo.

"I told you to stand down," the Senator said, almost apologetically.

"Asshole," Tom said, wiping the chafed mark on his cheek and spitting blood on the ground. He paused as he wiped his mouth and stared blankly at the Senator. "I meant him, not you, sir."

The Senator waved away the misdirected slight.

"You may be right, Tom, but you can't say I didn't warn you. Now, take a powder over by the cart while the grownups talk."

The agent moved away as the two older men watched. They could hear him muttering something under his breath.

"Don't make 'em like they used to, George," Bruce said. The wool scarf at his lips muffled the sound of his voice a bit. The rusty grey mustache fluttered as his lips moved.

"But they have to keep making them," the Senator replied.

"True…now what the hell are we doing here?"

"You know damn well what we're doing here."

"My man says there's others involved. People he doesn't know. And they've been getting in the way."

"What people? There aren't any other people," The Senator said.

12

"That's my question," Bruce said.

"This wasn't supposed to be so complicated," the Senator said, letting out a large frosty breath into the air.

"Then maybe we should have taken care of it when it was a simpler task," Bruce said.

"That wasn't my call," the Senator said.

"But you were there, and now you're the only one left," Bruce said.

The Senator broke out into a laugh.

"You think I'm doing this for me? Ha. I could give a rat's ass. If it had been up to me, I would have let them shout it from the rooftops. No…this isn't for me. It runs much deeper…higher too."

"How high?" Bruce said.

"I'm not even sure I know the answer to that…nor do I really want to know."

"Well, I've got my best man on it," Bruce said.

"He's been sloppy. If he's your best man, it's time to start recruiting again. It's getting into the news."

"That's your Dr. Taylor's fault," Bruce said.

"No…we intercepted all of his letters. But, one of the boys is wanted for questioning in a murder. If he was dead, we wouldn't be dealing with this."

"Who else could be after 'em? Who's fucking up what should have been a simple job?" Bruce asked.

"I…don't know," the Senator said.

"Don't know, or won't tell?"

"Don't fuck with me, Bruce. I didn't pay for an inquisition. Just get the job done."

Bruce stood up from the bench and turned to face the Senator.

"It's been a pleasure, George. I—"

The Senator looked up into the man's face. Bruce's eyes were wide and he lurched forward, coughing blood onto the Senator's face.

"What the fuck…Bruce?" the Senator could hardly react as the man fell into his arms, his eyes already rolling to the whites. He glanced over at Tom, only to find that the agent was lying prone in what could only be a pool of his own blood. He wasn't sure where it had come from, but the black sedan in the middle of the half-lit street sat motionless with a single tinted window rolled down. He saw the red fabric of a cuffed sleeve just before the muted flash of a muzzle cut into his last thoughts.

Chapter 3

James Masterson was up and moving toward the door well before he had time to understand what was happening. The sound of footsteps moving up the stairs of the room over the garage wasn't coming at a casual pace. There was motivation behind those steps. James dodged around the dinette that gracelessly adorned the center of the efficiency and reached out for the knob, only to discover that there was no lock. He stared at it in disbelief, just long enough to wonder who built an apartment with no locks. The door was thrust into him with force, throwing James back over one of the dinette chairs and onto the floor. The woman that stood in the doorway was a far cry from the woman he had met the night before.

They had spent less than twelve hours in the small Ohio apartment over the garage of Dr. Robert Paynter's former flame. She had been inviting, charming, and downright pleasant to the boys, all of which disturbed the hell out of James. James' brother, Doug Pederson, had protested James' guardedness the most.

"She's perfectly nice," Doug had said.

"She's too nice. There's something wrong. There's something she's hiding," James said.

"That's just how people in the Midwest are. Nice…for no reason," Doug said.

"That doesn't sell well in Jersey," James said.

"You're being paranoid," Paynter said

"Am I? Or is what happened between the two of you still festering?" James said.

"Water under the bridge," Paynter said.

"Yeah, she said that a lot tonight, didn't she," James said.

"You've been watching too many movies lately," Kevin said.

"Maybe it's the whole being shot at, accused of murder, chased, and having my girlfriend whisked away from an airfield in a fucking helicopter thing that has me a little more on edge than normal," James said.

"Keep your voice down," Paynter said.

"I don't trust her," James said.

"Ok, we get it. Can we go to bed now?" Doug said.

He settled down on the tired-looking mattress in the corner of the room and prodded it with his hands as if checking its stability. Apparently, it would do.

"Yes, but you're leaving early," James said.

"How early?" Doug asked.

"And why?" Kevin Powers, James' other brother, chimed in.

"Three AM. Because you've got a long way to go.

When Doug and Kevin left at three, James lifted his head just long enough to give them both a nod and wish them luck. For a moment, it had occurred to him that he and Paynter should leave as well. The moment passed as his head hit the pillow. Now, as he looked up into the double barrel of the

16

shotgun being aimed at him, he wished that sleep hadn't been so enticing.

Barbara Stewart stood over him in a state of barely contained madness. She was breathing heavily and her eyes grew wider with every breath. Her undone hair and tattered bathrobe that barely kept her modest simply added to the sense that Barbara had crossed over the edge. James looked into her eyes and back at the barrel that wavered before him.

"I'm getting real tired of this point of view," James said.

"Murderer," she spit through pursed lips.

Paynter ventured to stand, extending a hand toward her. She cocked the hammer of the gun; her eyes never leaving James as she spoke.

"Don't you dare. Don't you do it, you rotten son of a bitch. He's going to explain everything to me...and then…he can explain it to the police," she said.

"You didn't," James said.

Her momentary pause and the flicker of tension at the corner of her right eye was the only hope James had left. She either wasn't telling the truth, or she wasn't sure she had made the right decision. James was hoping for the former, though the potential that she had simply gone batshit crazy also crossed his mind.

"Turn on the TV," she said.

Paynter moved slowly over to the small tube TV that sat next to the bed. There was a loud electric crackle when he pushed the power button and a layer of dust seemed to rise up off its surface.

"The news," she said.

James thought Paynter clicked his way through the channels at a painfully slow pace. Then, he reached a news station. It read, in bold capped letters across the bottom of the screen, **U.S. SENATOR GEORGE McCLOUD GUNNED DOWN IN EARLY MORNING D.C. SHOOTING**. The video showed a blood covered park bench, a shopping cart full of towels, and playing fields in the background. Yellow tape cordoned off a major area and a detective was shown putting down markers in the street where they had apparently found bullet casings. Paynter shrugged, looked at James, then glanced at Barbara.

"Wait for it," she said.

It didn't take long. With a return to the studio, the woman newscaster's image shifted to the left and a picture of James materialized beside her.

"Oh, fuck me," James said.

"Turn up the volume," Barbara said.

Paynter obeyed and they listened, transfixed by the screen.

"Police and FBI operatives have been working closely with the Secret Service, as one of their own was also killed in the attack. Preliminary reports suggest this was a targeted assassination, though details are few. An anonymous source, however, suggests there may be a link between these killings and another that occurred in New Jersey three days ago. That murder has been directly linked to James Masterson, a 24-year-old New Jersey native with no previous record. Police have been unable to locate Masterson and are asking for the public's help in apprehending him. If you have information on his whereabouts, please call 9-1-1. He is considered armed and highly dangerous." The story moved on to a brief recent history of Senator McCloud and guest speakers were being introduced to discuss the possible motive of the killings."

"I am totally growing out my beard," James said absently.

He turned to Barbara meekly. The gun in her arms was looking heavy. The initial rush of adrenaline was fading.

"Explain," she said.

"How could that have been me? I was here!" James said.

"Maybe so, but what about the murder in New Jersey. Your neighbor. Why are you running? Why are you here? Did you murder that old man?"

"Do I look like a murderer?"

"Killers wear little-boy faces sometimes. You wouldn't be the first."

"I didn't murder Mr. Isaacson. He was a good friend and neighbor," James said.

"They said they were investigating the connection between that murder and one in Texas," Barbara said.

"Jesus, I've never even been to Texas. Listen, I know how this all must look, and I don't know how to convince you, but you need to believe me when I tell you it's not me. It's someone who kinda looks like me and sounds like me. And there's these people who are trying to frame me, but I wasn't anywhere near either of these crime scenes. I was in New Jersey when the Texas murder happened, near Pittsburgh when they killed Mr. Isaacson, and here in your house when they shot that Senator."

She lowered the barrel of the gun, which seemed to be as much a relief to her as it was to James.

"I'm sorry. This has affected a lot of people besides me and I really wish it hadn't," James said.

"I'm sorry too. You... you should have been up front about it all," she said and it was her turn to look meek.

"What did you tell them?" James asked.

"I told them there were some freeloaders in my garage," she said.

"You lied even after seeing that report?" James asked.

"I had a hard time believing Robert would bring someone like that into my home," she said.

"I appreciate that. Nevertheless, Dr. Paynter, we should pack our bags and start the car," James said.

"Don't. They'll be looking for that car. You've got about fifteen minutes. Nearest station is at least that far and they're not exactly quick around these parts. Take the truck out the side of the barn. The keys are in it and it's got a full tank of gas. Head out through the gate at the far end of the back fence. Stick to that trail. It's no four-lane highway, but it'll get you through the neighbors' farms and out of sight of any main road for a while. When it lets out, you hang a left and you stay straight for about a dozen miles to the interstate. Don't tell me where you're going. I'll tell them that, as far as I knew, you all left in the other car. Go on. You'd better go."

"For what it's worth, thank you. I hope I can make it up to you some day," James said.

"If they tell you to stop, you do it. Don't go dying for someone else's crimes," she said.

James nodded and dressed as quickly as he could. Paynter, who had slept in his clothes, moved gingerly in Barbara's direction. He stuck his hands in his pockets and glanced at the floor in a gesture that reminded James of being in high school.

"I trusted you," she said.

"I know," Paynter said.

"And you failed me… again," she said.

"I know," he said.

"You were dead to me two days ago. I shed those tears. I won't shed 'em again, Robert."

"I spent over twenty years hoping for another chance and… I failed when it finally came," he said.

She shook her head.

"You won't get another twenty," she said.

"When I come back, it'll be to stay," he said.

"If I'll have you," she said.

"Like you'll have a choice."

Chapter 4

It was after several attempts that Nicole realized blinking her eyes would not remedy her inability to see. This revelation came about the same moment she discovered that her hands and feet were bound together and a loose, but immovable gag had been tied to her mouth. Struggling against her bindings was useless. Instead, she focused on where she was and what she was doing. It came back slowly.

They had been at the hospital in Pennsylvania. She and Doug had found Dr. Paynter. But then she'd been caught by the creepy old guy in the red coat with the horrible breath. He'd pulled her hair so much she expected to find a bald spot. She'd been waved in front of James like a treat and the chase was on. That old man had been so strong! Then there was the airfield and a helicopter…and…and that was where things got fuzzy in Nicole's mind. They'd sedated her, she recognized that much. And now she was here, wherever that was.

She reached out with what few senses she had left. She could hear little, but when she shifted her weight, the scraping of the chair against the floor told her she was in a sparse room. There was little on the walls to reduce the echo of her heel tapping the floor. The floor was uneven and judging by the slightly cool temperature and musty smell that reached her nose, she wouldn't bet against being in a basement. An old basement. She shuddered, not from the cold, but from a sudden thought: bad things happened in old basements.

In a place that was dominated by only the white noise of silence, the sound of an opening door and footsteps somewhere above her head made Nicole flinch. There were several pairs of footsteps that moved across the floor in an inconsistent manner. Then, there was the sound of another door opening. This one was clearer. Footsteps were coming down stairs toward her. They were slow and deliberate. She couldn't help but hold her breath.

"Nicole?"

Tears filled her eyes at the sound of James' voice. She cried into the gag and shook with a mixture of fear and elation. She could feel his warmth as he approached, realizing for the first time just how cold she really was. He grasped her hands reassuringly before pulling the cloth from around her eyes. She breathed heavily through the gag, her tears blurring her vision. He smiled at her, working on the binding of her feet. He untied the gag around her mouth. She just wanted to hold him.

"Oh my god, James, how did you find me?"

"I have my ways," he said, working on the rope around her waist, but not looking at her.

"James, hold me...please...I...just hold me," she said.

He hesitated.

"Are they coming back? I can't believe you found me so quickly," she said.

He leaned in close to her in a half embrace. She pressed herself against him as best she could with her hands and midsection still restrained. He whispered in her ear.

"I would always come for you," he said.

She inhaled deeply of him and something clicked. His tone of voice, the ease with which he had entered the house, the hint of strange cologne, and the foreign scent that lay beneath it.

"Kiss me," she whispered.

Again, he hesitated, but she watched as he closed his eyes and moved in to kiss her. She quickly brought her feet up into his groin and placed the hardest part of her forehead into his nose; she couldn't be sure if the resounding crack that accompanied her action was her head or his. But, the result had been achieved. The man had fallen backward onto the ground, clutching his bleeding face.

"Get the fuck off me, asshole," she screamed, attempting to jump from her seat to continue the attack, this despite the stars that were now swirling in her vision.

She kicked out at him after failing to remove herself from the seat, the bond around her waist still very much secure.

"Fucking…asshole…who…the…hell…do you… think…you are?!" she said in rhythm with each kick.

"Enough!" came a commanding voice.

Two short men entered the room and quickly bound her back onto the chair. A redcoat lifted the not-James off the ground clutching his bleeding nose, fear spreading into his demeanor.

"She hit me!"

"Serves you right, you sick motherfucker!"

"It does serve him right, Nicole."

Nicole turned her head and stared at the man who addressed her. He moved down from the darkness of the steps toward her and into the glare of the single light bulb that hung above her. It was James again, only this time, he was older, the hint of grey beginning to touch the edges of his unruly hair. He showed the same cockeyed grin across his face that always won her over when she was pissed at James. And though she knew this wasn't him either, she felt her anger subside a little.

"Tell me, Nicole, what tipped you off? His looks? His clothes?"

"His stink. He smells like a French whorehouse."

There was a collective laugh from the men that was quickly silenced with a glance from this older not-James. He turned to assess his younger bleeding self and shook his head.

"All that training...and when it came time to perform, you failed," then turning to the two old men at Nicole's side, "You know what to do..."

"Sebastian, no! No, Sebastian! No! You can't do this! Sebastiaaaaan!" the young man screamed, garnering more from Sebastian's comments than Nicole could.

The young man was dragged out of the room and down the hall, his cries eventually dying out.

"Well, it seems you know my name now. Sebastian. Sebastian Walters."

"You're going to kill him," Nicole said.

"No, not at all. You wouldn't throw away something you've built just because it didn't work once. He needs discipline, that's all."

"I don't believe you," Nicole said

Sebastian stood closer to her and tapped a finger into her forehead as he spoke.

"Then you don't know me very well, sweetheart. But, don't worry... we'll become fast friends soon enough," he said.

Nicole lashed out at his hand with her teeth, making him flinch and giving him a momentary look of concern before he backed off. A wicked smile crept across his lips. He turned to the redcoat who smiled back at him.

"I like her. She's got spunk," he said.

"Who the hell do you think you are?" Nicole half-screamed at him.

"Haven't you guessed?"

"Another freak in the parade," Nicole said, resisting as best she could as the old men prepared to gag her once more. Sebastian crept closer and was mere inches from her face as they knotted the fabric tightly, making her eyes water.

"Not just another freak, sweetheart," he whispered. "You see, I'm the head freak. You could say...I'm James' father."

He smiled again and it was no longer any comfort to her. Then the hood was pulled back over her head and everything went dark once more.

Chapter 5

Doug leaned on his cane, staring up at the wall of snacks before him. His stomach told him to grab one of each. The five-dollar bill in his pocket, all that was left of the cash that was supposed to last him until Arizona, told him otherwise. Especially since they were only in Oklahoma.

The 24-hour box store at which they had stopped was nearly empty for that time of night. He'd left Kevin in the bathroom and, as he walked back, felt proud of the bounty that now lay in his basket. By his calculations, the three bags of chips and two candy bars would stretch all but two cents of his five dollars.

He pushed open the door and promptly dropped the basket at his feet. The red-jacketed old man was lifting Kevin off the ground by the collar of his shirt. The syringe in his hand was poised just inches from his neck.

Doug crossed the room with as much speed as his hip would allow, pinning the man's forearm, along with the syringe, against the wall. The man released Kevin's neck, eliciting a gasp and a colorful. With his free arm, the old man jabbed his elbow at Doug's head. Doug dodged just enough to avoid a blow to the eye, but held his ground, now shaking the hand that held the syringe. The old man lashed out with his elbow again but Doug was prepared. As Kevin slumped to the ground still gasping for breath, Doug grabbed the much smaller, though ridiculously strong man's arm. They were now in an intricate arm-over-arm struggle against the wall. The old man lashed out with his feet and caught Doug's bad leg hard enough for him to flinch. His hand that had pressed the unknown syringe against the wall released, but in such a violent fashion that it sent the syringe flying across the room. Kevin watched the weapon skitter across the room and land in the pile of potato chip bags and candy bars by the door.

"What, no Baby Ruth?" Kevin sputtered.

"Really?" Doug said through his clenched teeth.

Doug found himself pushed away from the wall now and facing an old man who was assuming some sort of attack stance. Kevin slunk away on the floor, a safe distance behind Doug.

"You may as well give up, dude. You'll never take us now," Doug said.

The old man's angry grimace slipped into a cruel smile.

"What makes you think I was here to take you?"

"You're..."

The man lashed out again at Doug's bad leg, clipping the thigh and forcing Doug to hunch over. The man swung with his left, which, though stunned, Doug reached up and easily deflected with a sturdy arm. The man was quick though and Doug knew that he would never be quick enough on his feet to connect at this range. He moved in closer, deflecting the frenzied blows the old man threw out. Doug sensed there was a weakening of his strength. He was starting to sweat and the rigor of his offense was lessening. He grabbed a soft right hook and held fast to the man's fist. Doug caught the man's glance over his shoulder.

"Kevin… the door," Doug said.

He could here Kevin move behind him to do so and watched as a rage crept back into the man's face.

"There's no lock!" Kevin shouted.

"Put something in front of it!"

"I've got some Funyons and a Snickers bar. Maybe they're allergic to peanuts," Kevin said.

With a cry, the old man leaped at Doug, but there was nothing left to his attack. Doug quickly reversed the blow and pulled the man into a half-nelson headlock. The two men struggled, the final bursts of adrenalin coursing through the old man's still powerful arms and legs, twisting Doug around and pressing him against the wall with his back.

"Little help here?" Doug grunted.

Kevin looked at him with some trepidation.

"I thought you had this," he said.

"Seriously? Can I get just a little help?"

"What do you want me to do?"

"Hit him, dammit!" Doug shouted.

He wiped his bloodied lip with his left hand and balled up his right, rearing back to strike the man in the face. That was when the old man raised his feet off the ground and struck out at Kevin, kicking him away and forcing Doug back into the hand dryer on the wall with an "Ooof!" It was enough of a jolt for Doug to release him. The man turned and cracked Doug across the head with a left. Doug caught the right in his hand with a solid "thwack!" much to the man's surprise. As Kevin lifted himself off the floor, he glanced down at the syringe the redcoat had dropped. He reached down to pick it up, just as Doug pushed the old man backward. The two fell down atop Kevin who cried out. There was a crack as the man's head caught the edge of sink at an odd angle.

"Jesus…Christ…get him off me," Kevin yelled.

"Gimme a minute…gimme a minute! I go down quick, but getting up is the hard part," Doug said, glancing around for his cane. He managed to use the edge of the sink to get himself back up.

"That's what he said," Kevin said, reaching out for Doug's extended hand.

"That son of a gun coulda killed us," Doug said, rubbing his hip.

"Son of a gun? Really? Your mom and dad aren't here now, it's ok to call him a son of a bitch. I won't tell," Kevin said.

Doug retrieved his cane from just beneath the bathroom stall where it had landed and sauntered back, leaning on it heavily. They looked down at the crumpled body of the man at their feet. His white pants were looking a bit dirty. His nicely pressed red sport coat was up around his shoulders and his untucked shirt exposed skin that nearly matched the white button-down he wore. The straw fedora was busted and a smudge of blood streaked the sink where he'd hit.

"Is he dead?" Kevin asked.

"I hope not," Doug said.

Kevin looked at him, shaking his head.

"The guy just tried to kill us!" Kevin said.

"Are you sure?" Doug asked.

"He had a syringe."

"He could have had a gun!"

"So, what are you saying?"

"I don't think they want to kill us, Kevin. They could have easily shot us all at the airport and been done with it," Doug said.

"Well, they have a funny way of trying to get us to come along peacefully. He didn't even say anything. Just snuck in and had me up against the wall like I was nothing."

"He was ridiculously strong," Doug said, rubbing his hip.

"You ok?" Kevin asked.

"I'll survive. You going to check for a pulse?" Doug asked, glancing down at the old man.

"Hell no! That's when the bad guy always jumps up and grabs the good guy in the movies," Kevin said, taking a step back.

"That's only in horror movies," Doug said, crouching down next to the motionless man.

"Have you taken a good look at these redcoats? They give me the goddamn willies," Kevin said and shivered for emphasis.

Doug stooped down with some difficulty and placed two fingers under the man's chin. Kevin stood with the syringe held out, bouncing up and down on his toes, as if something might happen. Doug pulled his fingers away and pulled at the man's coat. He rummaged through every pocket he could find. Each was empty.

"He's alive. Just knocked out. Nothing in his pockets. Not even a car key…," Doug said.

He looked at Kevin, who stared back fixedly.

"They're waiting for him outside," Kevin said.

"They would have come in by now," Doug said.

They moved to the door and Doug paused to put his snacks back into the basket. Kevin went out the door and then came back in when Doug didn't immediately follow.

"What are you doing?" Kevin asked, his voice high.

"Getting my snacks," Doug said.

"Douglas, we don't have time for your snacks," Kevin said, glancing nervously over his shoulder.

"Don't call me that. I need these. I'm starving," Doug said.

"You are far from needing those and, yes, that's a fat joke. Now leave the goddamn snacks and lets go before creepy wakes up or his friends come to fetch him," Kevin said.

Doug stood back up and stared longingly down at the snacks.

"I'll buy you a burger at the first In and Out we pass," Kevin said.

"You will?"

"Jesus… yes! Can we go now?"

They made their way through the store toward the exit.

"You promise?" Doug asked.

"Yes."

"With fries?"

"Are you just messing with me now? Are we really having this conversation?"

"I just want to know what my limits are," Doug said.

"Whatever your tummy desires big fella. Let's just get the hell out of here," Kevin said.

"Ok," Doug said.

"You're pathetic, you know that, right?"

"Shut up," Doug said.

"Shit… let's move," Kevin hissed.

At the far end of the massive checkout section, a redcoat was meandering down the aisle toward them. They saw one another at the same time, but Kevin and Doug were too close to the exit already. Even at a full run, and Doug's inability to move quickly, the redcoat wouldn't get to them before they left the building.

"Gimme the keys," Kevin said.

Doug tossed them to him and continued through the doorway as he watched Kevin race across the parking lot. He glanced over his shoulder. The redcoat pushed his way past an old man with a cart and made his way into the exit. Doug wasn't going to make it to the car. He turned and stood his ground. The redcoat sneered at him and slowed his approach.

35

The dull roar of carts was in Doug's ear. He could hear the engine from their car. Kevin wasn't going to make it. He raised his cane and held it mid-shaft, tapping the handle in his hand, as menacingly as he could manage. The redcoat rolled a sleeve on his coat, exposing a pale arm. They were less than ten feet away. The roar of the carts was almost on them.

"Excuse me!" came a shout and both he and the redcoat turned and watched as the caravan of carts slipped between them. There must've been over a hundred of them being prodded along by a motorized pusher.

It was all the hesitation he needed. The car slid in behind him with the passenger door open. Doug was barely in before it was taking off.

"You could wait for me to buckle," Doug said.

"He was about to scale that little Wall of China that was moving between you," Kevin said.

"Timing is everything," Doug said.

Chapter 6

"We should go in," James said.

James and Dr. Paynter had been sitting for a solid hour, watching the home of James' Uncle Ted. Set on a peninsula along the northeastern shore of the great Green Bay, the house looked out onto Lake Michigan, a mere 20 yards beyond the back of the house. The white stone driveway led up to the simple but clean two-story log cabin. To their right, a thin stretch of sandy-soil trees soon gave way to the sloping ground and the beginnings of a grassy dune. The calm cold waters lapped against the rocky beach. To the left of the house, the dense coastal forest sloped upward from near the back corner of the house like a great wave of green deciduous preparing to crash over the house and into the waters beyond. If it weren't for the situation, James thought, it might have been damn well serene.

It was those same woods that had frightened James as a child. Something the water had failed to do. No matter how his father and uncle had tried to instill in him a sensible fear of the water, it had never dissuaded him from jumping in. The water made sense to him. The woods held nothing but darkness and the unknown.

And now, as they surreally assessed the potential dangers of a place that had held mostly happy childhood memories, James watched those woods with trepidation. Despite his fear of seeing the place crawling with creepy old men in red coats, there was something even more chilling to find the homestead now completely abandoned. They had pulled in to the end of driveway far enough to see the house, but close enough to make a quick retreat. They had seen nothing except the movement of the screen door in the wind. No smoke rose from the chimney. No fishing gear on the porch. And no sign of Ted's car.

"We should," said Paynter.

"Glad we're in agreement this time," James said, unable to hold back the hint of anger.

"Oh, for Christ's sake…"

"Don't 'Oh, for Christ's sake' me!"

"You're not going to let it go, are you?"

"You just can't admit I was right, can you? It actually hurts to admit it, doesn't it?!"

"It pains me that it came to that, James. I really didn't think she would do something like that," Paynter said.

"But, you wouldn't have it when I suggested, before we even got there, I might add, that it was a bad idea. That we couldn't…shouldn't…trust anyone. And if I hadn't sent Doug and Kevin out in the middle of the night, where would we be? But, no. Apparently, my opinion is subject to review. And then she comes in first thing in the morning with a loaded shotgun in my face. Not a fan…in fact, not a fan of guns being pointed at me in general. Crazy…"

"You watch your tongue…" Paynter interrupted, raising a finger between them and glaring at James.

He looked away just as quickly and let out a long sigh.

"I'm sorry. It's just been a rough couple days… and the last thing I needed was her barging in looking like she wanted to put a hole in someone," James said.

"That she did."

"It might be none of my business, but what the hell happened between you two?"

"I never called," Paynter said.

"Hell hath no fury, as they say," James quipped.

"Pretty much."

They sat looking at the house again. James fidgeted in his seat.

"I don't think it's going anywhere, but…" James said.

Paynter reached into his pocket and slid out the dart gun. James gave it a sideways glance. Paynter shrugged.

"Better than nothing," Paynter said.

"I guess."

They approached the house slowly. To James, the sounds of their feet crunching the stones in the driveway beneath their feet was too loud. He glanced toward the small garage that hugged the shoreline; one bay on land, the other in the water. Uncle Ted's car was gone, the bay door still wide open. The other bay, if James remembered correctly, held his uncle's pride and joy: a 17-foot 1958 Chris-Craft Sportsman. On his few trips up north during the summer, James could always rely on finding his uncle waxing the mahogany beauty, unless there was wood to chop or some other mundane chore. The cold rush of winter wind and the slap of the screen door against the house pulled him back. They were on the doorstep and Paynter turned the handle of the front door. It opened easily and they were inside the kitchen.

Though not a typical "middle-of-the-woods" log cabin style, James had always appreciated the simplicity of the lake house. You walked into the kitchen from the front of the house. To the right, there was a combined dining/living area that extended the length of the house. To the left, there was a hall, an office, a foyer, and the stairs to the upper level. Paynter leveled his gun in each direction.

"Which way?"

"Shouldn't matter…nobody's here," James said.

They moved over to the doorway to the dining room and glanced in. That side of the house was empty. Not only was it empty, there was a sense of abandonment. Nothing had been disturbed. There had been no struggle, or if there had, it had been cleaned up in expert fashion. James shivered, despite the lack of a breeze of any type. Considering there was no heat running, the house was as tight as any traditionally stick-built home, if not better. Uncle Ted wouldn't have had it any other way. They made their way into the hallway and Paynter stopped before three doors, pointing at them.

"Office, closet, and cellar," James said.

"Cellar? So close to the lake?"

James shrugged. He'd never thought of it like that. But, like everything else, he knew that cellar was tight and as dry as any other room in the house. He watched as Paynter pulled open the closet door, giving it a once over; two identical coats and two pairs of boots. The office wasn't much better. An old phone stood guard alone atop the oak desk. There was a two-drawer file cabinet to the left and a lonely looking swivel chair in the middle of the room.

"Bit sparse," Paynter said.

"Looks the same as it did twenty years ago. Same phone too. That's just how Ted was…is…," James said.

"Let's take a look upstairs…then I want a look in that basement," Paynter said.

"What are you hoping to find?"

"Maybe something a little bigger than this," Paynter said, waving the dart gun.

"Doubtful…and even if he had a gun cabinet or something, it'd probably be locked," James said.

"Can you reign in your enthusiasm a bit, James?"

They glanced out the back of the house, which provided a nice view of the lake, before taking to the stairs. On the fifth step, Paynter stopped dead in front of James, throwing out his hand and half knocking him over. He raised a finger to his mouth at James' look of query. James could only hear the sound of his own pounding heart. Then he heard it as well. There was a faint tapping, like the knocking of wood on wood. James stopped breathing in order to hear better. Paynter turned around.

"It's not upstairs," he said and pushed past James back down to the hallway.

41

They stood, staring at one another in the hallway. The sound had stopped. Or was it there, just more faint? Paynter pulled open the cellar door. They stared down into the darkness. James' knees went a little weak when he heard the voice. Partly because he'd expected to find no one in the house and partly because it sounded so familiar.

"Help me…"

James threw the switch to the cellar light and bounded down the stairs.

"James! Stop! It could be a trap!"

James rounded the bottom of the stairs and saw him sitting in a chair he was bound to. The young man lifted his heels and let the wooden legs of the chair hit the floor, oblivious of James' presence. It was clear to him that it was another clone; another of the young men he was starting to call brothers. This one was not in good shape. Paynter slipped in behind James and let out a breath of air.

"Jesus Christ," he said.

A shaggy-haired, gaunt looking version of James, dried blood covered half his face and purple bruises covered the other half. The dirty gray hoodie he wore couldn't be warm enough for this time of year judging by his lack of shivering in the cool basement, it was a good bet he'd begun to freeze to death. James pulled off his coat and wrapped it around the man.

"He's cold to the touch," James said.

He went to the sink at the far wall and returned with a cup of warm water after a couple of minutes. James tilted the man's head back, letting a few drops fall into his mouth. He coughed on the second try.

"Hey man, you ok? Can you tell me what happened?"

Paynter worked on the ropes and the man nearly fell out of the chair. James supported him and gave him another sip.

"Who…who are you?"

"My name is James…and this is…Dr. Paynter. Can you tell us what happened here?" James.

"Where am I?"

"Uhh…Michigan…in the basement of my uncle's house. Ted Masterson?"

"Michigan? What the…fuck am I doing…in Michigan?"

"We were hoping you could tell us," James said.

The young man just shook his head in response. James looked up at Paynter, who looked confused.

"Which one is this?" James half-whispered. Paynter shrugged his shoulders and shook his head.

"Dude, what's your name?"

"Name?"

"Yeah…your name…what's your name?"

"It's Powers. Kevin Powers," he said, and his eyes rolled to the whites.

James stood up so quickly that he couldn't catch the man as he fell away from him and to the floor in a heap of unconsciousness. He looked back at Paynter, whose pallor was stark.

"Oh fuck."

Chapter 7

"What do you mean you can't be sure?"

James said through the strain of lifting. He considered the irony of having now carried two separate brothers named Kevin Powers in an unconscious state. The irony thinned a bit when he tried to wrap his head around what they were dealing with.

"I mean, I can't be sure…it's not like I followed each one of you every moment from birth. But…," Paynter's voice trailed off.

"But what?"

"But, this one fits some of the earlier descriptions I'd had of Kevin. Years before I contacted him. I just…assumed they'd been wrong," he said.

They placed the new Kevin on the couch in the living room and piled blankets on him. James fetched an old water bottle he knew his uncle kept in the kitchen, filled it, and slipped it under the still unconscious man. Paynter went about cleaning the man's wounds as best as he could. The wounds were ugly, but he determined that nothing was broken beyond a few blood vessels.

"Whoever did this…did just enough to hurt him. They knew we'd find him in time. Who are you calling?" Paynter said.

"Doug," James said.

"He might not be able to talk…," Paynter said.

"Doug! It's James. Call me as soon as you get this. It's important that Kevin's…not around when you call. We're at my uncle's place and shit's just gotten a whole lot weirder. I'm not sure Kevin's been telling the truth."

He hung up and paced away from Paynter and back.

"Dammit! If he's Kevin Powers, who the fuck is running around with Doug?"

"Someone's lying…," Paynter said.

"You think it's him?" James said, pointing to the unconscious man on the couch.

"I don't know, James."

"Really? You think the dying guy is lying? I've got a hard time swallowing that one."

"I'm just playing devil's advocate here."

"Well, this is just great. What do we do, leave this new Kevin here to die, just in case? God dammit! Twelve-hour drive just to go from the fryer into the fucking frying pan."

"James…breathe a little," Paynter said.

A flurry of expletives ran through James mind, but he knew they would be wasted breath. He walked the length of the room and out onto the back porch. The clouds that had appeared light near noon were now growing heavy. He could almost smell the snow in the afternoon air and the early winter night was creeping in from the east. The woods drew his eye again. He could imagine one of the red-coated old men watching this little glitch play out. That was what got him the most. Someone kept playing a joke and James was the recurring butt of it.

"I'm sorry," James said when he returned.

"I don't fault your anger, James," Paynter said.

"Yeah, well…I can't seem to think straight anymore. One thing after another. I just hate thinking that we're being strung along," James said.

"But we are, and we don't have much choice but to play along…for now," Paynter said.

They both turned as New Kevin grunted and opened his eyes a hair.

"He can't hurt us in his condition," Paynter said.

"And we can't just leave him, even if he is a plant," James said.

"He'll need a coat," Paynter said.

"Let's worry about him walking first," James said.

"I'll run a hot bath," Paynter said.

"Then what?" James asked.

"Then I'll bathe him," Paynter said.

"No, I mean…then what? Where do we go from here?"

"Oh, yeah…I don't know."

They went about the business of doing what they could for their new charge. James reluctantly helped bundle the naked body of his brother into the warm water of his uncle's large steel tub. If James had believed that this new version of him looked bad on the outside, it was only reinforced by seeing the young man naked. He had bruises forming across his neck and chest and the track marks that pocked each arm were too numerous to count. New Kevin stirred to his greatest level of consciousness since they had first seen him in the basement. He mumbled something incoherent and proceeded to urinate in the tub.

"Ohh…fucking lovely," James said, half-turning away.

"To be expected," Paynter said.

"Why am I wet?" New Kevin managed.

"It's called a bath. Ever heard of it?" James said, earning a stern look from Paynter.

"You got too cold down there in the basement," Paynter said.

"Basement? Where the fuck am I?"

"Michigan," James said.

New Kevin looked up slowly and his eyes briefly met James' before dropping back down into the water before him. James could read nothing of comprehension from them. It made him more and more nervous for Doug. This guy couldn't be that good.

"You think he can travel?"

"I don't think we have much choice," Paynter said.

"Hey! Hey, hey!" James shouted, snapping his finger to try and get New Kevin's attention. "What can you tell me about the people that did this to you?"

"James, jeez…the kid's barely…," Paynter began.

"Red coats," New Kevin said.

"No surprise there," Paynter said.

"Was there a girl and an old man here?"

"Lots of old men, no girl," he said.

"No girl?"

"James, settle down. You can't trust his memory at this point," Paynter said, raising an arm.

"We've got nothing else to go on," James said.

"It can wait until he's dressed," Paynter said.

"Why am I naked? You two aren't…assaulting me, are you?" New Kevin suddenly asked.

"No…or I guess this really would be a nightmare, huh," James said.

"Just give me five minutes. Toss in some clean clothes. Lots of layers. If I need you, you'll know," Paynter said.

"Nothing's going to fit him," James said.

"I don't think he'll care at this point. Just make sure you find a belt," Paynter said.

James closed the door and crossed the hall to his uncle's room. It was sparse, just like much of the rest of the house. There was a simple oak dresser against the far wall and a small square mirror that might just be big enough to adjust a tie in, not that his uncle ever wore them. James opened the top drawer and chuckled to himself. It was like a shelf in a department store. The socks were neatly rolled and organized by color; white and black. The underwear was stacked and folded as if they had just come out of the package. He pulled out a starkly white undershirt and some pressed boxers and placed them on top of the dresser. New Kevin would definitely be swimming in any of his uncle's extra-large clothing. The next drawer down had several immaculately folded pairs of pants and jeans; blue or black and a single pair of khakis. James pulled the latter out, not remembering ever having seen his uncle actually wear them. When he pulled out the final drawer, a chill caught hold of him. Here, amongst all of the near-clinical cleanliness, was a microcosm of disorder.

Of the three rows of waffle-knit and thermal tops, the third stack on the right was amiss. The shirts had been pushed aside from the far back corner and remained wrinkled and unfolded. He reached into the drawer and assessed the size of the space. He pulled out several shirts and placed them on top of the dresser, then opened up the jeans drawer again. His hand slid in beneath the pants in the back right and brushed something metallic. He flinched at first, then wrapped his hand around the butt end of the pistol and pulled it out. The gleaming black emblem on the stock said it was a Beretta. He opened the top drawer, not believing he would find another, but a part of him wasn't surprised when his hand grasped another gun handle. He stared back down at the bottom drawer.

"He knew they were coming," James said as he pushed his way back into the bathroom. New Kevin was now standing under his own power, if a little unsteadily, wrapped in several large pristinely white towels. He shivered as Paynter systematically went up and down his body in an attempt to dry him thoroughly.

"What?" Paynter asked.

"He knew. My uncle knew someone was coming," James said.

"How?"

"I don't know, but he took out one of his guns in a hurry. I found these," James said, pulling out both guns from his back waistband.

"Jesus, James…you want to shoot your ass off? I don't care if the safeties are on or not, you never stick a gun in your pants like that. The safeties are on, right?"

"Uhhh…yeah…I think," James said, glancing at the guns in his hands. The one was clearly not on and his effort to slide it into place did not go unnoticed.

"Put 'em down before you hurt someone," Paynter said.

New Kevin swayed, prompting a secure arm from Paynter.

"If he knew, that means someone called him," James said.

"He have a cell phone?" Paynter asked.

"You're lucky there's running water in the house," James said.

This elicited a soft chuckle from New Kevin, though it was hard to determine from his countenance whether he was laughing at what James had said, or whether it was some internal joke that had aroused his mirth. His unruly locks temporarily tamed by water and soap, he looked somewhat pathetic peering out from beneath the towels. Like a large sleepy child first thing after a bath. They were halfway through dressing him when James ventured a new question.

"Where are you from, Kevin?"

New Kevin blinked slowly, attempted to focus on James, then gave up as if it were too much effort. He closed his eyes and spoke.

"Philly."

"Do you know how you got here?"

He shook his head slowly, but spoke before James could ask another question.

"I was in the North End, doing some…business. I thought maybe that's why they took me. But, when they didn't kill me right away…I don't know. They sure didn't act or look like any drug dealers I'd seen before. Then they knocked me out and we were here…and there was a bunch of 'em all looked alike and…holy shit!"

New Kevin's eyes bulged wide and he pushed back away from both of them, half-falling backward into the empty tub.

"Holy shit!" he cried out again.

"What? What is it?!" James asked, left holding a shirt in his hands. Kevin struggled to put distance between himself and James, staring wildly at him.

"What the hell are you? Am I tripping…oh Jesus, I am tripping. Why the fuck do you look like me, dude?!"

"Oh shit," James murmured.

"James is your brother, Kevin. He's your twin brother. It's ok," Paynter said, reaching in to lift the man out of the tub.

New Kevin pulled his arms in close to his body, avoiding any such help that would bring him out and closer to James. His eyes darted to Paynter, but quickly returned to James.

"Fuck you. You're not real...none of this is real. I just smoked some bad shit and you're a fucking cartoon out of my head," New Kevin said.

"I promise you, this isn't a dream. I would've woken up a long time ago. A nightmare maybe, but not a dream," James said.

"Please, Kevin. We know you've been through a lot, but you've got to trust us...you don't have much choice," Paynter said, again extending a hand.

New Kevin glanced at Paynter's hand and stood himself back up, remaining in the tub. He finished cinching up his pants, pulling the belt all the way through to the last loop, where it still left the pants to hang precariously at his waist.

"Jesus, who the fuck belongs to these?" he said, still not taking his eyes off James. He scratched at the inside of his left elbow without thought.

"My uncle...the old man."

"He was one of the old men?"

"No, not the redcoats. He would have been tied up," James said.

"Oh, him," Kevin said.

"He was alive when you last saw him?"

"He...I think he was alive. I wasn't here long before they kicked my ass. And I didn't exactly see him. They had a cloth over my head, but there was definitely another voice that I hadn't heard."

He raised a hand to his bruised face for the first time, feeling along the swollen left side of his face. The swelling had subsided a little and the bruises were starting to come out in full, leaving his face a yellow and purple mess.

"Well, that's not exactly reassuring," James said.

"Sorry, man, it's a bit foggy still," New Kevin said.

James nodded, then turned quickly from the room and ran down the stairs. Paynter called after him.

"I've got an idea," James shouted back, reaching the phone in his Uncle's office. He lifted the receiver and pressed three buttons. "I don't know if this even still works."

The electronic operator came on and reported to James the number that had last dialed in to this line. James jotted in down, hung up, then quickly dialed the new number. It was six rings before a rough-voiced man answered the phone more loudly than necessary.

"Hangar!"

"I'm sorry?" James blurted out in response, responding in an equal volume.

"Jesus, you don't have to shout. I said, hangar. Johnson's Hangar. You called me, didn't ya?" the man said, not lowering his own voice.

"I'm sorry, can you give me directions?"

"Where ya comin' from?"

James was caught flat footed. They had just come down the road less than an hour before, but now the name was escaping him. He could hear the question building on the other end of the line.

"I'm on the south of the peninsula…by the Masterson place."

"The Masters…who the hell is this? How do you know Ted Masterson?"

"I'm his nephew," James said, not thinking to lie until after the fact. He was glad he hadn't.

"James? This is James? Damn boy, you scared the hell out of me. Jack Johnson. Happy to call your uncle a friend. What…why you callin' son?"

"Mr. Johnson, yours is the last number that called my uncle's house…and now he's missing," James said.

There was a palpable release of breath on the other end of the line. Then the man lowered his voice for the first time since the conversation had started.

"Damn…damn, damn. Damn it to hell. Have you called the police?"

"Given the circumstances, I'm not sure how much help they'd be, sir," James said.

"Knowing Ted, that doesn't surprise me. James, you write down these directions and come up and see me. I might be able to give you a lead."

"Thank you, Mr. Johnson."

"Jack, please."

When James hung up the phone, he turned to find Paynter and New Kevin standing in the doorway. Paynter looked curious. New Kevin looked like the trip down the stairs had taken all of his willpower.

"What was that about?"

"I was able to call back the last number to call in here. It came from Johnson's hangar. Safe to assume it's a small airport we passed on the way down the coast. I spoke to the owner. He seemed to know Ted pretty well. Said he might have some info."

"Sounds like someone we need to talk to," Paynter said.

"Think you can travel?" James asked New Kevin.

"If all I have to do is sit in the back of a car, I think I can handle that," he said.

"Let's hope that's all you have to do," James said.

It was another fifteen minutes before they'd gathered themselves. James and Paynter each took one of his uncle's pistols. Paynter was sure to check the safety on each gun before letting James take his. James decided that it wasn't worth getting upset over a gesture that just meant that Paynter cared whether he blew his own ass off or not. They wrapped New Kevin up in one of Ted's heaviest parkas from the closet. It was like bundling up a small child in his father's coat, but it would keep him warm no matter what happened.

"Ready?" Paynter asked.

"Yep," James said.

Paynter walked with New Kevin, directing him outside and steadying him on the gravel drive. James couldn't quite decide what to do with the door as he drew it closed behind him. It had been unlocked when they arrived and he'd never known Ted to lock up as a child. It just wasn't necessary in this part of the country. But, that had been then. He pushed the key into the locked and turned, testing the handle in each direction after he had done so. He backed away and pulled the screen door away from the house, pushing it hard enough to slam shut. It was during this action that his eye landed on a wire he had never seen before, leading away from the screen door latch. He watched, helplessly caught in the moment as the screen shut violently and a distinct little beep was emitted. James turned on his heels and shouted at the top of his lungs.

"Run!"

Chapter 8

"Gosh darn it!"

"Uh-oh, must be real bad," Kevin said.

"The message light on my phone just came on, but when I went to check my voice mail, it died," Doug said.

"Bummer. I'm guessing you didn't think to bring a car charger with you?" Kevin said.

"Not much use for a car charger when you have no car," Doug said.

"Oh, yeah…sorry," Kevin said.

"Maybe we can stop at a mall or something. If you see any signs, could we just stop for five minutes," Doug said.

Kevin glanced out the window, scanning the horizon in front of him.

"Not sure if you noticed, but we're kind in the middle of fucking nowhere," Kevin said.

"And where would that be exactly?"

"I think we crossed over into New Mexico a little while back," Kevin said.

As he spoke, they passed an interstate sign that read 40, and shortly thereafter, a sign that said Albuquerque was a little over 125 miles away. The barren red sand expanse ran out to the horizon to the northwest as a monolithic butte began to dominate their southwestern view.

"I don't think we should risk any big cities," Doug said.

"Not sure that Albuquerque qualifies, but I know what you mean. What's that?"

Kevin pointed at a dusty sign on the right hand side. It promised, "Homemade food. Cold beer. And the last clean bathroom 'til Albuquerque." Below it, the declaration was repeated in Spanish

"Sounds good to me. You got any cash left?" Doug asked.

"Dude…not if you're going to waste it on chips and cookies. I only got like twenty bucks left," Kevin said.

"I can't believe we had to leave that all behind," Doug said.

"I can always drop you by the side of the road. I'm sure those redcoats'll give you something to eat…before they shoot you. Jesus, all they need is a big ol' bag of pork rinds to draw you out," Kevin said.

"Shut up man. And don't say pork rinds…" Doug said, shifting in his seat and rubbing his stomach.

"Dude, seriously? You're pathetic."

"Just shut it. I can't help it…my blood sugar gets low. Too many two-bagel breakfasts and three-bagel lunches," Doug said.

"Jesus. Makes me sick just thinking about it," Kevin said.

"Makes me hungry. Can we change the conversation," Doug whispered, leaning back in the seat and closing his eyes.

"Alright. I'll stop. If you'll stop being a big fucking pussy," Kevin said.

"Fuck you, Kevin," Doug said, not opening his eyes.

"Holy shit. Now I know it's starting to affect your thinking. You'd better get something filling. Something with some goddamn protein. Is this what it's like to have a child? This must be what it's like to have a child."

"Do you ever shut up?"

Kevin guided the big white Lincoln off of the highway at the next exit. If this was civilization, it was only a hint of it. The little-traveled exit ramp let out onto a road that ran parallel with the interstate. A patch of red sand covered the road to their right. A sign in front of them identified the nearest town to be that of Cuervo.

Kevin slowed the car to a crawl as they approached the only building that might have represented a retail establishment of any kind; a blue aluminum-sided building with only a single filthy window. There appeared to be a beer sign in that window, but it was impossible to make out a brand due to the dust on the glass. Signs on either side of the solid wooden door advertised what the establishment offered. Most were in Spanish. A weathered sign over the door was in the same fashion as those on the road.

"Cuervo Goldie's," Doug read.

"Cute," Kevin said.

"Look, they even sell cell phones. Maybe they'll have my charger," Doug said.

"Dude…don't get your hopes up. By the looks of things, we might be lucky if they speak English. Jesus, look at these cars. It's like we slipped through a time warp getting off the highway."

"What do you mean? That Chevy is a classic," Doug said.

"So is the Dodge next to it and the Ford next to that!"

"Well, I wouldn't call an LTD a classic exactly," Doug said.

Kevin pulled the car into the last space in front of the store.

"Why is it so busy?" Doug asked.

"Maybe they all broke down here. Maybe it's a cursed lot. Maybe we're going to walk through that door and find a bunch of dusty corpses. The rest stop that time forgot!"

"You really are a jerk, you know that?" Doug said.

"Dude, look at this place…," Kevin said.

"Dude, I'm starving. If I have to eat my way out of there, I will."

They both turned as the door to the building opened. A Hispanic man in jeans and a blue shirt stepped out and squinted into the light of the afternoon sun. His face looked weathered by years of harsh desert air. He glanced over at the two young men in their car that stood out like a new penny amongst old. He shifted the belt at his waist and headed for his vehicle. Kevin might have been surprised that the vehicle started if he hadn't been so distracted by the large gun he'd seen on the man's hip.

"You ready?" Doug asked.

"Did you not see that?"

"See what?"

"The hand cannon on that guy's hip," Kevin said.

"Ummm…nope."

"They can do that here?"

"Did he have a badge?" Doug asked.

"I think I would have noticed that," Kevin said.

"C'mon, let's go. The sooner we get in, the sooner we can get back on the road," Doug said.

The two exited the car and braced themselves against the sudden gust of wind that swirled dust up into their faces. Doug moved slowly with his cane while Kevin ran for the door, pushed it open, and stumbled into the establishment, coughing and dusting himself off. Doug followed shortly. Doug paused mid-brush and stared blankly over Kevin's shoulder. It took a moment for Kevin to notice and when he did, he turned around slowly.

They stood beside an empty glass counter; the sparse boxes and thin layer of dust on the shelves and empty candy cartons suggested the supply had outweighed the demand. Beyond that, to their left, were several magazine racks, a stand that held various sizes of cheap-looking cowboy hats, and a rather large and a too-new-looking beef jerky display. To their right, and the focus of Kevin's attention, was what appeared to be a diner counter, lined with swivel stools ridden by men who looked as if Doug and Kevin had just interrupted a sacred ritual. A heavy smell of beef, beans, and peppers hung in the air. An old TV hung above the stove providing a grease-filtered image of CNN. Either the sound was turned off, or the ancient-looking unit no longer had the ability to express itself in an audible fashion.

Seven large men of Hispanic descent sat at the table, elbows on the counter, each one of them glancing backward to eye up Kevin and Doug. No expression was to be seen. A round-faced girl stood behind the counter in front of the stove. Her white apron was pristine. She stared through the two young men as if the door had blown open on its own and she was just waiting for it to blow back closed.

"Hola," Doug said.

One of the men at the counter sat up straight and swiveled slightly on his seat, exposing the gun and holster on his hip.

"Oh, Jesus...we're gonna die and it's gonna be your fault," Kevin said as low as he could. Doug held up his cell phone.

"Ummm...mi cellular telefono es muerto. Tiene un...um...charger?" Doug said, probably too loudly, wiggling his cell phone next to his head.

"Oh, they're definitely going to kill us now...you probably just told them you want to kill their grandmother...or shave their cats...or molest their..."

"Will you shut up...I know a little Spanish. It was my best course last year."

Whatever was frying on the stove made a crackling snap that seemed to cut the tension for the girl. She blinked heavily once.

"That's a shitty phone," she said, with only a hint of an accent. She then reached into her pocket and pulled out the exact same model.

"It was free," Doug said.

64

"I know," she said.

"So, do you have a charger?" Kevin asked. She didn't take her eyes off Doug, but nodded at him.

"It's cargador, by the way," she said.

"What?"

"Charger…in Spanish…it's cargador."

"Oh…thanks. Sorry. I didn't want to assume…you know…I…"

The man nearest to Doug turned away and said, "You ain't in Mexico, fool."

"Sorry…sorry 'bout that…rude of me…yeah…sorry," Doug said, watching as every man at the counter went back to his drink or plate of food.

The girl turned quickly, pulled something off the stove, slapped it on a plate and slid it in front of one of the men. She then turned back to Doug and waved him over to the counter. Doug approached the girl in a manner that suggested getting too close to the men might warrant some sort of attack. She reached out for his phone, which he willingly gave up. The hint of a smile flashed on the corner of her mouth and Kevin would swear that he saw some color enter Doug's cheek. She plugged his phone in, placed it on the counter and resumed looking at Doug. Doug, for his part, smiled and blushed, but couldn't seem to break away from the girl's gaze.

"Well, I'll just…ummm…check out the menu. Ooo… tacos. Doug? Are you…hungry?" Kevin offered.

"I'm starved, you know that."

"Then why don't you order something from the nice young lady," Kevin said.

"Order...right...I...oh. Mexican food always gives me heartburn," Doug said. Kevin slowly raised his fist to his forehead, closed his eyes, and turned away.

"Not my Mexican," the girl said.

"Not her Mexican," Doug said.

"Are you ok?" Kevin asked.

"Blood sugar is crashing pretty bad," Doug said.

"Can we just get a half dozen tacos to go?"

"Beef or chicken?" the girl asked.

"Beef."

"Crunchy or soft?"

"Crunchy."

"Mild, medium, or spicy."

"As mild as you can make it without insulting your heritage or upsetting my brother's sensitive tummy-tum," Kevin said.

There was general wave of mirth down the counter amongst the men. A few exchanged hushed one-liners in Spanish at which Doug and the girl frowned.

"I don't know that word, but I can guess it isn't very nice," Doug muttered.

"We're in a bit of a hurry, so...you know...," Kevin said, smiling and shrugging at the girl.

She gave Kevin a steely glance, but turned and proceeded to prepare the requested meal. Kevin paced up the space of the building, glancing at the handful of magazines left on the rack. Most were outdated by two to three months. A stack of newspapers was still in its plastic binding at the foot of the rack. A subscription flyer covered the front page. Kevin knelt down and pulled back the top page, surprised to find that it was that day's edition.

"Hey, mind if I open this?" he said over his shoulder.

The girl glanced over the counter frowning and shrugged her shoulders.

"Sure. Don't know why he still delivers. He just drops off a bundle and picks up the bundle from the day before," she said.

Kevin quickly snapped off the plastic wrappers, sliding out the top copy. He stood up and unfolded the paper before him, then, seeing what was on the front cover, quickly crumpled it back onto itself and looked around. Only Doug had noticed his strange behavior. And now Kevin stared him down, gesturing to the paper and motioning toward the door.

"How are those tacos coming?" Doug asked.

"Almost ready…but your phone. Ten minutes won't charge it for shit," she said.

"Ooo…it'll have to do. We're in a bit of a hurry. How much for all of these?" Kevin said, holding the entire pile of papers in his hand.

She stared at Kevin, then at the pile of papers, then back at Kevin.

"Fifty cents each, twenty-five to a bundle. Umm…"

"Twelve fifty," Doug said.

Kevin looked at him.

"First Spanish, now math? Do I know you?"

"Obviously not," Doug said. The girl beamed at him as she handed him his cell phone and a bag with the tacos in it.

"How much for the tacos?" Kevin asked.

"Dollar each."

"Perfect. Keep…uhhh…the change. Doug, let's go."

Doug followed Kevin's wide eyes and spotted the television in the corner. There, with the word "ASSASSIN" in bold letters above, was a picture of what could have been either one of them. Kevin was pulling on his arm. Neither had to look back to see that some recognition was occurring between what was being seen on the TV and the two young men in the room. Kevin nearly pushed Doug out the door as the latter had trouble navigating the exit door with his cane. He hobbled to the car behind Kevin who stood at his door bouncing back and forth on his feet. They were in before Kevin reached down and picked up one of the papers he had thrown to the floor.

"Get us the hell out of here!" he shouted.

He waved the paper in Doug's face, half attempting to pull the seatbelt across his chest with one hand. He shook it again for emphasis as Doug maneuvered past one of the men who had run out after them. Doug downshifted the automatic and floored it, jerking the car around, but accomplishing what he'd hoped; a large plume of red dust billowed up behind him as they pulled away.

"Why is our face on a newspaper? Why were we on the news like that? It said assassin in big letters!"

Kevin scanned the front page quickly, between glances in the side-view mirror. No ancient car or pickup took up the pursuit.

"Jesus, It's James. They're accusing him of assassinating the state senator from Michigan. Wait…there were no witnesses, but they found evidence that linked this to the murder in NJ…James' neighbor. A secret service agent and a homeless man were killed along with the Senator. Jesus…"

"Oh my gosh…James would never kill a bum…"

Kevin stared at Doug as they made their way back onto the highway. He glanced over his shoulder, checking again to see if they were being pursued.

"Dude…James wouldn't kill anyone…well, maybe one of those old dudes, but…c'mon."

"We're not going to be able to stop anywhere anymore, huh," Doug said.

"No…I think we got lucky there," Kevin said.

"Lucky? You call that lucky?"

"Ummm…lemme think. While your little senorita was undressing you with her eyes…don't argue…she was too…and while she was doing that, she was too damn distracted…along with all of those other hombres. She made you food. She charged your freaking phone for Christ's sake. And it wasn't until they posted that big fucking mug shot of James…which, by the way…where the hell did they even get that? It wasn't

69

until they posted that shot that the single brain synapse that the entire room shared seemed to kick in and they recognized us. Oh, and no one decided to play hometown hero and shoot out our tires as we drove away. Yeah…damn lucky I'd say."

"Are you done?" Doug asked.

"Yes."

"Feel better?"

"No."

"Can I have a taco now?"

"Yeah…I'm not very hungry anymore."

"Can I have yours?"

"Shut up and drive."

Chapter 9

"Nicole?"

Nicole's dreams had ranged from vivid to vague and based on how frightening the vivid parts were, she was comforted by not quite having a grasp on all that had passed through her mind. Her first instinct was to move quickly when she realized her bonds were no longer restricting her movement, but the simple act of raising her head seemed to cause her pain. She opened her eyes and tried to focus on the face above her. It was not another James. The face was hard, but the eyes that looked down on her were soft, despite the nasty gash over his left eye.

"Uncle Ted?"

"Hello Nicole," he said.

"Where are we?"

"I'm not quite sure," he said.

She sat up slowly and glanced around the unfamiliar room. For all she knew, they were in the same house she had woken up in last time. It was a small office-sized space with no window. She lay on the only piece of furniture in the room; a single mattress with a fitted sheet on a short frame and no pillow. She rubbed at her wrists and flinched as her fingers crossed over the raw abrasions that decorated each. She pulled the ragged cuffs of her grey sweatshirt down over them.

"You ok?" Ted asked.

"Nothing on the outside that won't heal," she said.

"I'm so sorry about all this, Nicole. I don't know if I could've prevented it, but maybe you could've been better prepared," Ted said.

Nicole looked down into her lap at her hands. She rubbed the palm of her hand with her thumb.

"I just don't understand. Why did that man know who you were? Why did he tell James to find you? I don't understand anything that happened."

Ted turned to face the empty adjacent wall. The large man took up a third of the edge of the bed and running his hand through his hair seemed to be an effort in self-importance to which he was unaccustomed.

"The last thing I ever wanted was to hurt James. And now…what a mess. A smarter man would have seen this coming. A smarter man would have dealt with his problems when he had a chance. Instead…I don't know. People are dying…and it's my fault."

Nicole heard a rip and looked down to find that Uncle Ted was gripping the edge of the mattress so hard that the fabric of the fitted sheet had begun to tear. She placed a hand on the white-knuckled fist. The tension seemed to run out of the man.

"So, you're not really a carpenter," Nicole said.

"Not really…I mean…I taught myself to be a carpenter, but that was a long time after I'd quit my day job," Ted said.

"And that's why these men are using you to get to James," she said.

"I hate to break it to you, but they're using *you* to get to James. As much as I know he'd come after me, he probably wouldn't go to quite the extreme if it were *just* me. They know that," Ted said.

"James loves you very much," Nicole said.

"I know he does. He's a good boy…a fine young man. He's the best thing that ever happened to my brother. I promised Maggie I would always look after him…and now look," he said.

"Who promised to look after you?" Nicole said with slight smile.

Ted managed to smile back at her.

"Stories aren't supposed to work this way. Fate's got it all wrong," Ted said.

"I don't see you as a big believer in fate, Uncle Ted," Nicole said.

"Is it that obvious?"

Nicole shrugged, then nodded.

"When I was a boy, I had a lot of…anger. Passed down from our father. Now, he never laid a hand on any of us, but I seem to remember patching a lot of holes in walls and doors in that house. He'd fought in the last world war. I was two when he left; five when he came back. His wife, our mother, died when William was just a little guy. I was ten. Father never breathed a word about the war to us. But, there were times, mostly when he was tired or when he only had a few years left, when I'd catch him, hands clenched, lips pursed, sweat on his

73

brow, staring off at a spot that might have burned from the heat in his eyes. Sometimes, I'd just stand and watch him, waiting to see if something would finally come out. Sometimes, he'd realize I was there and he'd snap out of it and slowly deflate. But if I ever startled him, which was usually my own damn fault, those clenched fists would slam onto whatever was closest and he'd curse me a blue streak for sneaking up on him, even if I'd come charging into the room. Billy'd get away with a less profane rendition, but neither of us ever escaped his wrath if we disturbed him. Dream time we came to call it. Don't mess with pop when he's in dream time. Even on his death bed, he wouldn't tell me what the hell it was. Hell of a way to go through life, but there you have it."

"Anyway, William had a tendency to channel that anger into a positive energy. Me, not so much. All I knew was this sort of brooding anger without reason. I just figured that's how I was supposed to act. Well, it landed me in a lot of trouble. Military seemed to be the way to go. I joined up and made a life out of it. They gave me tests and taught me everything my brain could handle, which, in military terms, was quite a bit, I guess. The Navy determined that I was a cut above the rest, so I became a SEAL. I did 8 tours in Vietnam. They gave me the hardest tasks and I got them done. When the war was over, I stuck around and did Cold War operations into the 80s."

There was a sudden pounding on the door and a voice shouted instructions.

74

"Stay on the bed! Dearest Uncle, you be a good boy and you'll both be fine. We're not going to hurt anyone. Am I understood? Be a good boy now. Theodore? Am I clear?"

"Yes," Ted said, his large hands wrapping around the edge of the mattress beneath them. He nodded to Nicole.

The door opened and a redcoat with a pistol entered, the barrel clearly pointed at Uncle Ted's head.

"If that finger slips, you better kill me outright, or you'll wish you had," Ted growled.

"Not to mention how pissed I'll be at getting blood and brains on my nice white walls," came a voice from the hallway.

Sebastian entered the doorway and gave the redcoat a look. The man lowered his arm, but didn't quite take the gun off of Ted.

"Apologies. You just can't get good help these days. My name is Sebastian and you are my guests," Sebastian said, his smile going unreturned.

"What do you want with us?" Nicole asked standing up.

"Such fire! I like you. I knew I kept you alive for a reason."

"Fuck you," Nicole said lunging and throwing a fist at Sebastian's head.

Sebastian caught the wrist of her extended arm with his left and stopped the strike inches from its target. He smiled at her as he easily caught her other fist as it came around.

"You are lively, I'll give you that, but you're wasting your energy. I can feel it sapping out of you by the moment. You haven't eaten in days now and we can't have you just expiring on me, now can we? That might make your boyfriend mad enough to…well, to kill me…and that's no good. Ah-ah-ah…" Sebastian was looking over Nicole's shoulder now, presumably at Uncle Ted.

"Don't do anything we'd both regret. I'm just defending myself here. Tell her to calm down," Sebastian said.

"Nicole…honey, do as he says," Ted said.

Nicole struggled against the man for one last moment.

"When he finds you…and he will…he's going to kill you," she said, feeling her knees give out beneath her. She slumped on the ground at his feet, trying to stave off the tears that were coming to her eyes.

"Oh, foolish girl, I have no doubt James will find us. You must realize, that's been the plan all along. He's going to help bring in the rest of his brothers. And then, he's going to do one more thing for me before I'm done with him."

"He'll do nothing of the kind…he won't…" Sebastian reached into his back pocket and produced a rolled up newspaper. He unfolded it with relish and smacked at the front cover, his fingers slapping the image of James and the bold headline that was bringing on a feeling of nausea in Nicole; SENATOR ASSASSINATED.

"That's a lie," Uncle Ted whispered, rising slowly and placing a hand on Nicole's shoulder.

"Is it, Ted? Or is it just the truth finally rearing its ugly head."

"James didn't do that," Nicole said.

"You know that…and I know that, but by the time I'm finished with all of them, they'll swear the lies are truth and the truth, lies. Your faithful government started this bullshit for the exact purpose for which I now use it. And now, their little joke isn't so funny."

"He's as much a victim as you are," Ted protested.

The rage was evident on Sebastian's face and Nicole flinched as the newspaper flew over her shoulder at Uncle Ted. She cowered back toward the bed as the man's shouts reverberated in the small room.

"He had his life! He knew a loving family! He cheated his fate and you helped! I gave everything to my country thinking I would make the world a better place and they shit on that dream, just like they did on yours."

"We gave it up willingly," Uncle Ted said.

"I gave it…willingly. Ha. Yes…yes I did. Then they proceeded to kill that man. No, I take that back. They would have been better off killing me. Instead, they turned me into an enemy of the state. They stripped me of my life and threw me in a cell. Did you know that your country did that, young lady? Did you know that we lock up our own citizens in a place where no one will think to look. Yes, my country tis' of thee," Sebastian said.

He attempted to regain his composure by straightening the collar of his tweed coat and taking a step back, much to Nicole's relief. She was trembling despite the assuring grip that

Uncle Ted had on her shoulder. She just wanted to go home, and the frightening reality that that might not happen now was beginning to creep into her thoughts. She might die here, wherever here was. She might never see her parents again. And, perhaps worst of all, her last memories of James might not even be of him, but of this older version of him screaming in her face. She shuddered and looked away from him.

"They told me you died," Uncle Ted said.

"Don't patronize me, Ted. You knew the truth," Sebastian said.

"I never said I didn't. But, they still told me you'd died," Uncle Ted said.

"An elaborate ruse," Sebastian said.

"A clone," Nicole offered.

"Clever girl. One of the other early models that didn't quite work out. That batch had a short life expectancy, so we traded places. Hard to do when you're a nameless man in a nameless place, but where there's a will, well…you know the rest."

"And now you think James will just jump up and volunteer to do your bidding? He's not a fool," Nicole said, venturing once more to look at Sebastian.

His eyes were empty to her. Devoid of feeling anything but anger. It was something she'd never seen in James and she now found it hard to maintain eye contact. He smiled at her wanly.

"Oh, I know he's not a fool. My own flesh and blood! But, I know how to pull a man's strings. It's something I'm good at."

"He'll do nothing for you," Nicole hissed.

"And you may be right, but he will do it for you and he'll do it for dear Uncle Ted. He'd kill for you. In fact, I'm betting on it. James Masterson will kill the man I tell him to because he'll believe he's going to be saving you all. And his name will go down in infamy. Maybe even more famous than Booth!"

Nicole took in his words and looked up into Sebastian's growing Cheshire smile. He folded his arms across his chest and smiled up at the ceiling, as if he was preparing to tell the cleverest punch line to a joke.

"Why would he be more famous than Booth?"

"Thanks for tossing me the easy one, my dear, but it should be pretty clear. James is going to kill the President of the United States."

Chapter 10

Jack Johnson hung up the receiver and rested his trembling hand on the phone. He'd known Ted Masterson for twenty-plus years. A good man. A smart man. A man who had, in his own words, a past that was better left in the past. But, a man who was to be trusted. And now, he was in trouble. Ted Masterson was in trouble because his trusted friend had let him down. Jack had let his sense of trust overwhelm his gut feeling that these 'friends' of his were up to no good. And, despite his warning call to Ted, the man had gone missing.

He slammed his other fist against the aluminum siding of the hangar.

"You old goddamned fool!"

He picked the receiver back up and punched some numbers into the phone.

"Hey, Maddy. It's Jack over at the airfield. Doin' ok. Hey, is Pete in? Can you do me a favor and have him stop by in his travels. I'd like to have a word..."

He waited for a response. There was none.

"Maddy?"

Jack repeated himself again, only louder than normal, then stared at the phone. He tapped the hook. There was nothing. In all his years at the airfield, the worst of blizzards had failed to take out the phones. It was plain to Jack that someone had just cut the line. He looked around him. The hangar bay was empty. The door to the far bay was open and he eyed it warily. If they had cut the line, they could be down the road, or on the other side of the far wall. He backed in through the office door, refusing to look away before he was able to close it. In years past, the 12-gauge rosewood-stocked pump-action double-barrel shotgun had seen use every winter. Now, it was lucky to get the dust blown off it once every spring. He checked the chamber and slipped two shells in, pumping it once.

The door to the office creaked loudly as he pushed it back open. He knew it had to be doubly loud if he could hear it. Pressing the stock into the crook of his shoulder, Jack moved out into the expanse of the empty hangar, his eyes glued to the open bay door. Perhaps that's why he didn't notice the man in the red coat, white shirt and slacks, straw fedora, and thick black glasses standing next to the tool chest in the hangar. Perhaps more so he reacted the way he did when the man spoke.

"Now, what are you going to do with…Jesus!"

Jack spun on his heels and let fly a round at the man, clipping his right leg. Then, the gun that had served him so well for so many years failed him. He tried to pump the second shell in and the gun jammed. The man in the red coat stared at him in disbelief, raising his own gun. Jack threw the shotgun at the man and turned to run for the open bay door. A shot rang out and Jack's hand snapped to the spot where the shot had grazed the side of his neck. He knew it was blood he was feeling slide on his fingertips, but the light of day was motivating his movement now along with the knowledge that the man in the red coat would probably not miss again. He

82

reached the edge of the open hangar door and ran smack into an anomaly.

"And where do you think you're going?"

The man who spoke was identical to the one he'd left behind in the hangar. It occurred to him that the only thing missing were the bottle-cap glasses. Then the second shot rang out and found its mark, searing through his right shoulder and knocking him forward, into the man in front of him, who looked just as shocked as Jack felt.

"What the fuck are you trying to do, kill me? He wasn't going anywhere. You could have waited until I was out of the way. Jesus…gah…"

Falling forward, Jack had grabbed the man's collar, but instead of going down, he used the last of his strength to swing a right hook at the man. It landed squarely, but hadn't done what he'd hoped. The old man had a much firmer jaw than he'd expected. Jack clung to him now, knowing that a third shot would be especially difficult.

"Let him go!" said the man behind Jack.

"I'm…not…holding him!"

"Bastard fucking well shot me!"

"Not a nice feeling, is it! Get off me!"

The second man pried Jack's hands from his coat and tossed him to the ground with ease. He'd never been a particularly big man, but Jack had gone toe to toe with bigger men than this in his time and come out on top. How this old scrawny prick was tossing him like a doll was beyond him.

But, a lot was beyond him at that moment. The wound in his shoulder was burning and he was finding it harder to breathe. The bullet must've found something important. He was on his knees now, both hands on the ground. He didn't want to die on his knees. He'd worked too hard. He raised one foot up and struggled to put his weight on it. His body was failing him.

"Tough old fuck."

"Just get it done with."

"God damn…"

"How bad is it?"

"Don't know…bad enough. Ruined a good pair of pants."

"Fuck you," Jack said gaining his feet, if not unsteadily.

"You know, I usually shoot most folks in the head. Get it done quick. Not you. You're going to suffer. Maybe get a nice woodland beasty to come out here and nibble on your old sorry ass."

"You do like to hear yourself talk, don't you," Jack said.

"Not particularly."

"Well, then–"

But Jack never finished the sentence. The man quickly raised his pistol and shot him in the back. Jack fell to the ground unceremoniously.

"I thought you were going to make him suffer?"

"Changed my mind."

"Mid sentence…that's cold."

"I'm bleeding here and he was starting to bore me."

"What now?"

"Well, your wiring is obviously suspect, so we go back and finish the job."

"I wanted to wire the porch. You said to do the screen door. Sounds like your problem not mine."

"It'll be both of our asses if any of them die."

A resounding BOOM! made them both flinch. To the southwest, a black cloud rose up from over the trees. Birds went up from the forest into the gray sky.

"What the fuck…"

"You told me to use it all."

"Are you fucking deaf? I told you to put it in the hall, this way, at worst, it would kill the kid in the basement. I ought to shoot you right now and save Sebastian the trouble of doing it himself. God dammit!"

"I clearly heard you say all. Son of a bitch."

"Are you a fucking idiot? Half a pound of C4 and you thought I said all? You're fucking dense! We'll be picking up their goddamn pieces if we're lucky. You dumb prick! Let's go."

"What about him?"

"What about him. He ain't going anywhere and, at this point, he's not my biggest concern. You shouldn't be worried about him either."

"Sebastian's going to kill me, isn't he."

"If they're dead, you'd better have a backup plan."

"You'd give me a head start?"

"And have to explain to him that you somehow got away? Doubtful. Like I said, you'd better have a backup plan."

"Maybe they're not dead."

They both looked back over the trees at the billowing black cloud rising into the sky.

"I hope you got something better than maybes. Let's go."

Chapter 11

New Kevin and Paynter had made it about half the distance between the house and the car. James had crossed about half the distance to both of them, but his warning of flight had done nothing but make them pause in their tracks. It was this action that he was about to verbally berate when the bomb wiped out, in a matter of seconds, what had taken Ted Masterson 18 months, 6 days, 12 hours, and 42 minutes to complete by himself. James was lifted off of his feet and enveloped in a deafening cavalcade that cancelled out all other sound. He felt his arms flail out for something as the world turned over, before landing hard onto the gravel drive on his left side. James' arm came up between his face and the ground, protecting him from taking one in the teeth, and the impact knocked the wind out of him. He instinctively covered his head and gulped at the dust-filled air. He could hear nothing but ringing and his eyes were watering as he choked on the air.

James felt something hard slap him in back and roll off. Debris was coming down from the blast and there was nothing he could do to protect himself. He just cowered further under his own arm trying to take in air.

He was unsure of how much time passed before the hands reached under each of his arms and pulled him to his feet. The pain that shot up his left arm made him wince and the arm that was under that side loosened its grip. The hint of voices were starting to come through the overwhelming sounds of ringing. He blinked at tears still in his eyes and brought a shaking hand up to his eyes and probably put as much dirt in as water he wiped out. His hand hurt and he held it up to examine it more closely.

"That ain't good," he said, staring at the crooked middle finger on his left hand.

The words seemed hollow, even in his own throat, as if spoken by someone else, in a cave, far away. He turned to find Paynter standing on his left. Other than a raw scratch above his left eye and a layer of dust, he looked no worse for wear. He looked at James with some concern and he might have spoken something, but the ringing in James' ears was reaching a sudden and painful aftershock crescendo. He closed his eyes against the pain. Turning to his right, he found New Kevin. To James, there was a distinct possibility that the blast had improved his appearance. Perhaps it had scared some color into spots where there had been none. He was wiggling a finger in his ear and opening his mouth, as if he'd simply experienced a pressure change.

He turned back to Paynter who was examining James' hand gingerly, particularly the finger that wasn't quite right. Paynter looked up at him, then pointed over James' shoulder. His lips moved, but James couldn't hear what he was saying. When James finally glanced over his shoulder, he felt Paynter grasp his hand firmly. The pain that followed made everything else disappear. He whipped away his hand and doubled over it, clutching the finger and resisting the urge to vomit.

"Can you stand?"

"What the fuck was that about? What the fuck did you do to my hand? God damn that hurt. God dammit."

"I fixed it," Paynter said, helping New Kevin lift James back to his feet again.

James uncovered the hand he'd been clutching, half expecting to now see blood. Though there were some abrasions he hadn't seen earlier, his finger was now perfectly straight, if not a little sore and swollen. He clenched a fist, repeatedly testing the hand. The remaining pains began to stream back into his consciousness. He wiped his eyes again and turned to look back at where the house had been.

A smoldering grove of broken logs was all that was left. There was no evidence there had ever been a second story. It seemed to James, among the smoke and flames, that the only thing remaining was the desk that had stood in his uncle's office.

"Bastards," James said, sticking a finger in his ear at an equally futile attempt to hear better.

"That ain't the half of it," Paynter said.

"Huh?" James said.

Both New Kevin and Paynter were facing the other way. James turned.

"Fuck me," James said.

Equidistant as the house had been to them, the pickup sat in the middle of the gravel driveway, a smoking mess in its own right. As if tossed there by a giant playing lawn darts, a solitary log had impaled itself through the hood of Barbara's truck.

"How does that even happen, man?" New Kevin asked.

"Couldn't do it if you tried," Paynter said.

"Fuck me," James hissed again.

"James, what's in that boat house?"

"Ummm...whaddya think? A boat?" James said, not turning from the wreckage of the car.

"And the keys for that boat?"

"On a hook, just inside the boat house door, where they always were," James said.

"C'mon," Paynter said.

"Where are we going? How the hell are we going to get anywhere in a boat?"

"It's a big lake, we'll find something. Point is, we can't stay here. Even out here, someone will have heard or seen that. Not long before something resembling the authorities will be here."

James turned back to the house. He reached down suddenly, grabbed a handful of gravel and threw it at the house.

"You...bastards! Mother...fucking...bastards!"

"Easy, man," New Kevin said as he pulled James back from grabbing another handful. "Nothing you can do about it now."

"They're taking everything I've ever cared about and destroying it, right in front of my eyes. Why?"

"Because you have so much to destroy," New Kevin said.

James turned and looked into his brother's eyes. They were void of anything resembling emotion. He'd said it not out of a sense of knowing, but as a matter of fact.

"How can you say that? You don't even know me," James said.

Through busted lips, New Kevin smiled for the first time since James had met him.

"I know what you're not," New Kevin said.

James just frowned back at him and turned to Paynter. They made their way through a field of debris, past several remnants of window and even what appeared to be a part of the kitchen sink.

"Just had to close that screen door, didn't you," Paynter muttered.

"That supposed to be funny?" James asked.

"Kevin's not here…," Paynter started, then cut his sentence short.

"Huh?" New Kevin said.

"Nothing," James said.

Despite its distance from the blast, the boat house had not come through the blast unscathed. Each of the small windows in the door and the side of the small building had blown out. James reached for the door, only to have Paynter stay his hand.

"Let's not tempt fate," Paynter said.

"You're gonna give me a complex," James said.

"At least you'll be alive."

They examined the doorway and surrounding siding, searching for any sign of wires or explosives. There were none. Still, James now hesitated as he as he reached for the door again. He waited for the beep, knowing that the ringing in his ears would drown out any sound that faint. The blast would be mercifully quick in dispatching him. It didn't come. They'd obviously determined that one explosion should do the trick.

James stepped into a wholly unfamiliar environment. The boat house, which had always been capable of housing multiple boats, was now filled to capacity, but not with any kind of boat he had ever seen before. Paynter and New Kevin stepped in behind him.

"What the fuck is this?" James asked.

A large tarp stretched from one side of the house to the other, obscuring whatever lie in the middle. James moved around on the walkway to the far side of the room, ducking under bungees and ropes that hung down and supported the tarp. He pulled at one, letting the tarp fall, revealing what was clearly the tail of a plane.

"What the fuck is this?" James repeated.

"Looks like a plane," New Kevin said.

They coordinated to pull off the remainder of the tarp, which slipped into the water at the side of the seaplane. The bright yellow plane dominated the building and James had a hard time believing it could even fit out of the doors to the lake. James ran his hand across the smooth, immaculate edge of the wing closest to him.

"I didn't know Ted could fly," James said to no one.

"There's probably a lot you didn't know about your uncle," Paynter said.

"Apparently," James said.

"What do we do now?" New Kevin asked.

"We fly," Paynter said.

"No thanks. I'd rather die quickly here on the ground than screaming all the way to it."

"It's not that hard," Paynter said, hopping over to the pontoon on the pilot's side.

"You gotta be kidding me," James said.

"Get the doors," Paynter said, sliding up into the seat and getting a feel for the location of the instruments.

"You're telling me you can fly a plane," James said.

Paynter stopped what he was doing and turned to face James.

"When you're chased for twenty years, you learn how to run any way you can."

Chapter 12

"James isn't going to kill anyone," Ted said.

He was sitting across from Nicole at a small folding table. The table and the two chairs in which they sat were the only objects that seemed out of place in the middle of the small barn they had been taken too. She blinked tears out of her eyes back at him and reached down to shift the ankle monitor that had been so unceremoniously clamped to her leg. She looked away from Ted and glanced around the barn. The earth beneath their feet was near stone after years of foot traffic. There was still hay in some of the stalls. A sturdy ladder led up into a loft that ran the width of the building. Blindfolded and marched across what Nicole could only describe as a wide-open space, she and Ted had been unblinded, unshackled, and given the anklets. She wiped away a tear on her sleeve.

"If you had told me that five days ago, I would have said you needed treatment. Today, I'm not so sure," Nicole said.

"Sebastian doesn't have that kind of power," Ted said.

"Doesn't he? He's killed a bunch of people, including a U.S. Senator, and managed to blame James each time! Doesn't that show just a little bit of control and power? He's assembled a small army here and worked in anonymity. And now he has James by...," Nicole said.

"...the balls," Ted finished.

The door to the barn swung open and both Nicole and Uncle Ted started out of their chairs.

"Don't get up," the redcoat, who had pushed the door in, said.

Two men, both dressed in white and an inch shorter than Nicole, followed behind him. One carried linen and the other carried what appeared to Nicole to be place settings. The redcoat remained by the door, his arms folded across his chest. He glanced at Nicole before looking away with what might have been a blush. He pulled his hat tighter to his brow. She watched as the two men approached the table and set it, as if they were in a restaurant. They muttered to one another in a low tone in French and neither man made eye contact with either Nicole or Uncle Ted. Nicole saw Ted's eyes follow the round-tip butter knives to the table. She was sure he could probably kill both men with or without a blunt metal instrument, but they both knew it would get them nowhere. The table cloth was pristine and stark against the rustic surroundings. The two men disappeared back around the doorway and returned a moment later carrying silver serving trays. They placed the trays in their respective places and poured glasses of water and what appeared to be red wine. They then pulled out the chairs.

"Mademoiselle," the man closest to her said, gesturing to the chair.

Nicole stared at him, but he refused to meet her gaze. She looked over at Uncle Ted who shrugged and invited her to sit. She did so and flinched a bit as the man swooped in and deftly placed the napkin on her lap. They both made a short bow.

"Bon a petit," they said in unison.

They turned and left the barn, muttering again in French. The redcoat pulled the barn door closed behind him as they left without another word.

"It smells magnificent," Nicole said.

"I haven't had a warm meal in almost two days now," Uncle Ted said.

"You think it's drugged?" Nicole asked.

"I wouldn't bet against it, but I'm not sure they'd need to bother at this point," Uncle Ted said.

"Not like I'm hiding anything. And, it's not like we can go anywhere," she said.

Ted lifted the lid on his tray. A cloud of steam revealed a plate of carrots, rice pilaf, and what appeared to be a beef stew. He lifted a fork and prodded the beef.

"Hopefully not made from the last captive," Uncle Ted said, raising an eyebrow.

"My mouth is watering. This is cruel. No! Wait!"

Nicole raised her hand to her mouth to stifle a small scream as Ted had speared a piece of the meat and quickly shoved it in his mouth. He chewed thoughtfully and swallowed with a sound of contentment, licking his lips. He glanced at Nicole and raised his glass of water.

"If it's poison, it's the slow kind," he said.

"That's not funny," she said still looking at him with unease.

"Nicole, I'm fine. You heard him. They need us…for now. Why bother with the ruse of anklets if they're going to poison us?"

Nicole whipped the cover off of her plate and lifted her fork. Steamed broccoli, mashed potatoes, and grilled chicken. They ate with silence of speech and noise of voracity. When she felt that the bite on the fork would no longer fit, she glanced sideways at the glass of wine.

"Maybe just a sip," she said.

"All you. I quit the stuff years ago," Uncle Ted said.

Nicole raised the glass to her lips and sniffed before taking a small sip and swishing it around her mouth. She swallowed and felt the warmth of the liquid run through her. She took another larger sip. She knew it was a lie her body was telling her, but she felt good. An ounce of the tension came out of her shoulders with each sip and it was hard to put the glass down for what it offered. Drinking suddenly made more sense to her now than it ever had; if she could just keep this feeling, it would all be better. It was the biggest lie of all.

She finished the glass and accepted when Uncle Ted offered her his glass. They both sat back in their chairs. The silence was broken by the clatter of the wooden barn doors being pushed open. The two men came in to the barn pushing a small cart on whose wheels rattled against the packed dirt floor. They moved swiftly around the table and cleared it to the cart. One eyed the full glass of wine before reaching for it.

Nicole raised her hand for him to leave it and he did. The two men left again just as quickly as they had come.

The redcoat came in just after they had passed out of sight.

"Sebastian would like a word," he said.

"A king who asks permission from the prisoners in his own dungeon stinks of insincerity," Nicole said.

"What she said," Ted answered.

"I'll take that as a no," the redcoat said, and moved to close the doors.

Nicole chuckled.

"What's he playing at? If he wants a word, he can take it or not. It's not like we're going anywhere," she said.

She felt the warmth of the wine feeding her words. She was feeling sleepy and a bit drunk and the total absurdity of everything that had happened and that was possibly *going* to happen was beginning to sink in. Their captor was crazy and they were all caught up in this madness he had created.

"Bring him in for Christ's sake! Let's have a little entertainment before bed!" she shouted, surprising the redcoat and Ted.

Sebastian entered, having been waiting just around the corner. He was smiling at Nicole as if amused by her outburst. He'd changed since their last meeting. He wore worn blue jeans and several cream-colored thermal tops covered by a thickly-padded burnt orange vest. When he stopped next to the table, he placed one tired-looking brown boot up on the chair seat next to Nicole. He leaned down on his knee, still smiling.

"Well?" Nicole asked.

"I can see why he likes you. You're everything he isn't. Spit and fire on the surface to cover up the calculating interior monologue," he said.

"You've got it all figured out, don't you?" she said.

"No. That's the best part. I'm not much of a planner. I actually make up most of it as I go along. Make a move and see what presents itself. So much easier than hoping something works out the way you planned, especially when it most often doesn't," Sebastian said.

"Commitment issues. I get it," she said.

He laughed.

"Ever the analyst, aren't you? What next? Mommy didn't hug me enough? Daddy didn't care? If only my youth had been given a little more guidance, we wouldn't be here right now," Sebastian said.

"No, I don't blame your parents. Some people manage fucked up all on their lonesome," Nicole said, the corner of her mouth rising slightly.

Ted made an effort to cough over his snicker, but it didn't fool anyone.

"I'm glad you've managed to keep your humor through this," Sebastian said, the once-colorful air now gone from his tone.

"You either laugh or cry, right?" she said.

She picked up the glass of wine and raised it to Sebastian in a silent mock toast before taking a large mouthful, swishing it across her tongue, and swallowing with a look of pleasure. She wiped her mouth with the back of her hand more for effect than anything else. Sebastian's demeanor did not change. He cleared his throat before speaking.

"You've been outfitted with tracking devices. Should you leave the property, the devices will allow us to track you down to within five feet," he said.

"Impressive," Ted said.

"However, you've got full reign of the farm. I have no locked doors. No authorized personnel signs to be seen. You'll find no resistance from any of the men on the farm. If you do, I want you to report them to me. Despite what you may think, you're my guests and you'll be treated as such," he said.

"Don't fool yourself. Guests don't wear collars," Nicole said.

"I'll admit, that's a bit unorthodox. Perhaps there will come a day when I care little whether you run away, but that day is not now. You're my insurance plan," he said.

"Said the man who claims to not have a plan," Nicole said.

"I may not have a plan, but I like to stack the deck in my favor. There's a difference. Anyway, there it is. If you need me, you only have to ask. There's two beds in the loft above. Should be private enough, but let me know," Sebastian said, his tone returning to one of casual indifference.

"Can we expect room service every day?" Ted asked.

"Unless it bothers you, the men eat in the mess hall. It's the building at the far end of the compound. Breakfast is at 7. Lunch at noon. Dinner at 5."

"Sans the steak and wine," Nicole said, pretending to pout a little.

"True. The fatted calf was killed to honor your arrival. Maybe we'll throw another little party when James arrives."

She was surprised at how easily the glass shattered against the table as she brought it down upon the edge, but she was even more surprised at how quickly Sebastian grabbed her arm as she swung the ragged stem at his head. His thumb pressed in against the bones in her wrist and he twisted, forcing her down toward the ground. She screamed.

"You're breaking my wrist!"

"Drop it," he said calmly.

"You're hurting me," she screamed again.

"Ted, remain seated. Nicole, for the love of God, drop the glass," Sebastian said.

She obeyed and he released her arm and took a step back. He adjusted his vest and pulled at the cuffs of his shirt. Nicole rubbed her wrist and backed away. The redcoat had advanced to Ted's side of the table, but held his ground. Apparently, he knew when his boss needed his help and when he didn't.

"Well, now, I knew you were spirited, but a killer? Interesting. I have pushed you to the edge, haven't I? Fair enough. I won't hold it against you. Just do me a favor? Don't go around trying to kill anyone else, hmmm? They might be prone to give you more than a bruised arm for your efforts," he said.

"Don't believe for one moment that I will treat you like anything other than a captor. If I get another chance to hurt you, you can be certain I'll take it," Nicole said.

"Noted," Sebastian said.

He turned and left the barn without a word. The redcoat only hesitated momentarily before doing the same. It was only after she was positive they had walked away from the barn that she ran into Ted's arms and began to sob into his chest.

Chapter 13

The next day, Nicole and Ted made their way across the dimly-lit compound to the building that had been identified as the mess hall. Even though it was not quite 7 AM, the compound was still. However, as soon as they opened the door to the hall, they were met with the sound of chatter and laughter. A redcoat seated at a desk just inside the door barely looked up when they entered.

Nicole couldn't help but take a moment to stare in wonder at the man who sat at the desk. It was the first time she'd seen one of them without their hat and coat on. It was hard for her to comprehend that this person was actually younger than James; younger than her. He sat staring at a computer monitor in the same fashion she'd seen her grandfather do it. Biting his bottom lip, he tilted his head up to look through the bottom of the glasses perched precariously on his nose. She glanced at the screen, realizing that he'd increased the size of the font to the point of ridicule. She could have read the screen from across the room and here he was squinting at it from a foot away.

"Fuckin' Yankees," he muttered before turning quickly in her direction. "Help you?"

"Umm...no. Breakfast is that way?" Nicole said, somewhat embarrassed that she'd been caught.

"Yep. Better get in there. Sixty boys don't leave too many leftovers," he said, pushing his glasses back up his nose.

"Sifty? Six-oh? Sifty boys?" Nicole said.

"Give or take a boy. Some of 'em don't look like boys anymore, but you can bet they are. Not quite as handsome as me, but there's barely a man amongst 'em," he said, smiling with perfect dentures.

Nicole returned to Ted who had moved toward the doorway to the cafeteria. She hesitated toward the door when Ted moved.

"You ok?" he asked.

"I'm not sure I want to see what's in there," she said.

"Boys. Little boys," he said.

She took a deep breath and stepped forward as Ted pulled the door open. The effect was immediate. The chatter stopped and, for Nicole, it felt as if the heat had been turned up. She stopped a step inside the doorway and glanced around the room at the eyes that were fixed on her; nearly fifty pairs. She had expected to see more James clones. She just hadn't expected to see quite the range of ages. There he was as a ten-year-old, a few pimple-faced teens, some sporting the first signs of facial hair. And one, just near the back of the room that looked just as he had on the day they had met. She wanted to smile at him, but memories of her encounter in the basement were too fresh. Though the incident had disturbed her, she quietly hoped that boy was still alive in this room. The cynic in her said told her that he was elsewhere.

There were also several "not James" in the room. All with a slightly familiar look to them. A table of what appeared to be older men at the far side of the room pulled the hoods from their sweatshirts up over their heads and avoided looking her way. At the head of the table, Sebastian stood up and gestured to two empty seats at a table adjacent to his. Nicole made her way around the tables of quietly staring boys. As she passed, a young boy, who looked about ten reached out and touched her hand as she passed. The reaction around him was immediate. Apparently, they had been warned about touching the guests. Nicole glanced quickly at Sebastian for a response, but his face was blank and he stood with a mild look of amusement on his face. Nicole turned back to the book and took his hand into hers.

"How do you do," she said.

The boy squeezed her hand gently, but in a way that told her that his intention was to feel her hand and the act of shaking it was a perfectly acceptable method to do so. He released her hand as quickly as he had grasped it, but made an effort to let his fingers linger across her palm as he withdrew his hand.

"My name's Nicole," she said.

He stared up into her face, appearing to take it all in.

"I'm sorry," he said, in a manner that was too old for the body that she saw before her.

"Why?" Nicole asked.

"My brothers shouldn't stare. We don't get many visitors," he said.

His articulation was like that of some professors she'd had in college. She tried not to think about it.

"It's ok. It doesn't bother me," she said.

"You're very beautiful," he said.

Nicole blushed. Apparently, the sweet-talking gene was strong.

"What's your name?" she asked.

"Tollgate, uh…Tollgate. Yeah, Tollgate," he said.

"Tollgate, hmm? Well, Tollgate, it was a pleasure to meet you," Nicole said.

He smiled and Nicole suddenly felt very lonely. She turned away from the boy and continued on to the seat Sebastian had indicated. Only after she had sat down did the room begin to murmur again. In moments, it was almost back to the dull roar she had heard upon entering the room. The occasional head would pop up at the table and glance at her. The boys nearest to her kept their heads and eyes down and fixed on the food on their plate. The smell of bacon returned her focus to how hungry she was. As if on cue, the two men in white who had served them the night before appeared with piled-high plates, cups, and a jug of orange juice.

"Coffee monsieur? No? Mademoiselle?"

"Yes, thanks," Nicole said.

"Oui, Madame," he said.

Nicole watched as Ted dug into the food before him. He kept his head down and focused his energy on his task. He had a bit of a nervous energy about him that Nicole had never seen before. She turned her head and caught Sebastian watching her and smiling. She frowned and turned her attention back to Ted.

A bead of sweat was beginning to form at the edge of his temple.

"Are you ok?"

Ted's eyes darted Nicole's way but quickly returned to his plate.

"It's like a bad dream come true," Ted muttered as close to under his breath as he could.

"But you knew about this," Nicole said.

"Not this many and not this young. He's obviously still producing, which means he's got an active lab. And those boys with the hoods. I've seen every one of those faces before. They couldn't hide 'em quick enough. Presidents, vice presidents, premiers," Ted said.

"Boys?" Nicole asked.

She glanced back over at the head table as she put a forkful of egg into her mouth. They all sat with the same posture; hunched over their plate with their hood pulled far over their head. But, their bodies didn't match the visage. They were lean and long. They were James. They were James with different faces. She shivered and had a hard time swallowing the food in her mouth.

"What has he done?" she hissed.

A boy next to her gave her a look of concern, but looked away again immediately.

"It's what they were planning," Ted said.

"I don't understand," Nicole said.

"Now isn't the time," he said.

Nicole put her fork down and took a sip from her coffee. A chime sounded and the clatter of utensils hitting the plate was nearly in unison. Every boy in the room stood at the same time, turned from their chair, pushed it in, picked up their plate and stood patiently in line to put them on trays near the kitchen. Every boy filed out of the room and Nicole, Ted, and Sebastian.

"Not hungry?" Sebastian said.

"You're a monster," she said.

Sebastian stood up from his chair and pushed it back under the table. He drummed his fingers on the back of the chair.

"You'd rather see them in a government lab?" he proposed.

"Do they know? Do they understand what you're turning them into? Do they understand you're turning them into pawns?"

"Does a child know it's being taught to walk?"

"You disgust me," she said.

"I'm sorry you don't see things my way yet," he said.

"You're walking a dangerous line," Ted chimed in.

"Dangerous," Sebastian mocked. "The U.S. government didn't seem to find it dangerous. I didn't make the toys, I just stole them."

"You're playing God," Nicole said.

"Don't you dare talk to me about playing God, young lady! You seem to be forgetting who the first victim was here. But, I'm not looking for any tears here. Those days are done."

She wanted to push him some more. Wanted to see the layers slowly peel away from the calm exterior and expose the vulnerability.

"So, you've moved on from the anger, but when it came time to negotiate your anger, you chose the opposite path of integration," she said.

His left eyebrow rose and Nicole couldn't help but see James. She looked away from him.

"You think you've got it all figured out, don't you? So smart. So sure of yourself. But, you seem to forget who has the position of power here. In more ways than one. I can look at you with complete disregard for who you are. You're just another pawn in my game. You, on the other hand…you can't look at me without seeing him, can you? We even have some of the same ticks and nuances. Amazing, isn't it? Kinda creepy even. Try surrounding yourself with fifty replicas. You'll have a grasp of what creepy really means. My point is this. You may raise the dagger to my eye, but would you be able to follow through? Would you be able to strike down the likeness of your lover? And, if so…how do you think you'd react the next time you saw him? How do you think it would make you feel?"

"Wanna find out?" Nicole hissed.

"Not today," Sebastian said.

Nicole watched him walk across the room toward the doors before he turned back to them.

"You are still my guests, despite your lack of cordiality. You still have all of the freedom that the property provides. I

111

hope you'll take a look around and see what we do here," he said and left before either Ted or Nicole had a chance to respond.

Ted wiped his forehead with a napkin and sat back in his seat. He sighed deeply and looked more tired than Nicole had ever seen him. He cleared his throat.

"Sitting here, knowing what he's doing...I could have stopped it all," he said.

"You can't blame yourself," she said, reaching across the table and placing her hand on his. It was clammy.

"I've lived with the guilt of those days on my head for a long time, but sitting in this room...surrounded by those boys. I...it was like an old nightmare come true," he said.

They turned at the sound of the door they had entered through, but there was no one there. The door eased back into place with little more than a metallic squeak.

"Hello?" Nicole called.

"I think it's time for us to go," Ted said.

"Wait, tell me about those others. Why did they look like that? Those faces. You said presidents and vice presidents?" Nicole asked.

"They're replacements, Nicole. He's molding them to look like world leaders so that he can replace them," he said.

She allowed the words to sink into her head. It was laughable. It wasn't possible. You just couldn't swap people out.

"He can't," Nicole said.

112

"You don't sound so sure," Ted said.

"It's not possible," she said.

"I don't think he shares your opinion," he said.

"He's already done it, you know."

The high-pitched voice came at them so unexpectedly that they both jumped. The small boy standing over Nicole's shoulder looked fixedly at her without expression.

"Tollgate? You're probably not supposed to be here…wait…what?" Nicole said.

"You're not supposed to be here either," the boy said nodding his head vigorously, but still not changing his expression.

"What was that other bit you said?" Ted asked.

The boy didn't take his gaze off of Nicole.

"He's already done it. He's sent some of the older boys out. Some of the boys with the other faces," Tollgate said.

"Where?" Nicole asked.

"Everywhere," Tollgate said.

Chapter 14

It was 7:53 AM when the sun peeked up over the dash of the car and into Norris' eyes. He glanced at his watch and determined that he had managed about five hours of sleep since stopping. Sitting up, he assessed his surroundings. The rest area just off of interstate 65 near Munfordville, Kentucky, had seemed like a beacon in the night when he'd seen the signs. He was exhausted and though he could have easily kept sleeping, he knew they had to keep moving; *he* had to keep moving. If he was still moving, he wasn't dead.

Taylor was still out and the man in black was feigning sleep in the back seat. He was leaning awkwardly in the corner, his arms still cuffed behind his back. He hadn't resisted Norris after their scuffle in the back seat, but it didn't make him any more trustworthy.

"You can stop the act," Norris said, eyeing him in the rear view mirror.

The man didn't open his eyes, but a crooked smile flash across his face.

"Could never fool you, Rich."

"Try as you might."

"What are you gonna do with me, Rich? You can't turn me in. You've got nothing on me. We both know that. And you can't keep me forever," the man said.

"Can't I?"

"I'd outlive you."

"Not if I can help it."

"Rich, you've spent the last thirty years hating my guts. Why?"

Norris turned in his seat and looked back at the man. The question had sounded sincere and the look on the man's face read the same. He turned back to the wheel and drummed it quietly with his thumbs.

"You don't deserve an answer."

"I don't think you have one," the man said.

Norris smiled despite himself.

"You think I'm a machine? That I haven't taken a moment to examine my own life and what it means? Or are you just afraid I won't tell…"

"Rich, we both already know you're a machine. An old and broken machine, but a machine nonetheless."

"You know enough about me to know why I entered the academy. Just like every other young prick, I started out seeking justice," Norris said.

"Until you found out justice was bullshit."

"Justice, in the sense that everyone imagines, is bullshit. And the kind of justice that isn't bullshit, well, they're not concerned with."

"Only if it affects the bottom line," the man said.

"I lost that drive and you gave it back to me," Norris said.

"But you'd lost that drive long before Maggie," the man said, leaning forward in the back seat.

116

"Maybe I had, but you certainly helped to reinforce what I'd learned. Gave me a goal. Gave me a reason to get up in the morning."

"And Liz was lost in all that," the man said.

"Liz had been lost to me long before that, but you didn't help. I let you consume me because I needed a way out. It was easy to blame you, but I knew it was just a cover."

"Jesus, Rich…"

"Oh, don't pretend that you care. Don't even!"

At this, Dr. Taylor startled awake in the seat next to Norris. He looked around as if he expected the men to be locked in combat again.

"You didn't always hate me, Rich. And, yeah… maybe I've given you no reason to care, but it's a bit hard to think that you blamed me for your woes because you needed a fucking grail to crusade for. I had to leave the goddamn country because of you. You just wouldn't let it go… and for what? Not because you wanted justice served, even in your own warped definition of the word, but because you needed a reason to fucking well live. I may have been a bastard, but I never pretended to be something I wasn't. And even after all these years, I never took what you did to me personally. I guess I was wrong. That's pretty fucking low."

Norris spun around in his seat, pulled the revolver from his jacket pocket, and pointed it at the man.

"So would killing an unarmed, cuffed man in the backseat of his own car. Conversation over."

117

"Am I interrupting something?" Dr. Taylor asked.

"You're shouting again, Doc!" The man in black said.

"You're not interrupting anything, Dr. Taylor. We were just…reminiscing," Norris said.

"The good old days," the man said from the back seat.

"Some memories are best left alone," Norris said.

"That's ok, I was done with the small talk. Now I gotta piss like a racehorse," the man said.

"Forget it," Norris said.

"You're seriously going to let me piss myself? In my own back seat? You're a colder bastard than I thought, Rich."

Norris looked back over his shoulder, then turned back and considered his hands on the wheel.

"Would stink the place up something fierce, I'm sure," Norris said.

This was followed by a short laugh that quickly turned into a series of coughs. Norris struggled to find his remaining handkerchief and pressed it against his mouth, clinging to the steering wheel for added support as the fit wracked his body. When it had passed, he glanced into the folded cloth in his hand out of habit and quickly tucked it into his coat pocket, no longer fearing what he might see, but not wanting to share the discovery either. He caught Dr. Taylor looking away quickly out of the corner of his eye.

"What?" Norris said.

"Nothing, but if you're done, I still gotta piss."

"Fuck you and your bladder," Norris said.

But, glancing in the rearview mirror he could see that the man had begun to rock ever so slightly and sweat was forming at his temple. And, as much as this gave him great pleasure, he also knew that a mess wasn't what he needed right now.

"Doc? I imagine you might have to use the facilities as well?"

Dr. Taylor nodded.

"Ok. We're gonna play this like we're just a couple of agents escorting a prisoner. Any funny business and I shoot you, got it?" Norris said.

"Did you just say you'd shoot me?" Dr. Taylor asked.

"Him, Dr. Taylor. Not you," Norris said, raising his voice and thumbing in the direction of the back seat.

"I hear you. Let's go… please," the man said.

"Please? Jesus Christ… now I've heard it all."

Norris and Dr. Taylor got out of the car. The rest area was vast and pretty empty of cars. The truck parking lot, on the other hand was well stocked. Red, yellow, blue, black, and even green trailers were scattered amongst the sea of eighteen wheelers idling on the other side of the flat median. Between the two lots were an information center and a rest room on either side. Norris had been sure to park close to the nearest rest room. He stepped around to Taylor's side and assessed the distance from the car to the rest room door. He reached in and pulled Taylor's seat forward, grabbing the man's feet where he had tied them. He glanced at the man and cut the large plastic zip-tie with the knife from his pocket and retrieved three more

119

zip-ties. He attached one around one ankle, then one around the other and connected the two with the third, giving the man enough room to step, but not enough to run. He then hauled the man up from behind the seat, allowing him to lean on him.

"Glad you keep a stash of ties in the trunk. See, we do have something in common. Let's go."

The three men moved quickly to the door of the rest room with Dr. Taylor in the lead. Apparently, his desire to use the restroom was bordering on that of their captive. When the door opened, they were met with an overwhelming air of feces.

"Oh, I'm so glad I have some friends to share this experience with," the man said.

"Shut up and get to your business," Norris said, pointing to the urinal.

They watched as Taylor slipped into one of the stalls, followed by the sound of a zipper and belt buckle. Norris watched as the man in black turned to face him.

"You gonna pull down my fly and pop my dick out of my pants?"

"God dammit," Norris said.

"Not to mention that, but… I think I might need to drop a deuce," the man said.

"You've got such a way with words," Norris said.

"Well, it's gonna be a moot fucking point in a minute. For fuck's sake, I'm starting to get emotional here!"

Norris thought a moment, then gestured to the second stall.

"Get in the stall, close the door and squat down so I can cut the tie. Do your business and we'll repeat the process before you come out. You touch that door before I get the cuffs back on you and I'll shoot you. Am I understood?"

But, the man had already entered the stall and followed his instructions by the time he finished speaking. Norris located the gun in his coat pocket for his own sense of security and withdrew the knife. He reached down and slipped the blade across the plastic tie. What followed was a comedy of sounds involving zippers and belts and groans and considerable splashing and an audible whisper of "That was fucking close." For a brief moment, Norris considered taking a moment to complete his business, but decided that he would feel better doing so once the man was back in the car and secured. That was when the trucker walked in.

Norris wasn't sure, but it could have been that the man had to duck upon entering the rest room. His John Deere hat sat atop a head of curly brown hair. He was easily seven foot tall and weighed, in Norris' estimation, over 300 pounds. His jean jacket had a Harley Davidson logo on the shoulder and the matching t-shirt beneath it bulged at the man's enormous waistline, which was adorned with a belt buckle the size of Norris' head. The stitching on the breast pocket of the jacket told everyone his name was Jim. Jim did a double take at seeing Norris leaning against one of the sinks outside the stall.

"Mornin'," he said.

"Uh…mornin'," Norris echoed.

Norris glanced at the stalls nervously. All sound had ceased from the man's stall and he heard the familiar sound of a toilet tissue roll issuing from Dr. Taylor's. His hand went back into the coat pocket to find the revolver. Trucker Jim gave Norris another look, looked over to the stalls, and apparently satisfied, stepped up to a urinal. What followed reminded Norris of using a garden hose to wash his car. As the hose sound tapered off, there was a moment of silence in the small odiferous bathroom, right before Dr. Taylor hit the floor.

It was so quick that all Norris heard was the thud of Taylor's head against the side of the stall, followed quickly by the slap of the side of his face smacking the brick colored tile floor. The tinkle of glass and the air going out of the doctor's lungs quickly followed. Norris jumped and immediately slammed himself against the door to the man's stall. It was locked. Norris had been distracted enough to let him lock it without notice. He backed up and kicked at it, but the force simply jarred the neighboring door open, revealing a pants-down, boxers thankfully up, semiconscious Dr. Taylor being dragged feet first into the next stall; the man's hands grabbing for Dr. Taylor's coat pocket. The one, Norris was realizing, that carried the gun from the man's glove compartment.

Norris threw himself into the stall, kicking at the man's hand, and pulling back on Dr. Taylor before a large hand pushed him to the back of the stall. He stood, frozen, staring back at the imposing man who looked at him, dumbfounded.

"I knew it. A bunch of faggots! What in God's holy name are you faggots doin'?!"

Without waiting for an answer, the trucker reached in and, with one jerk, removed Norris bodily from the stall, tossing him into the corner by the sink. He then opened the neighboring stall door with little effort and caught the man in black by the collar in mid-leap. The man appeared to be somewhat surprised by the size of his new foe, but recovered quickly enough to reengage. He swung both arms down, chopping the giant man's neck on either side. And, while an average-sized man might have collapsed under such blows, or at least dropped his prey, Trucker Jim merely grew angrier. He reared back his free hand to strike, which was when Norris saw his opening. He didn't usually resort to such tactics, but it wasn't often he had a raging bull as an opponent. His well-aimed kick succeeded where the man's blows had not. Big Jim gagged hard, throwing the man in black to the ground in violent response. His hands flew to his groin and he sputtered obscenities at them as he sank to his knees.

"Fucking faggots…oh, God. Uhnnn!"

The man in black found himself on top of Dr. Taylor and by the time Norris had his gun out, they were standing, face-to-face, guns drawn on one another.

"Son of a bitch," Norris said.

"Is that the best you have for me, you old fuck?"

"Cocksucker," Norris said.

"That's a little more like it. But, we wouldn't want to give big Jim here the wrong impression, would we? Oh, wait… he's already gotten the wrong impression. Haven't you, big Jim!"

Jim groaned in response.

"You're not getting your car back," Norris said.

"You can have it. I'm taking the rest of this trip in style… aren't I, Jim."

Trucker Jim seemed to have caught on to the gist of the conversation and swung a meaty fist in the direction of the man in black. The man was ready, however, and caught the hand and quickly put it behind Trucker Jim's back all while keeping his gun aimed at Norris. Even Norris had to admit the man had talent. And poor Trucker Jim seemed to have lost all of his fight.

"You really did a number on him, Rich. Poor big dumb ox. He was only trying to do God's work. You know, stopping a bunch of faggots from fuckin' in a rest area. Can't have faggots running around rest stops dirtying the place up."

He followed this comment with a deep inhale of breath.

"Yep, it was smelling like roses in here before we came in and faggoted the place all up. Which truck is yours, Jimbo?"

"Fuck you," Trucker Jim said.

The man cupped one hand and quickly slapped Trucker's Jim's right ear, sending the big man sideways with a wail of pain.

"Now, I know it's out there running. Which one is it, and what's your security code? C'mon, chubby britches. Before I do something I regret. No one's paying me to kill you, but it wouldn't be the first time I worked all pro bono like."

"Fuck...Aigh!"

At the sound of the letter *f* coming out of Trucker Jim's mouth, the man's gun hand flashed down and a round was deposited into the meaty flesh of the back of Trucker Jim's right calf. The report was like a cannon going off in the small, highly acoustic room. At this, he rolled over, clutching the leg and howling in pain.

"Aw, shut up ya big fuckin' sissy. Jesus Christ, who the hell are you calling faggots? I bet I didn't even hit bone."

The man raised the gun at Norris and took a step forward.

"You tell him to do what I say, or I'll make it worse for all of you," the man said.

"Jim, you got insurance?" Norris asked.

The big man appeared to nod.

"Tell him what he wants. You'll get your truck back and then some. It ain't worth it."

"Just... jus' leave the picture of ma wife and kids."

"Aw, now don't try and make me feel bad," the man said.

"That would require a heart," Norris said.

"You wound me, Rich. Right here," he said, tapping his chest.

The man in black crouched down and watched Norris as Trucker Jim relayed his details. He then stood and backed his way to the door. He adjusted the newsboy cap on his head and Norris could see the crooked smile return.

125

"I'm behind schedule, Rich. No time to fuck around anymore. I'll see you in Nawlins, I'm sure."

"Right before the flash," Norris said.

The man in black winked at him and ducked out the door to the rest room. Norris lowered his shaking arm and slipped the pistol back into his pocket. He surveyed the scene before him. Dr. Taylor was still lying face down. Norris considered the fact that he was blinking a good sign. Trucker Jim had regained some of his composure and was pulling a cell phone out of his pocket. He caught Norris looking at him.

"You a cop?"

"FBI."

"I fucked up, didn't I."

"I think it was a combined effort."

"Why the hell didn't you just shoot him?"

Norris shook his head and turned his palms up, his voice failing in his throat. Trucker Jim wouldn't understand the truth. Norris wasn't sure he even understood it, but the words came out anyway.

"Cuz he's the last fox…after that, I'll just be chasing my own tail."

Chapter 15

Christopher Collingswood stared at the handwritten note his mother had left him. It was on the kitchen counter and he scratched his ass as he read it. "Chris, please remember to take out the garbage. And, make sure Murphy doesn't crap on the back doormat again when you let him out. I found another turd there yesterday! Sunday's leftovers are in the fridge. I'll be back tomorrow night. Maybe look through the want ads if you get a chance. Love you. MOM."

Chris turned and looked down at the Bassett Hound at his feet. The dog looked up at him in mournful adulation.

"I thought we had a deal, Murph? No more shittin' on the back step," he said.

The dog merely wagged his tale in anticipation. Chris scratched the dog's head and went to the fridge. He cocked back the milk carton and wiped the white froth from his lip with the neck of the t-shirt he wore. The black shirt was splashed with an angry blond boy with spiky hair in an orange jumpsuit, proclaiming an apparently loud anime phrase.

"C'mon, Murph," Chris said, and the little dog followed him to the back door.

"Now, go on, go do your business out on the rocks," he said and pointed across the back yard.

The dog stepped over his petrified stool from the previous day and trotted out, around the natural form in-ground pool, to the rocks that made up the "yard." He sniffed around the base of the cactus by the fence.

Chris shivered, and rubbed his arm a little. It wasn't what he'd call cold, but upper fifties was still a bit chilly to be out in boxers and a t-shirt. "C'mon, Murph! That cactus smells just like it did yesterday…like your piss! Stupid—"

The ring of the doorbell made him jump. He waved off the dog, leaving the door open enough for him to nose in, and plunged back through the house, searching for a pair of pants.

"Just a minute!" The bell rang again. "Hold on! I'll be right there!" He slipped into the wind pants as he arrived at the door. Peeking through the peephole, he stepped back, rubbed his eyes, then looked again. The two men were saying something low under their breath, but both had turned away. Not Jehovah's witnesses, he thought. Not today. But, he pulled open the door, despite his uncertainty. Murphy bellowed from the back yard. His mother had called him, at times, the worst watch dog on the face of the planet…and the best. Angry hordes could be knocking on the door, threatening rape and abuse and the dog would sit and wag his tale perpetually. But, the moment the threshold was breached by friend or foe, the dog would go into full guardian mode.

Chris pulled open the door, waiting for the dog to come charging in from outside. With little legs, it might take him a bit longer than normal. But, Chris dropped his guard immediately as he stared at the two men who had turned to face him on the porch. The smaller of the two men was smiling somewhat sheepishly, and Chris returned the smile and chuckled.

"Fuck me...I've been cloned," he said.

Kevin's smile withered a bit and he looked at Doug, who was looking over Chris' shoulder in anticipation. Then they stepped into the house, forcing Chris to back away. They closed the door behind themselves. "This is some kind of joke, right? Pat set this up? You guys are from some talent agency? C'mon. That's some awesome makeup."

Doug shook his head without looking at him, but Kevin spoke first.

"We don't really have time to explain, Christopher. I'm your brother, Kevin. The big guy," At this Doug frowned at Kevin, who seemed to be having a laugh, "is your brother Doug. Our other brother, James, is up north trying to save his girlfriend from some angry clones who got the short end of the stick in the looks department. But, no...you haven't *been* cloned. You *are* a clone. Or, more precisely, you're a clone of someone else. I'm still not clear on that part of the story, so you'll have to just trust me."

"Right. Trust you...sure," Chris said, not really hearing the words come out.

"You got a dog?" Doug said, and looked somewhat anxiously at Chris, then over at Kevin, who looked back at his brother and mouthed, "Really?"

"I...what? C'mon...you're...how'd you know my name? Pat set you up to this...he must've laid out some cash for this one. I mean...you guys look good. The big guy's a bit of a stretch, but...you—" Chris said, pointing to Kevin.

"Jesus," Doug said, surprising Chris. "I'm not that big! I'm perfectly healthy for my height." Then he turned to Kevin, who was smiling, and whispered, "Jerk."

"Chris? Can I call you Chris? Listen…like I said, we really don't have a lot of time. You see…there are some people who would rather not have us around, soooo…if we don't get you out of here in, say, thirty minutes or less. Well, there's a pretty good chance that someone might be shooting at us soon."

"I wouldn't even give 'em that long, Kev. Ten minutes tops…whoa!"

Murphy rammed the back door with his full weight and the little dog bounded around the corner, little legs digging furiously at the wooden flooring in a vain attempt to gain traction. He screeched to halt, dropping his back end to aid in stopping, a few feet in front of Doug and bellowed at him, BAWOOOO!

"Murph! Stuff it!" Chris said.

"Nice dog," Kevin said.

Doug simply put his hands in his pockets and pressed himself back against the door. The little dog, sensing weakness, shuffled his butt on the floor and bellowed at Doug again.

"You have got to be kidding me," Kevin said, and put a palm-up hand down to the dog. Murphy snuffed at Doug, then turned to the hand, giving it a thorough sniff before allowing its owner to scratch him behind the ears.

"Some watch dog, huh?" Chris said.

"He's a beast. Some brother, huh? And he's supposed to be the muscle. You're a disgrace, man."

"I don't like dogs, ok?" Doug said. Murphy turned to bark at him again and now Doug was at the door, one hand on the knob.

"So, anyway," Kevin said. "We need you to come with us…strength in numbers. You know"

"You're serious about this…aren't you," Chris said.

"Brother, I wouldn't be here if I weren't," Kevin said.

"Let me get some things…and leave my mom a note…where are we going?"

"New Orleans," Doug said, which prompted a short WUFF from Murphy.

"Nawlens! Nice!"

"Been there?" Kevin asked.

"Are you kidding…I've never been out of Arizona," Chris said.

"Now you are kidding," Kevin said.

"Nope," Chris said, walking back into the house. "Come in, sit if you like."

"You're twenty-four and you've never been anywhere? Last time I checked, Arizona isn't an island."

"I…no. It's sorta complicated," Chris said, from a room beyond the kitchen. Kevin walked into the living room and glanced around. It was nicely furnished. A cozy Arizona home for all he knew. What looked to be a fake cactus leaned haphazardly in the corner. A photo on the mantel drew his attention.

"This your mom?" he said, looking at the photo. She was an attractive woman, with a smile that seemed to radiate beyond the frame.

"Ummm…yeah, adoptive…I guess you know," he said.

"Yeah…she's kinda hot…if you don't mind my saying," Kevin said.

"Jeez, Kev," Doug said from the hallway.

Murphy had taken a seat, about three feet from Doug in the hallway. He had stopped the barking, but kept a wary eye on Doug, who returned the favor. Chris walked back into the room, wearing a light jacket over his t-shirt. He'd changed into jeans and sneakers.

"Yeah, I hear that a lot," he said.

"She married?"

"No…not anymore…"

"Divorce?"

"Yeah, you could say that…" Chris said.

"Kevin, give the guy a break…he just met us. Maybe he doesn't—"

"No, it's ok…it's better to tell you than to have you wondering." He sighed and Kevin immediately regretted digging.

"When I was ten my adoptive Dad…stole me. Took me out into the middle of nowhere A-Z…which isn't too hard to do. We lived there for almost eight years. I never went to

132

school. According to the cops, he called my mom on a regular basis and told her he'd send me back to her in pieces one day. Of course, he never let any of this on to me…told me she was making me sick. That he and I were going to show her. He didn't bad mouth her a lot, but when he did, he'd usually end with and we're gonna show your momma. We moved a lot…for reasons that only became obvious to me much later. He tried to teach me as much as he could. Don't get me wrong…he was a good dad…in his own way. Then they caught him…and he decided that he couldn't live without me, whether it was in jail or out…so he killed himself. Hung himself with his bed sheets. They got me all sorts of counseling. Figured he must've abused me while we were out there. I'm not sure they ever really believed that he didn't. My mom and I had it rough there for a while. A lot changes in eight years. I had to deconstruct some walls she'd built assuming I was going to come back as her enemy. Like I was going to be some sort of extension of him. I was just a dumb kid. All I ever thought was mom and dad are fighting and I hope it ends soon. I guess maybe I would have wizened up eventually. Who knows."

The words hung in the air and were only broken by the slow click-clack of Murphy's claws as he padded his way across the floor to his master. He sat at Chris' feet without a word. Chris looked down and scratched the dog's head.

"So, who's up for New Orleans?" Chris asked brightly.

Chapter 16

Norris had forgotten how flat it was. Some would even call it concave. And, in a sense, they were right. With an elevation that ranges from below sea level to a mere twenty feet above, one might call it a bowl. New Orleans was really just a slip of land separating Lake Pontchartrain from the Mississippi River.

"Ever been to New Orleans, Doc?" Norris asked.

"No, this was one of Dr. Paynter's stops. Not my kind of place, really."

"Oh, we all have a little New Orleans in us somewhere, Doc."

"Guess I never found mine," Taylor said.

"No time to party when you're running, huh."

"Got so used to it that staying in one place gave me nausea," Taylor said.

"That's why you sent the letters," Norris said.

"One of the reasons. When you spend the best years of your life working on something, you want someone to know about it. Even if it's wrong. If you tell your story and the audience walks out, it's one thing. If you never have an audience, it's something completely different," Taylor said.

"You'd think we'd have heard by now," Norris said.

"I thought they might be intercepted, but I planned for that," Taylor said.

Norris looked at Taylor and raised an eyebrow.

"You knew they'd get your mailings?"

"I expected it, so I planned on it…probably hoped for it in a way. The first mailing was aimed at the big names. New York Times. Los Angeles Times. Chicago Tribune. I threw in USA Today for fun. I created huge envelopes filled mostly with crap. Even if they had made it through to those venues, they probably wouldn't have seen the light of day. I also sent them priority. Like I was in a rush after all this time. The second mailing went out two days ago. Much quieter locales, with enough clout to get the necessary attention. Smaller packages with USB data cards. Sent slow boat through standard mail. Some may reach their destination as soon as today."

"Throw enough shit, somethin's bound to stick, eh?" Norris said.

"Not quite what I was thinking, but the concept is the same," Taylor said.

"Might not help that boy James any. He's already in a shit storm."

"It certainly wasn't my intention to do them harm, but it seems like things can't get any worse for them, can they?"

"Never say never, Doc. Bottom is only a state of mind. It can always get worse. Just look at me," Norris said. His laugh led to a cough, which led to a fit that nearly forced him off the road. He swerved slightly trying to retrieve the handkerchief from his pocket. The bloodied spots on the white cloth were getting harder to hide. When he'd finished, Taylor spoke.

"You should really see a doctor."

"So he can tell me what I already know?"

"So you can get some meds."

"Not like I can pop a pill and make this go away, Doc."

"So, you've accepted your fate then? Just going to hope it doesn't kill you before you finish the job?"

"Something like that."

"So you'd rather kill yourself than take a break and possibly lose a chance at revenge," Taylor said.

"Not a fan of that word, Doc. Retribution. Retaliation. Vengeance. Yeah, vengeance. I like that one," Norris said.

"You're a fool, you know that?"

"You have your story, Doc. You've got your audience too. Me, I've got to finish the story and to be honest, I don't care if anyone ever hears it told, so long as the ending is mine."

They passed along Route 10, across a narrow strip of Lake Pontchartrain and into the last vestiges of bayou before entering the northeast corner of the sprawling city of New Orleans. Taylor pulled a scrap of paper from his coat.

"You trust those directions?" Norris asked.

"Paynter did his best to get them to me, but it's been twenty plus years," Taylor said.

"And I'm guessing my black-coated friend has slightly more up-to-date info," Norris said.

"And a head start," Taylor said.

The directions led them off of Route 10 and into the densely populated neighborhoods north of the city center. A left and a right and, to Norris, each road looked like the last.

Row upon row of single-story shotgun-style houses, with as little as eight feet between, lined each avenue. They entered an area called Bywater, a neighborhood situated just to the east of the infamous French Quarter and whose southern boundary was the Mississippi River.

"Not quite the neighborhood that I was expecting," Taylor said.

"A bit too dark for your liking, Doc?" Norris said.

"I…that's not what I meant," Taylor said.

"Of course not. You just wouldn't want to live here," Norris said

"Not if I had a choice," Taylor said.

"Yeah, well…what most people don't get is, neither would they," Norris said.

"I think we're here," Taylor said, pointing out the window.

"Oh Christ," Norris said, pulling the car to a stop at the curb.

"Literally," Taylor said.

There was nothing particularly extraordinary about the house at first glance. On a street with a dozen other houses on the block, it had no particular amenity above the others. What it did have was crucifixes, Christ figures, and an assortment of other Christian paraphernalia. The piece de resistance, for Norris, was a tossup between the stick-on stained glass in the windows and the hand-painted Madonna with the lazy eye on the front door.

"You're sure this is it," Norris said.

"This is it…I guess," Taylor said.

Norris turned off the engine and the two men stood on the sidewalk, examining the residence before them. Norris couldn't help but shake his head.

"I guess if it makes you feel better, it can't be that bad, right?" Norris said.

They climbed the steps and he pressed the doorbell. A tinny version of the hallelujah chorus from Handel's Messiah called out to them. Attempting to stifle a laugh forced a cough into the back of Norris' throat and he quickly pulled out the handkerchief and turned away from the door, his mouth filling with blood and a hot searing pain piercing his chest. He staggered down the steps behind Taylor. He could barely make out the conversation over his shoulder and he turned the corner to spit onto the ground. A crimson streak spattered the sidewalk and the white paint of the house foundation. He dabbed the foot of a crucifix that had been nailed to the nearby siding. It occurred to him that he wouldn't want to leave behind any accidental stigmata.

When the fit had passed, he returned back up the stairs. A small plump woman with a gentle, but vapid looking face stared wide-eyed at him. She was wringing her thick-fingered hands in a dish towel that was hanging from the apron around her waist. Her round face seemed particularly taught due to the bun in her hair. She blinked at Norris.

"Afternoon, Ma'am. Agent Norris, FBI," Norris said.

"Mrs. Paul was just telling me that her son isn't here," Taylor said.

"When was the last time you saw Peter, Mrs. Paul?" Norris asked, hiding the handkerchief away and pulling out his badge which she regarded with indifference.

"I…earlier today. He was here for lunch, but he goes into town in the afternoons most days. Either to the library or…to church."

There was a noise that came down the hallway behind her. Norris looked over the woman's shoulder, but she moved as if to block his view. Norris smiled at her.

"Is Mr. Paul home?" he asked.

"Ummm…no…Mr. Paul has, by the Grace of God, left us. It's just the dog," Mrs. Paul said.

"Oh, my condolences," Taylor said.

"Oh, he's not dead…he just left. God guided him away from us…and that was for the best," Mrs. Paul said. She said this with such emphasis, which made her cheeks shake.

"Right. Funny thing…a dog that doesn't bark at the door bell," Norris said.

"I…," Mrs. Paul hesitated.

"Mrs. Paul, we're here to help your son…," Norris said, raising his voice in volume, but not intensity.

"That's what that other man said. He had a wicked face though. The Devil himself had written on that man's face," Mrs Paul said, her face reddening.

140

Norris flinched at the mention of the man in black and looked over his shoulder to the road, knowing he would see nothing. The street was quiet.

"I know that man, Mrs. Paul, and the fact that he didn't just take what he wanted was a gift to you. A brief window of opportunity for your son," Norris said.

"Well, I told my son the same thing and he's left," she said.

"I don't want you to have to keep lying to me, Mrs. Paul. I'm not much of a liar myself, but your son has to realize that the other man is out to harm him and will do so if given the opportunity. I can't guarantee your son's safety, but I can guarantee he isn't safe at home or on his own."

Mrs. Paul shifted on her feet and Norris spotted the edge of the boy's face peering out from behind a door jamb just down the hall.

"Peter!" Norris cried out.

"Leave me alone!" the young man shouted and he stumbled from his hiding spot down the hallway to the back of the house, plowing through a swinging door and into the kitchen.

"Excuse me, Ma'am," Norris said as he beat her to the screen door and threw it open.

She crossed herself and leaned back against the wall as Norris and Taylor made their way past her and pursued Peter down the hall. The inside of the house made a mockery of the outside. There was no angle to turn to without being confronted by a saint, angel, or Christ figure. Even the wallpaper was adorned with a cloying repetition of fat cherubs looking misty eyed at an equally misty-eyed Virgin Mary. Taylor nearly stopped in his tracks.

"C'mon, Doc. You can get decorating tips the next time you're in town," Norris said as he pushed his way into the kitchen.

The back door was still somewhat ajar and he saw through the window as Peter made his way across the small lot to a small brick wall that he judged to be about five feet high. His black unbuttoned trench coat flapped like the wings of a dying bird and the red and blue backpack on his shoulders seemed to be weighing him down. Then, in one motion, he climbed two stacked milk crates and threw himself at the wall in what, Norris could only imagine, must have been an attempt to hurdle the wall. He missed badly, half-slamming into the side of the wall, his right foot not even close to the top of the wall.

"Ouch," Taylor said.

"He's a bit bigger than the others, huh? Peter, please stop!" Norris said.

Peter recovered quickly, pulled his backpack off and threw it over the wall, then managed to hoist himself up and over the wall. Norris was just reaching the wall when the last piece of black trench coat fabric slipped over the top. They watched as Peter made his way through the next couple of yards and out of sight. Norris stared at the wall for a moment.

"I'm getting too old for this kind of bullshit, Doc."

Norris turned to find Mrs. Paul standing in the window of the closed back door. She appeared to be dabbing at tears on her cheek. He heard the click of the bolt being turned on the door.

"Oh, fuck me," Norris murmured.

He moved through the yard, careful to step around a miniature crucifix on a mound. It was surrounded by what appeared to be plastic action figures painted to look like Roman soldiers and sporting bloodied spears.

"Mrs. Paul! Mrs. Paul. Please. You've got to believe me that we're here to help your son. Where does he go? Is there somewhere we might find him?"

Mrs. Paul let the curtain go, but Norris could tell she hadn't moved from doorway. He moved up the steps and spoke to the door.

"Your son is running from the wrong people, Mrs. Paul. I can't help him if I can't find him. It's very important. You obviously care a great deal about him. Let me help him. Mrs. Paul?"

"St Louis!" she shouted unnecessarily.

"St. Louis. What does that mean?"

She pulled back the curtain, her face red and strained. Her small eyes staring through Norris one moment, then off into space the net.

"St. Louis Cathedral! It's on Chartres Street, near Jackson Square," she said, again too loudly.

"Thank you, Mrs. Paul," Norris said.

"You keep my boy safe, Agent Norris. May God keep you all safe," she said.

Norris nodded to her through the glass, then turned to Taylor who had a skeptical look on his face.

"C'mon, Doc. You, me, and God have a kid to find."

Chapter 17

The straightest and shortest route from the Bywater section of New Orleans to St Louis Cathedral was to hook up with Royal St. to the South and follow it all the way into the French Quarter. But Norris didn't think this was the kind of kid who would run without thinking. He hadn't been caught unawares. He had his coat, despite the warmth, and bag at the ready. Why he'd waited for a return visit was beyond Norris, but that didn't matter now. What did matter was that the kid was out of reach for the moment and the man in black was as close as they were, if not closer, to catching him. He refused to think of where failure would lead him. In Norris' mind, failure was always a possible end result, but never something to dwell on. You acknowledged the possibility, but then just as quickly struck it from your mind. Overthink it and it was natural to find yourself headed down that path. He turned a corner and continued his zigzag maneuvers through the streets in a gradual movement westward.

"You don't think he went straight there?" Taylor asked loudly.

"Shouting again, Doc. No. I don't think he did," Norris answered.

"Path of least resistance?" Taylor asked, apparently more conscious of the volume of his voice.

"Not always the easiest way though. And in a big city like this? Easy to get lost, especially if he knows his way around,

145

which he apparently does. Besides, he headed North out the back."

"He could've just headed West from there," Taylor said.

"Well, even if we go halfway like this, and straight the rest of the way, we should still beat him there on foot. That's assuming that he's heading to the church, of course, which is why we need to intercept him."

"The man...he's close, isn't he," Taylor said.

"Yes. If I had to dare a guess, he was watching that whole scene play out back at Peter's house. I'm just glad it didn't seem to be from the end of a scope," Norris said.

"I—," Taylor began, then stopped, staring past Norris.

"What?" Norris said, bringing the car to a stop.

"I don't know, it might have been nothing," Taylor said, continuing to squint beyond Norris at a spot down the cross street they had just edged across.

"Doc, we're looking for a kid in a city. Need I remind you of the needle in a haystack analogy? Pretty much the same thing here. If it's shiny, we've got to check it out," Norris said.

"It might have been the back of his coat, as if he slipped in between two houses on the run," Taylor said.

"Good enough for me," Norris said, throwing the car into reverse and turning down the road toward the spot where Taylor continued to stare.

"There," Taylor said, pointing.

The alley between the houses was no more than seven feet wide, but it was completely empty. Norris brought the car to a stop and watched. He watched as the chain link fence at the back of the property shuddered violently for no reason apparent to his line of sight. In his mind, he saw Peter at the far most edge of the yard, throwing himself against the fence in another vain attempt at scaling the obstacle before him.

"He's there. We'll round the block and wait for him to come out the other side," Norris said.

He moved slowly down to the corner, signaled, and turned down the long edge of the block. A few cars were parked along the sidewalk, but most looked as if they had been there for a while and none were running. Norris knew the man wouldn't place himself into the path of pursuit. He'd be behind them, waiting for the right moment. He edged the car to the curb at the end of the block and turned the engine off. Both men slipped from the car, carefully closing the doors behind them.

"Doc, you watch to the South. I'll keep an eye East and North. He'll have to come through sooner or later."

They waited and watched. Norris heard him before he saw him. He tapped Taylor on the shoulder and gestured up the block. The good doctor probably wouldn't be able to hear, but someone was breathing heavy and muttering in something above a stage whisper. The kid's intentions of getting away had been solid, but his skills at remaining hidden were a little suspect. By the sound of it, the young man was just one house down. Norris could just make out what sounded like a self-rallying pep talk.

"C'mon…just another block. Please dear Jesus, just another block," Peter said.

Then he was out into the road, doing his best to sprint across the street. It was a tired, lagging effort. Norris ran after him.

"Peter, please stop! I'm an FBI agent. My name is Richard Norris. I'm here to help you. Peter!"

"Get away from me, man! I don't know you. Why are you all after me?"

"Peter, you're not getting away again," Norris said, reaching out and grabbing the back of the boy's backpack, which tore away with a Velcro-like ripping sound. Norris was left standing, holding what seemed to be an almost empty bag, and watching Peter continue at his full pace to the next gap between houses.

Norris picked up the pace again, just in time to see Peter come face-to-face with another fence; that of the black steel kind with nasty looking pointed tops. The boy's shoulders slumped and he raised his head up to the sky. He was trapped, but Norris gave him some room.

"Peter, please understand…we're really here to help you," Norris said.

"If the good Lord wanted me to get away, this gate wouldn't be here," Peter said.

"I imagine not. Do you want this back?" Norris said, lifting the empty bag.

Peter took it from him, careful not to make eye contact. He merely glanced in Taylor's direction, then returned his focus to Norris' person. To Norris, Peter was a bit of an anomaly. His features were stretched by the significant weight difference between himself and the other boys he had seen. Peter was a chubby caricature of them both. Red-faced and still breathing heavy, Peter pulled a handkerchief from his pocket and wiped his brow. Definitely an anomaly, Norris thought.

"You've been chased before," Norris said.

Peter smirked without humor, as if the statement were a moot point.

"I'm not exactly the popular kid, Agent Norris. You know that some lizards can release their tails if caught? Grow it right back later on. People tend to grab the first thing within reach. I've never put a single thing of value in that bag."

"Fascinating. Listen, I don't want to rush things, but it's kind of important for us to keep moving. So, if you wouldn't mind," Norris said, pointing back toward the car.

"You still haven't told me why so many people are suddenly trying to find me. I haven't done anything," Peter said.

"It's...a bit complicated. The important thing to know is that the other man who came to your house is here to kill you and I'm here to make sure he doesn't," Norris said.

"Sweet Mother above," Peter said, crossing himself and raising his eyes to the sky again.

"Seriously?" Taylor said a bit too loudly, but Peter either wasn't paying attention, or didn't care.

"I can explain in the car, but we have to hurry. He'll be watching and if he doesn't make his move now, it won't be long from now," Norris said.

Norris turned and edged his way to the corner of the building. He knew that they would have little time. The hair on the back of his neck stood up despite the heat. His stomach reminded him that food hadn't been a priority over the last couple of days. Suddenly, the distance between them and the car seemed insurmountable. There was no way they would make it back and he was a fool to have given the man that much separation. His head swam and the tearing he felt at the back of his throat might have been more from the rising bile than from that which was killing him.

"Agent Norris?" Peter asked.

Seconds had passed and the longer they stood there, the greater the possible danger they would face. Norris shook his head, which did nothing but increase the dizziness he was feeling. But somehow he found his voice.

"The car is just around that corner. Run...now!" he said, pushing both Peter and Taylor ahead of him into the street. He didn't want them to see him draw his weapon.

Norris was only a couple steps behind Peter when he stopped in the middle of the road. He had known it was coming, so it wasn't the sound of the engine that had stopped him. It was the type of engine. The diesel had roared to life right on cue, but the ferocity had suggested something much more sinister than Norris had prepared for in his head. Like the howl of an unleashed beast, Trucker Jim's black semi cab tore rubber around the corner a block up with more nimbleness than Norris had ever seen in a truck that size. The gun felt limp in his hand, but he managed to shout out his previous orders.

"Run…now!"

They would make it. He might not…and it occurred to him in that moment that he'd die in the middle of the street with the keys to the car in his pocket, subsequently dooming his companions. He was going to fail in the last thing that meant anything to him. And failure was hurtling at him in the form of a 10-ton chrome-covered man in black.

He raised his pistol, knowing that even if he hit the man, it probably wouldn't do anything to change the truck's current path. But as he made to squeeze the trigger, the shot that rang out wasn't his own. Its effect, however, was immediate, rupturing the front left tire and forcing the vehicle into an arch around Norris, who could only watch as the metallic beast screeched around him in a blur of painted steel and churning rubber. It was so clean he could see his own wide eyes staring back at him in the chrome as it passed. Then he saw the car that had slipped in behind him. A scoped pistol was still sticking out the back passenger window. The red cuffed arm was flinching and there seemed now to be some desperation to avoid the wounded trucked that was now bearing down on them. It was all happening too fast. There was no time for a second shot. They hadn't anticipated the man's driving ability and now they were going to pay dearly. The front of the cab caught the tail end of the sedan and threw it around like a toy, knocking one of the doors open. The truck came to a halt and the entire mess lay steaming in the middle of the intersection. Norris' body seemed to react quicker than his mind and he was running toward Taylor, shouting as loudly as he could.

"Get in the car! Get in the goddamn car!"

He ran around the corner, all the while looking over his shoulder and holding the gun at the truck. Norris threw open the door, slipped into the driver's seat, and started the car. Taylor was sitting in the passenger seat, but the back seat was empty. Norris looked in the back and back at Taylor, dumbfounded.

"Where the fuck is Peter!?"

"He...I...I dunno," stammered Taylor, raising his hands as if Peter had actually slipped from his grasp.

"Doc, where the fuck did he go?"

"I don't know. I turned...the wreck. I don't think he stopped. Just kept running. I didn't even see which way. He was just gone," Taylor said, still staring out the front window at the scene before them.

A door to the sedan opened slowly. Norris decided not to wait around to see what condition its occupants were in. Some nearby residents were coming out of their homes. He cut the wheel and headed back the way they had come.

"We had him and they know it and now this and we should still have him, but the fool only knows how to run on what God gave him," Norris said.

"Why does that surprise you?" Taylor asked.

"It doesn't surprise me! It pisses me the hell off!"

Then the coughing fit that had repressed itself in his moment of greatest stress finally released and he had to bring the car to a near complete stop before continuing on.

"Where are we headed?" Taylor asked.

"The church. They won't hesitate to stalk him there. Neither should we."

Chapter 18

Doug stared at his phone, listening to the voice mail girl go through his options now that the message had played. Press 1 to save the message; he wasn't sure that was such a good idea. Two to forward it to someone; there was no one else who would care, or understand. Three to play it again; as good as it had been to hear James' voice, he didn't need to hear that message again. It was bad enough he was wishing he'd never heard it to begin with. Seven to delete; his finger punched the button so quickly that he didn't have time to stop himself. It occurred to him that someone was talking to him. Not talking. Shouting.

"What?" Doug asked.

"C'mon! Remember? Little old men in red coats who want to kill us? What are you doing? Was it James?" Kevin called from the car.

Chris sat in the back seat looking like an eager dog who knows he's going to the park for a walk.

"It was nothing," Doug said, telling himself that the answer wasn't really a lie, even if that's what the situation called for. But he didn't want to start sweating because that's what happened when he lied. And, now, in the heat of the Phoenix sun, he could feel the sweat beginning to form because despite his avoidance of the lie, he knew that he was still lying to himself. His head spun a bit and he leaned heavily on his cane.

"C'mon, Doug! It's not a difficult decision. In the car or out of the car. You want me to drive? I can—"

"No!" Doug said and shuffled over to the driver's side.

"Well, I'm glad to see something got a response. The heat getting to you?"

Doug put his seat belt on, pretended to adjust the rearview mirror, then turned and stared at Kevin. Kevin could only hold his gaze for so long before laughing.

"You're not going to touch my face, are you?"

Doug broke his stare.

"Chris, what's the best way to Louisiana do you think?"

"Well, that's not the kind of question you hear every day. Through New Mexico and Texas, I guess. We gotta get to 10. That runs all the way to Florida."

"So, would that be a left or right out of the driveway," Doug said, managing a smile.

In no time, they were stuck in traffic on Route 17 heading toward Phoenix. Doug focused on his mirrors, trying to take his mind off of James' message. It wasn't working. How could there be two Kevins? But there weren't; that was abundantly clear. One of them was lying and the possibility that it was his Kevin was excruciating. It couldn't be his, though. They'd fought together, slept in the car together, shared so much in the last couple of days. If he was putting on a show, it was a damned good one, Doug thought.

"This normal?" Kevin asked.

"Welcome to my desert paradise. Apparently, even in the middle of the day, people just *have* to be somewhere else. This is worse than normal though, so it might be an accident," Chris said.

"Somebody better be dead," Doug said.

"Whoa, big fella...that's a bit harsh," Kevin said.

"We're sitting ducks here," Doug said.

"If we're stuck in it, so are they," Kevin said.

"Yeah, well, they seem to have gotten through before," Doug said.

"How do they keep finding you?" Chris asked.

"I don't know. I wonder how they keep finding us," Doug said, unable to prevent the inflection in his voice or the accusatory look he shot Kevin.

"What the hell does that mean?" Kevin asked.

"Nothing, nevermind," Doug muttered.

"Nothing? I don't think so..."

"Kevin, c'mon man..." Chris said.

"No, I wanna hear this. That wasn't nothing. There was some accusation in there and I want to know why."

Doug wrapped his hands around the steering wheel, flexing his fingers. He cursed his weakness.

"It's just funny that they keep finding us," Doug said.

"They haven't found us since the Super Mart! That was two days ago...and they haven't found us since."

"But they found us in Ohio...and they found us in Pennsylvania," Doug said.

"Ohio was that crazy woman that Paynter took us to! And Pennsylvania…wait…are you blaming me? You seriously think I'm bringing them to us? Are you out of your mind?"

"Maybe. And maybe I'm wondering how come you and the redcoat were having a quiet moment in the bathroom."

"A quiet moment! Are you fucking serious? You're fucking serious! You've fucking lost it, dude! His thumb was pressed against my larynx, or don't you remember that part. Maybe that explains why we were having a quiet moment. Did that chick slip some peyote into your burritos this morning? Good God! After the last couple of days, you're gonna sit there and accuse me of narc-ing us out? You've got quite a set on ya, Doug. Quite a set."

"Fuck me," Doug said.

"Oh, you can curse! Nice to see that this trip is completely warping your mind. What the—"

With little space to maneuver, Doug had suddenly accelerated between two cars, essentially making his own lane. He swerved again, bringing the car into middle lane, just ahead of a tractor trailer.

"Doug, what the heck?" called Chris.

"Redcoat…on a bike," Doug said, wedging the large white car begrudgingly into the slow lane. He smiled and waved back at the driver whose middle finger was raised.

"Bikes? You gotta be…kidding me…," Kevin said, looking in the side view mirror.

Sure enough, about a half mile back, two red motorcycles, one with a red-jacketed rider, were weaving through the traffic behind them. They had about thirty seconds.

"Shit's illegal," Kevin said.

"Really?" Doug said.

"Happens all the time around here. You sure it's your guys?" Chris asked.

"Not many motorcyclists wear red sport coats, white pants, and white straw fedoras," Kevin said.

"Seriously?" Chris said.

"Seriously. We need to get off this highway," Doug said.

"There's an exit ramp on the northbound side up ahead. No median. Not much traffic going North," Kevin said.

"I got all the way to the right just to have you tell me to get to the left?" Doug asked.

"Yes…it's all part of my plan of getting caught,remember?" Kevin said, giving a stone-faced look to Doug.

"Amazing that they found us again, though, isn't it?" Doug said.

"No, it isn't, is it," Kevin said.

"Hold on," Doug said.

He floored the pedal and shot through a gap that had reappeared to his left. His next maneuver wasn't as clean, as the fender caught the back left of a car to his right. The bikes were gaining on them quickly now, having spotted their startled prey. The rest of the trip to the left hand lane involved

159

much grinding, scratching, swearing, and cringing on the part of Kevin. A pristine red BMW convertable purposely placed itself into Doug's way, the driver shouting at the top of his lungs.

"You'd better have a good fucking lawyer, buddy," the man said, smiling in a way that only motivated Doug more. Doug rolled down his window.

"You got a gun in that car?"

The man's smile wavered for a moment before he responded.

"No! Of course not!"

"Well, they do…," Doug said, gesturing behind him before flooring the pedal and slamming into the car in front of him and effectively pushing him out of the way. Closing the window only slightly muffled the high pitched screams and curses being emitted by its owner.

"He deserved that," Doug muttered.

The white car pitched out into the northbound lane and raced across, just ahead of a produce truck, and onto the exit ramp. They could hear the whine of engines behind them as Doug maneuvered down the narrow ramp.

"Where the hell are we?" Doug asked.

"Beats me," Chris said.

"You live here!" Kevin yelled as they rounded a 180-degree turn, wheels squealing.

"I never went down this street! Wait…that's a president. Turn left here!"

Doug didn't hesitate and went through the red light and across two lanes into the eastbound lane.

"Jesus, they're still right behind us!" Chris called out.

"How the hell does he keep that hat on?" Kevin wondered aloud.

"You can ask him when they catch us," Doug said, swerving in and out of the less dense traffic.

"Hang a right at 7th," Chris said.

"Why?" Doug asked.

"I've got an idea," Chris said.

The car lurched again as Doug just missed ramming a car in the slow lane. Horns blared as they made their way, all the time the bikes behind them were gaining.

"If they don't get us, the cops will," Doug said.

"What cops?" Kevin asked.

"Oh, c'mon! Even if I hadn't pissed off Beemer boy, I scratched one too many fenders back there. We're not gonna make it out of the state in this car," Doug said.

"Let's worry about that if we're still alive," Kevin said.

Doug floated the car into a sliding turn at 7th without losing much momentum while avoiding any further collisions. The bikes were hard pressed to do the same and slipped between a couple of cars of their own.

"Left at the light!"

"Ooo! A light…there's a novel way of crossing a highway," Doug said.

"Is that…? Hey, it was the best possible way at the time, ok?" Kevin shouted.

"Trick with lights is when they're red and you need them to be green," Chris said.

"Yeah…about that," Doug said.

Though there were no cars in the turn lane, there were plenty of cars obstructing a clean passage to the far side. Doug didn't slow down as he approached.

"Jesus, man…what are you doing?" Chris screamed.

"Doug?" Kevin said, raising his hand to grip the handle above his seat.

"There's a gap, trust me, there's always a gap," Doug said, and with that he sent the car into the intersection and pulled on the steering wheel as quickly as he could, making sure to not over-turn the wheel and slow them down more than was necessary. Kevin and Chris let out a collective scream and covered their heads. It all happened so quickly and at such a high rate of speed that the oncoming drivers didn't react until after the car had slid past them. They were across and accelerating when Doug allowed himself a victorious giggle.

"Where the hell did you learn to drive like that?" Chris asked.

"Playstation."

"We really gotta talk about your definition of a gap," Kevin said.

"Hey, that sign said authorized personnel only beyond this point. Where the hell are we?" Doug asked.

"Rail yard," Chris said.

"As in freight trains?" Kevin asked.

"Yep. You said we had to ditch the car," Chris said.

"Yeah, but this isn't the old West, Chris, or the roaring '20s. You can't just hop on a train like a hobo anymore."

"Who says? Just because not as many people do it, doesn't mean it isn't done. It'll take us as far as San Manuel," Chris said.

"Listen, I don't know if you noticed, but running and hopping on a train might be wishful thinking on my part," Doug said.

"And what makes you think no one will notice us just getting out of car and climbing on a moving train?" Kevin asked.

"Listen, I never said it was a good idea, I just said I had an idea and no one seemed to object. Besides, they're still right behind us!"

Doug maneuvered around a corner and into the main freight yard. There had to be over thirty rail lines and most of them appeared to be filled to capacity. He crossed over one track and took the road that ran parallel to the lines through the complex. Behind him, the bikes were back with a vengeance, but were joined by a white SUV with a flashing blue light on the top.

"Police?"

"Freight bulls, more likely. Train cops. Not real cops, but not real nice either. They get paid to be assholes. Look for somewhere to cut across the tracks," Chris said.

"Uh...ok!" Doug said

The bikes were right behind them. He saw the one rider reach inside his coat and pull out something black.

"Gun!" Doug shouted, swerving into the path of the biker and laying on the brakes. The redcoat was quick, but not quick enough. He saw the maneuver happening, but couldn't slow down quickly enough. He put the bike into a skid to avoid slamming into the back of the car.

"One down...oh crap. Down!," Doug said, reaching over and pushing Kevin's head to the seat. The passenger side window shattered and glass scattered onto the dash. A large hole was torn into the radio. Doug swerved back to the right to deter a second shot. The bike wobbled, but fell back enough to avoid a collision. Doug floored the pedal to put some distance between them, but they were running out of yard. The road was coming to a split. They would either cut across the tracks or continue out of the yard. Doug hesitated.

"Do it," came Chris' voice from the back seat.

"There's no crossing lights here, Chris. I won't know if one's coming or not until it's too late."

"That's what I'm planning on," Chris said.

"I'm liking this plan less and less," Doug said.

"We're already up to our asses. What's a little train chicken now?" Kevin said.

"I hope you're right," Doug said and hung the left into the yard, running perpendicular across the tracks.

"If the yard master knows we're here, they'll have stopped all of the trains except the ones already leaving the yard. But, if there's a wreck, they might put more in motion."

"And what if there isn't a wreck? You know…luck?"

"Three vehicles moving through a train yard in close quarters at a high rate of speed? It's almost certain," Chris said.

"I'm worried about your confidence in that matter," Doug said.

"I'm worried about the one in three chance of it being us," Kevin said. They passed by the first train parked along the cross road. There was nothing beyond it, but Doug leaned to the right, just in case. There were several in a row and Doug watched as the bike and SUV kept pace. They heard the train before they saw it. Doug slipped past a parked engine when, out from beyond it, a pusher glided out just behind the white car's bumper.

"Holy shit!"

The bike slammed into the side of the passing train as evidenced by the spray of metal and fire that appeared on the other side. Doug slammed on the brakes, bringing the white car to rest in front of a parked engine. They could just make out the SUV beyond the passing train as it spun sideways to avoid the wreck.

"Now what?" Doug asked.

"I can't believe it worked," Chris said.

"Fucking unbelievable. We should be dead. No way that happened. No fucking way," Kevin said.

"Calm down, dude," Chris said.

"Calm down? I'm pretty fucking calm for almost having lost my life. Your ideas need a serious vetting process going forward," Kevin said.

"Now what!?" Doug reiterated.

"We get out. There…over there. That one's just starting to move. Let's go."

The three young men exited the car. They could hear the train involved in the wreck was coming to a stop. Beyond that, they could see that more vehicles had arrived and several had red and blue flashing lights.

"Best make our exit while they're preoccupied," Kevin said.

"Think that guy's dead?" Doug said, staring back at the train, cane in hand.

"Live by the sword," Kevin said.

"That's why I don't," Doug said.

"Train's not gonna get any slower, folks!" Chris shouted.

They moved past the white car, around another parked train and to the side of the departing train. It was particularly long and mostly made up of tanker cars. Several freight containers had been tacked on the end. Kevin and Doug watched as Chris demonstrated the timing and grab. Doug slipped on his approach and the jump sent a shot of pain into his hip, but he used his cane as a hook and grabbed on with all

166

of his strength. He had caught the car just behind Chris, and Kevin caught the next one. They were all on and they were getting away from the redcoats once again.

"For now," whispered Doug to no one as he watched the rail yard and the city slip away into distance.

Chapter 19

"Are you sure about this?" James shouted.

James had just shoved the floating plane away from the boat shed and jumped back into the copilot's seat. He glanced over his shoulder at New Kevin. Despite his foggy disposition, there was a look of wariness about him and he gave James a quick look of apprehension. He fumbled with the four-point harness in the passenger seat.

"It's been a while…and I don't think I ever took off from water, but…," Paynter said, shrugging.

"What's that mean? You can't just shrug and leave it at that!" James said.

He slipped the headset on and hoping that he didn't look as foolish as he felt. Paynter's voice came through the headset much clearer over the roar of the engine, though it was still all filtered through the cotton that seemed to have lodged in his ears since the house blast.

"You got a better idea?" Paynter offered.

"Yeah, one that doesn't involve a long drop and a quick stop," James said.

They both heard New Kevin chuckle and turned to find him adjusting his own headset gingerly on his head.

"Was starting to feel left out. Dr. Paynter, I got faith in you. Let's go before that changes," he said.

"Yeah, it might be a good idea to get going…like now," James said and pointed over New Kevin's shoulder.

The others turned and saw the car maneuvering around the pierced truck at the top of the driveway, pulling to a stop amidst the debris. The first redcoat out of the car had his gun drawn and was headed their way.

Paynter wasted no time and pushed the throttle forward. The engine whined into a roar and the seaplane lurched forward. Despite the apparent calmness of water, they found that even the smallest chops caused the plane to buck. They were no more than a hundred feet from the shed when the first shot rang out clearly over the roar of the engine. They all flinched and New Kevin covered his head and ducked below the window.

"Did he hit anything?"

"No," New Kevin said, his voice muffled by the hood of his oversized coat.

"All the gauges still look good," Paynter said.

A second shot rang out, this time clearly putting a hole in the wall behind New Kevin's seat. He waved without lifting his head.

"I'll take that to mean you're ok?" James said.

"I think it might've hit the back of the bench. It moved!"

"Keep low, we're gaining speed and distance. Another couple hundred feet and they won't be able to hit us," Paynter said.

"If I had an oar, I'd get out and row," James said.

"I'll second that," New Kevin said.

"Hold on," Paynter said.

The plane was beginning to gain more and more speed, which meant they were hitting the cresting waves harder and harder. The spray was so thick that James could no longer see out the side windows. There was no looking back now. The last shot ricocheted off of the underside of the wing, tearing a hole in the fabric.

"That a problem?"

"Not the best thing for aerodynamics, but she'll hold...I think...c'mon baby...," Paynter said and pulled back on the controls.

James' stomach leapt. In one moment, he had the sensation of lifting off, followed immediately by the sense that they were going back down. He braced himself for the impact that never happened. They weren't exactly climbing with speed, but the plane had broken free from the water and was now gliding above the waves, slowly gaining height. James looked out his side window and watched as the water and shoreline began to get further away. The smoke from his Uncle's house was still clear even at this distance and probably would be for several hours. He wondered if anyone else really cared.

"Now, where the hell is this airfield?" Paynter asked.

"He only gave me street directions, but it wasn't overly complicated. We probably passed it on the way down. We'll have to follow the main road up a couple miles, but it should be pretty clear," James said.

"Ever tried to spot something from a plane?" Paynter asked.

"Well…no," James said.

"Even an airfield?" New Kevin piped up.

"Even an airfield. Keep your eyes peeled," Paynter said.

He banked the plane to the right and brought them to the southern-most tip of the peninsula. Paynter had leveled out their ascent and was content to fly at a height just a hundred feet or so above the trees. They easily picked up the road again and followed it to the top of the peninsula. James was glad that Paynter kept the plane low. He hadn't been kidding with seeing things from the air. Any higher and he'd barely be able to follow the road.

"It should be to our right, to the east. It's between the road and the water, essentially," James said.

They scanned the right hand horizon for a moment.

"There," Kevin said.

James followed his outstretched finger and saw the bright orange wind flag.

"I'm going to have to make a pass and come back around. We're coming at the wrong angle to land," Paynter said.

"This thing does have wheels, right?" James asked.

"C'mon, James…I'm not the sharpest tool, but I can still cut paper," Paynter said.

He tapped his hand on a lever below the throttle. James could see an image that showed wheels coming out of the floats. He glanced out the window as if he might be able to inspect them by doing so.

"Hope they're in working condition!"

"I trust your uncle, James. He wouldn't leave something like landing gear to chance," Paynter said.

"Sorry, but you're talking about a man who, a few days ago, I thought could possibly build a nice deck given some wood and a hammer, not fly a plane or fight a war or whatever it is he really did...does," James said.

"Your Uncle always had a knack for making something out of nothing. Probably could have made a bomb out of some chewing gum and a paper clip," Paynter said.

"Sounds like a guy who'd be fun at parties," New Kevin said. Paynter smirked.

"Not quite," James said.

"Look!" New Kevin was pointing down to the ground out the left side as Paynter prepared to bank over the airfield.

"I can't see. What is it?"

"That's not good," Paynter said, glancing down.

"I have a feeling he ain't napping," New Kevin said.

"What?"

"It's gotta be your Mr. Johnson. Looks like someone got to him," Paynter said.

"I don't see anyone else down there," New Kevin said.

"Stay sharp. I'm going to keep the idle high in case we have to do a touch and go. When we land, the engine isn't going off.

"Jesus, I just talked to him," James said.

"We don't know he's dead," Paynter said.

"They could be waiting down there...," James said.

173

"Not many places to hide, unless they're in that hangar," New Kevin broke in.

The plane came around, giving them a wide view of the narrow runway and the lonely looking double-bay hangar and office. There was a small, white, utility pickup parked in front of the office. James could now see the man's prone body near the corner of the hangar bay door.

"I'm not betting against the worst," James muttered.

"We've got to check. Least we can do is call it in," Paynter said.

"Then what?" James asked.

"Ontario," New Kevin said.

James turned in his seat and stared hard at New Kevin. New Kevin blinked hard then looked away and massaged a raw-looking spot on his temple.

"They thought I was out a lot more than I was. Or, maybe…maybe they didn't care because they thought I'd be dead soon," New Kevin said.

"And they mentioned Ontario. It's a big province, y'know," James said, still not taking his eyes off of New Kevin.

"Well, I'm not sure. The one was talking about the farm and how much he liked it and when things blew over, he'd like to get a farm in the area and the other said something about not being able to show his face in the Sudbury area for a while. I think—"

He said this as if the act of remembering the words hurt. James turned back in his seat as the plane touched down. He looked over to Paynter, then back out the front window.

"Pretty goddamn specific memory you have there, Kevin. Pretty good for a guy who's just had his ass kicked to hell," James said.

"Well, I could be wrong…"

"We'll worry about that later. Keep your eyes peeled, both of you. I'm going to bring it in as close to the hangar as possible. We check on him, then we get the hell out of here."

The plane came to a stop within twenty feet of the man on the ground. He was perfectly still and now that they were closer, James could see that the grass at the edge of the man's burnt orange parka was red. He'd been bleeding for some time. A wound at his shoulder was made apparent from the bloodied stuffing that had come out of his jacket.

James reached into his pocket and pulled out his Uncle's pistol. He turned it to one side and slid the safety off. He then drew back the slide, cocking the hammer. He felt Paynter's stare before he saw it.

"Typically, the only people who get shot are ones carrying guns," Paynter said.

"I seem to get shot at whether I'm carrying or not. Might as well have something to answer back with," James said.

"Ever fired one?" Paynter asked.

"No, but there's a first time for everything," James said.

"Maybe I'll just stay in the plane," New Kevin said.

"Let's go," James said.

Paynter lowered the throttle slightly as they exited the plane. James and New Kevin crossed to the man and stood there. They could see no obvious sign of life.

"Well?" New Kevin asked.

"Well? Check him out. See if he's dead," James said, keeping an eye on the open hangar bay door in front of him. He took a couple of steps toward the opening.

"I...he looks dead. I don't think he's breathing," New Kevin said.

James looked back over his shoulder.

"Seriously? If he'd dead, he ain't gonna hurt you. If he's alive, I'm pretty sure he might thank you. Just check him."

New Kevin stared down at the dead man and then back at James, shrugging his shoulders.

"How?"

"Really?" James said.

He turned the gun in his hand and switched the safety back on. Then, he knelt down by the man, reached in to the side of his neck and pressed his first two fingers against the man's throat. James' first reaction was of surprise at the warmth of the man's neck. The second was surprise at the pulse his fingers detected. The third was abject horror at how quickly the man had grabbed his wrist. James heard the little cry that New Kevin made as he nearly fell backward onto the ground.

"Thought you'd killed me, didn't you ya sorry son of a bitch!" the dead man screamed, turning James' hand backward in such a fashion that forced him lower and closer to the man's face.

Pale, with dried blood plastering some of the hair on his forehead, the man's eyes were wild with rage. He was near to foaming at the mouth when he spoke again.

"Takes more than two bullets to take down a Johnson, boy!"

"Mister Johnson! It wasn't me! I'm here to help."

"The fuck you are…shot me in the back…you… coward…"

The man's grip slackened, his eyes rolled into the back of his head and he slumped back to the ground.

"Ok, I'm gonna have nightmares. Can we go now?" New Kevin said, backing away from the scene towards the plane.

"No! He's not dead…we can help him."

"Dude, he thinks you shot him!"

"Dude, he's delusional. He's lost a lot of blood," James said.

He rolled the man gently onto his back. There was clearly an exit wound in the man's abdomen and the wound to his shoulder was much clearer.

"I don't know if there's anything we can do though," James said.

He pressed his fingers against the man's neck again. The pulse was still there, but faint. The man needed medical attention and quickly.

"Hey! Wrap it up!"

Paynter's shout came at them from the passenger seat of the plane. He was pointing to the far end of the field and a cloud of dust that was coming toward them up the lone road to the airfield.

"You think it's them? The redcoats?" James shouted.

"Can't see! Don't want to find out. Let's go!"

New Kevin ran toward the plane. James looked down at the man. His eyes were open and he was staring up past James. James knelt down and leaned close to him. He spoke into his ear.

"I don't know if you can understand me, but I'm James Masterson and I'm sorry that our paths have crossed this way. I'm not the one who shot you, but I'm going to find the men that did."

The man smiled vaguely and spoke.

"You're Ted's…of course. He's a good friend. We used to fish together….boat…on the lake…"

The man's voice faded and James stood up. Turning toward the road, James reached into his pocket and gripped the gun. He pulled it out and flicked the safety back off. He moved toward the edge of the building, the cries of Paynter and New Kevin going unheeded. He watched as the cloud of dust made its way closer. Then, the top of the car appeared above the berm that ran along the length of the road. It was not what he had expected. He turned and ran quickly back to the plane, pointing to the end of the runway.

"Go, go, go!"

"What changed your mind?" Paynter asked as James slammed his door closed. He pushed the throttle full forward and released the brakes.

"It's a cop!"

Chapter 20

Norris followed Royal St. until he reached St. Anne Street. As they reached Chartres and the turn they would take to reach the front of the cathedral, Norris cursed under his breath. A sign placed squarely in the middle of the road indicated that beyond it was a pedestrian mall. Vendors lined the traffic-free lane with nearly every type of hand-made art known to man; all with the aim of freeing the tourists from some more of their hard-earned cash. He kept going the only way he could, parking in the first spot he could find. It was still further away than he would have liked. He didn't want to have a repeat performance. Taylor looked over at him as if the same thought had entered his mind.

"It's not ideal, but I don't know what else to do," Norris said.

"Not ideal…not ideal at all," Taylor said.

Norris pulled the gun out of his pocket, opened the cylinder, then popped it back into place.

"Just remember, they'll have the same disadvantage," Norris said.

"If they're not all dead," Taylor said.

"He's not dead yet. He's not allowed," Norris said.

They made their way cautiously up the street. In a time that now seemed to be someone else's life, he had strolled through the streets of New Orleans, admiring the architecture, ornate balconies on every block, the near-constant sounds of live music, zydeco rhythms at every turn, and the alluring smell of Cajun food. Now, as he stood at the corner, assessing the situation, he wished that there were fewer ornate balconies and a little less distracting music.

The area in front of the cathedral was a spot called Jackson Square. And though the trees provided adequate coverage from the majority of the street, it still left them wide open to a long-range attack. There was just too much open space. If someone really wanted to prevent their escape, they had only to set themselves up on the rooftop of an adjacent street. But, were they so well organized as to have planned the failure of one group and set up shop with a second. It all made Norris very nervous.

"How the hell are they always one step ahead, Dr. Taylor?"

"That's easy. Better intelligence," Taylor said.

"More manpower doesn't hurt either. These guys seem to be everywhere at once," Norris said.

"Not moving doesn't improve the situation," Taylor said.

"I know. It's just…that's a big fucking church," Norris said.

"Cathedral," Taylor said.

"Toe-may-toe…toe-mah-toe. Let's go," Norris said.

With that, he broke out into a jog toward the front steps of the building. He weaved his way in and out of the artists with their canvases sprawled before him and the potential patrons who looked over works as if they were assessing the Mona Lisa in the Louvre. By the time they reached the front doors,

Norris was wheezing and needlessly fighting back the cough that was coming. He pulled out his bloodied hanky and pressed it against his mouth with one hand while the other pressed against one of the white pillars that adorned the front of the building. He could just make out Taylor behind him, breathing heavily. He wasn't focused on Norris; his gaze was elsewhere, but Norris would have to wait until the fit subsided. Time seemed to speed up. They were going to be caught. And if not during this fit, then the next. It was only a matter of time.

The urge subsided and he wiped his eyes on the back of his sleeve, only realizing then how filthy his coat had become in the last week. He gazed into the handkerchief. Not as bad as last time, but he knew it was a fool who held on to the dream that something like what he had would get better and just go away.

"You ready?" Taylor asked.

"No, but I don't have much choice, do I?" Norris said.

Taylor shook his head. He moved a step forward and pulled open the door to the narthex. As Norris' eyes adjusted to the change in lighting, he was greeted by two cherub-like angels holding bowls of holy water. He watched as Taylor dipped the tips of his fingers into the water and made the sign of the cross.

"No offense, Doc, but I wouldn't figure you for a man of God," Norris said.

"Old habits die hard," Taylor said.

"That's what the nuns say."

"What?"

"Never mind," Norris said.

They stood at the end of the pews, taking in the scene. Fifty foot tall ceilings were decorated with innumerable saints and scenes from the bible. Colorful stained glass windows glowed on the Western side of the building. Flags ran along each side of the walls. Some, apparently nationalities. Others, Norris assumed were state or perhaps Parish flags. The altar was marble and surrounded by objects and walls that were gilded in gold. The alternating black and white tile floor made stealthy movement nearly impossible.

There were, perhaps, a half dozen people praying quietly, none of whom looked like Peter. Instinctively, Norris moved toward the darkness of the aisle along the wall. It would give him the best vantage point and the best means of not being seen. He moved to the first pillar and jumped a little as he heard the front doors creak open. He had almost pulled the gun out of his pocket when the two women stepped out from the narthex, cameras in hand. They pointed and spoke a little too loudly for being in a cathedral. Their entrance produced a couple of turned heads from the front pews. Two ancient-looking women seemed particularly disturbed by the vocal entrance and were quick to say so to one another in stage whispers that were equal to those of the intruders.

Norris moved on to the next pillar, but it was becoming clearer by the moment that Peter was not in plain view. That he had expected him to be, made Norris shake his head a little. Of course the boy wouldn't be in plain view. This was his second home. These priests had probably visited his home on a regular basis. He probably had his own room for Christ's sake. Norris flinched when the priest spoke to them.

"Can I help you gentlemen?"

A small, well-tanned, middle-aged man with a pleasant smile stood before them. His glasses rested just at the tip of a long, thin nose and his bright eyes moved back and forth between the two men. His hands were pressed somewhat nervously against a Bible he held against his chest.

"Good…morning, father. I'm hoping you can help us. My name is Norris. Federal Agent Richard Norris," Norris said.

He fumbled for the badge in the inside pocket of his coat.

"Agent, my name is Father Daniel. I'll do what I can," he said.

"We're looking for someone who is in danger," Norris said.

"You realize that if he has chosen this house of worship to find solace, that he will have it," Father Daniel said.

"I appreciate that, Father, but I never said it was a he," Norris said.

The priest's cheeks flushed visibly.

"There are men after Peter Paul who will not think twice about desecrating the sanctity of your cathedral in order to get what they're after. I know you want to protect him, but these walls will be his tomb," Norris said.

"It's unwise to believe that you can stop the hand of death," Father Daniel asked.

"The good Lord gave us brains, Father, and the wherewithal to use them. Peter has the instinct to run, which is good, but he hasn't run far enough. Staying here is like the mouse sitting on the trap, hoping it never springs shut," Norris said.

"Then that's his decision," Father Daniel said.

"And you're comfortable with being witness to his execution?"

Taylor's hand on his shoulder told Norris everything he needed to know. His last words were still reverberating through the cavernous interior. He didn't have to turn his head to feel the stares he was getting.

"Have a good day, Agent Norris. Any further disruption of my Father's house and I will be forced to call the police.," Father Daniel said.

"I…," Norris began, but he faltered at the return of Taylor's hand to his shoulder, this time more firmly.

"Thank you for your time, Father," Taylor said and turned, half pulling on Norris' coat.

When Norris finally turned, he made for the entrance at a double pace, making sure to slap his shoes against the linoleum with extra force. Taylor had to trot to keep up with him. When Norris reached the arch, he stopped dead in his tracks and spun on his heels so quickly that Taylor almost bowled him over. Norris gazed up into the rafters and the railed-off choir lofts

186

that were situated above the altar. He was just quick enough to see Peter's head pop back behind the corner of a wall.

"Little fool," Norris hissed before turning back toward the door, Taylor in hot pursuit.

Standing on the front steps of the Cathedral, Norris stretched his arms out at his sides, then shrugged, letting them go limp. He sat down on the first step.

"What are you doing?" Taylor asked.

"Taking a breather. Let the little fucker die. I don't know if I care anymore," Norris said.

For the first time in years, he wanted a cigarette. A cigarette, an everything bagel with lox, and a nap. A nap sounded like such a good idea. Norris was tired. His body had given out long ago and no matter the fuel he put in it, it was still a clunker running on borrowed time. He glanced down the length of the small step. About thirty feet down, a homeless man was wrapped up in a coat that could have been Norris' if he'd been dragged through a trash heap.

"Sometimes I envy them, y'know," Norris said.

"No you don't...not really," Taylor said.

"Sure I do. They've made the ultimate escape whether they think so or not. They've returned to the most basic form of living. Two concerns; eating and finding shelter," Norris said.

He stood up, took his coat off and walked to where the man lay, curled up on the step. He was an older black man with a face that was probably weather worn to look as old as it did. In reality, the man was probably Norris' age. He cracked an eye as Norris approached. Norris didn't say anything, but dropped his coat in front of the man, nodded to him, and walked away, stuffing his belongings into his pants pockets.

They reached the corner and Norris suddenly grabbed a lamp post like it was going to fall over without his help.

"You ok?" he said.

"Do you really want to get into that, Doc?"

"No, not really."

"Then I'm just dandy. Thank you for your concern," he said and straightened himself up.

"What next?" Taylor asked.

"As much as I say I could care less about that little bastard, letting him die, or worse…letting *them* get to him…well, I can't allow that to happen."

"So, what do we do?"

"Find a back door."

"Naturally. And then?" Taylor asked.

"And then drag the little pecker wood out by the short hairs if we have to. Let's go."

Chapter 21

Nicole watched the little James, the one who called himself Tollgate, stride confidently next to her. He'd grasped her hand as they left the building as if it was a perfectly natural thing to do. He revealed no emotion through the action except through the flexing grasp of his hand around hers. It was as if he were blind and trying to memorize how her hand felt; and like he was afraid that if he let it go, he'd forget. For a moment, as the three strolled across the compound, it had a fleeting feeling of normalness.

Then she saw all of the other Jameses running around the fields and the bizarre reality overwhelmed any sense of normality. Bundled in identical heavy, dark blue winter coats, the boys were scattered about the complex. Nicole noted the lack of any of the hooded boys. A group of them were jogging along a well-worn oval path. Some of the older boys were using spades to try and dig trenches into the dirt. Others were chopping logs.

"Why do they call you Tollgate?" Nicole asked.

"I watch the gate," he said, as if the answer might have been obvious.

"Do you charge?" Ted asked, slightly bemused.

"Once. When Sebastian was returning from town," he said.

"Bet he didn't like that," Nicole said, giving him a sly look.

Tollgate frowned a little and shrugged it off.

"He said it was resourceful. Said it showed I wasn't afraid of him. Showed that I had something the other boys didn't. Something he called kahoniss," Tollgate said.

"Kahoniss?" Ted said, glancing at Nicole.

"*Cajones*," she said.

"Oh. Heh," Ted said.

"So, he's a good… leader," Nicole said.

At this, Tollgate stopped in his tracks and turned, looking at Nicole. He still had no emotion on his face. It was a look she had rarely seen in James, but this little man had perfected the poker face.

"Leader. Why do you use that word?"

"That's not what he is?"

"Do you have a family, Nicole?"

"Sure."

"Does your family have a leader?"

"Well, not exactly. My parents raised me and guide me even now," she said.

"And why do you think that is?" Tollgate asked, squeezing her hand as if reassuring an old friend.

"Because they're older and have experience," Nicole said.

"And so it is in my family. Sebastian is the eldest brother. He raises and guides all of us down to the youngest," he said.

"Has he told you this?" Nicole asked.

"In not so many words," Tollgate said.

"He was right, you know," she said.

"About what?"

"You are special," Nicole said.

She reached up and pushed a stray hair from his forehead, sensing the slightest pressure from him gently leaning into her hand. She tried her hardest to read his expression. There was no fear. He was just a boy who was fully aware of his position within the hierarchy that had been created around him.

"I like you. He's a very lucky brother, you know. Your James," he said.

It was Nicole's turn to frown.

"What do you know about James?" she asked.

"He's one of the first six. Next to Sebastian, they're the next eldest brothers. They have a major role to play in his plans," Tollgate said.

"And just what are his plans?" Ted asked.

Tollgate smirked.

"But you already know the answer to that, Uncle," he said.

"Do I?" Ted said.

"It's not like we're hiding anything here, Uncle. We haven't barred any doors or covered up plans. You've seen everything," Tollgate asked.

At this, Ted moved closer to the boy, towering over him. His chin quivered and when he spoke, it was through pursed lips.

"What I've seen is a blasphemy against humanity. What I've seen is a disregard for established society—," he managed before being cut off by the 8-year-old.

"Established society? Is that what you call it? Are you forgetting who started this all? Your so-called established society. You of all people should be speaking out against them Uncle, not for them. You were told to kill children—"

"Enough! You freakish little parrot!" Ted screamed.

Nicole jumped at the outburst. Ted's face was strained and sanity was not visible in his eyes as he menaced over the boy, his hands clenching at his sides. She moved toward him, placing herself ever so slightly between him and Tollgate.

"Ted," she said, reaching out and taking one of his hands.

A moment of resistance gave way to resignation and the look of madness washed away to one of regret and distance. She looked beyond him and found that every boy in the compound had stopped to spectate. There was no sound but the crunching of the hard soil beneath her feet.

"You should go lie down," she said.

"Yes. It's been…," he murmured, not looking at either of them.

"Quite a day so far," she said.

"Yes. I'll be in the barn. Resting," he said.

He turned and walked away from them toward the red barn, his head down and his hands by his side. He still seemed to be making fists as he walked away. The other boys all returned to their tasks as soon as he did so. The show was over.

Nicole turned back to Tollgate. He stood with his hands in his pockets, rocking ever so slightly onto his heels. She could tell he was waiting for her to say something. How a boy of his age could manipulate them so easily frightened her. But, she wasn't without her own cunning. She resisted the urge to speak and, instead, extended her hand toward him. A momentary curl of his brow was followed by a coy look before he reached out and took her hand again. She tried to avoid shuddering as he took it. There was something about him that bothered her. He was calculating and assessing her at every move in a way that even most adults didn't. She was not so sure that Tollgate had come to them on his own; he could have been planted. For what purpose, it wasn't quite clear, but Nicole felt the claims of total transparency falling down around her.

Nicole glanced over her shoulder and watched as Ted neared the barn.

"Tell me. What happened to the boy from the basement?"

"Basement?"

"Yesterday, when I was first brought…wherever *here* is, I was in a basement and they…they tried to pass off one of your brothers as James. It didn't work."

"That's terrible. Why would they do that?" Tollgate said.

"Oh, come now. Who's being coy?"

"Interesting. I guess that explains what happened after your arrival," Tollgate said.

"What became of him?"

"He was punished and given a new assignment. He was part of the group sent to bring in James. He's the best shot we've got. A real wizard with a sidearm," Tollgate said.

"But, they're not going to kill him, right?" Nicole said and she hated the sense of helplessness that came through in her voice.

"No! That would ruin Sebastian's plans. He's to be a guest with us. Just like you and Uncle. At least until he's reassigned. I think he'll like it here," Tollgate said.

"I don't think you know James very well," Nicole said.

"He's still a brother, and family comes first, right?"

"He's really warped your sense of what's right and wrong."

"I don't know. From what I've seen, I might have a better grasp of things than most kids."

Nicole could only shake her head. He wasn't completely wrong and it was apparently no use openly arguing with this hyper-intelligent, self-aware, little boy. She wasn't going to get anything else to work with, so she would continue to work the only angle she knew. She reached back out for his hand again, which he took.

"I'd like to show you something," he said.

He led her along the edge of the tree line to a well-worn path. She noted how the clutching of his hand had relaxed a bit. The path was a straight line and they walked for two minutes before coming into another wide clearing. A strip of asphalt, about thirty feet wide and cleared of snow, ran along the center of the clearing and beyond. It looked like a landing strip. Across the field, a concrete building with a single door stood alone with what looked to be a spinning radar dish on its roof.

A small wooden building lay directly in front of them, flanked by what looked to be two fuel trucks. A strange sort of ragged white tarp was suspended above it all.

"What's that, hanging overhead?" she asked.

"It's like camouflage for buildings. We change it depending on the season. You'd have to be a hundred feet right overhead to see it and even closer to realize what it was. Uncle found it. He knew where it was before we got to him."

"I don't understand," Nicole said.

"Do you really think he's been ignorant of everything? Do you really think that a man that smart, with that many connections from the past would hide away from the world and, by chance, be just a stone's throw away from here?"

He watched Nicole's face and she could tell that he was reading her reaction. It was hard to hide her anger and confusion. It was his turn to shake his head.

"You might not approve of the world I live in, but I can tell it's filled with a lot more honesty than yours. And for that, I feel sorry for you," Tollgate said.

"He knew about all this?" she asked.

"He knew enough," he said.

"I don't believe you," she said.

He released her hand and walked to the front of the little building. She trailed along behind as they rounded to the other side. There, beneath another length of ragged tarps were two red and black helicopters, much like the one in which she had been taken. An open spot indicated that one was missing.

Beyond that, Nicole spotted a stack of sandbags in a small, circular pattern, stacked about four feet high. It too had a small tarp hanging over it.

"What the hell's that?"

"Anti-aircraft gun," Tollgate said.

Nicole waited for some sort of reaction. She was tempted to just turn and walk away. She knew that he wanted her to react. She knew that he was pushing her buttons at this point. And she knew that by reacting, she would be allowing him to win. Which was exactly what she wanted him to think.

"This is complete insanity, Tollgate! An anti-aircraft gun? To shoot down what? Are you kidding me? I'll take my world of lies and false normality over hiding in the woods with a bunch of kids waiting for the final battle any day."

She turned and walked away as briskly as she could. She listened for footsteps behind her, and was a little disappointed that there weren't any. That was ok, she thought. She could keep up this game for as long as it took.

Chapter 22

"Do you feel that?"

Sitting against a wooden crate, Doug wiped the sweat from his brow for the hundredth time since they'd climbed inside of the freight car. The heat of the morning had only increased as the day went on and, despite the fact that it was late December, the Arizona sun had born down on the steel container with all of its fury.

"The pounds of weight I'm losing sitting absolutely still? Yes...yes I do," Doug said.

"No," Kevin said.

"The train...it's slowing down," Chris said.

"Shit," Kevin said, jumping to his feet.

"You think they figured it out?" Doug asked.

"I think it's surprising it took them this long," Chris said.

He threw his weight into the door, sliding it back about a foot with a screech. He stood at an angle to the door, making quick glances ahead. They were now deep into the desert and sand blew in through the door.

"What do you see?" Kevin asked.

"Hard to tell. We're heading into a dust storm. The head of the train is only a mile off of it," Chris said.

"Would they slow the train for that?" Doug asked.

"They might. I guess they could slip a rail if they were going too fast and it was covered in sand," Chris said.

"But, wouldn't loss of momentum be another problem? I mean, in Philly, if it was wet enough, the train couldn't get up even a small slope from a full stop," Kevin said.

"The question is, are we slowing down, or are we stopping?" Doug asked.

"I can't see far enough ahead to see if there's a town…or a way station," Chris said.

"I thought you've taken this trip before?" Kevin said.

"I have, but we're only half way at most and I never had a reason to stick my head out before. I usually jotted down lyrics …or read a book or something," Chris said.

"At this rate, if we keep slowing down, we'll be completely stopped in a couple of minutes," Kevin said.

"More. Takes a long time to slow something this big to a complete stop," Chris said.

"But if we wait too long, it might be too late, no?" Kevin asked.

"But, jumping out now almost guarantees a broken bone…or worse," Chris said.

"Just what we need," Kevin said.

"No thanks," Doug said.

They could feel the hot sand beginning to get in through the door. Chris stood back and slid the door back into place. The sound of the wind and sand beginning to pelt the freight car made hearing anything else next to impossible, but what they felt next made hearing unnecessary. The train lurched.

"They're stopping. Goddamn it!" Chris said.

"Is it safe enough to jump yet?" Doug asked.

"It's never safe enough to jump from a moving fucking train!" Kevin said.

"It's safer than it was thirty seconds ago and the closer we get to stopping, the closer we get to being dead meat anyway!" Chris said.

"Let's get this over with then!" Doug shouted, waving his cane.

Chris reached over and threw back the door as wide as he could. They were greeted with a face full of wind and sand, forcing each of them to turn away, covering their eyes. It was like opening a window onto a blank sand-colored canvas. They could make out neither earth nor sky.

"This is crazy! What the hell do we do out there!" Doug shouted over the wind.

"We're sitting ducks in here if we stay!" Chris said.

"There could be a big fucking rock right there for all I know…or a hole…or a fucking river half a mile down!" Kevin said.

"It's either that or get caught…or killed. I'm gonna jump!" Chris said

He didn't hesitate. The words were fresh from his lips when he jumped into the void. Kevin and Doug stared after him, waiting for something. Anything.

"Fuck me!" Kevin shouted.

"I don't know if I can do this!" Doug said, holding his arm at eye level to block the sand.

"You can…and you will. I know you don't trust me right now, but I'm here with you. We can do this. We're gonna survive."

"I'd feel a lot better if you went first," Doug said.

"I was afraid you were going to say that," Kevin said.

"I'll be right behind you," Doug said.

"If I survive, you promise to trust me?"

"I can't promise that, but if you die, I'll feel really bad," Doug said.

"Thanks! I'm feeling the love…you asshole," Kevin said, a smirk creeping onto his lips.

"Get going! Chris will be waiting! Cover your head!"

Kevin stepped back, then leapt out of the opening, screaming.

"Geroni-fucking-moooooooo!"

The sound of his scream disappeared with the sand. Leaping out probably wasn't the best plan, Doug thought. He made his way to the edge. The train lurched again and his decision had been made for him; he was falling out. He pushed off just enough with the one foot that was close enough to touch the floor. He wouldn't see just how close he'd come to falling under the train's wheels. He barely had time to raise his arms to his face before he was making contact with the ground. It was both softer and harder than he had expected. He rolled several times before coming to a rest, his cane still clutched in his hand. For a moment, he wasn't sure if he'd landed face up or face down as his view hadn't changed from the blank slate of sand. Then he realized that he couldn't breathe. He scrambled with his hands, trying to orient himself. He opened his mouth to gasp for breath, but found sand instead of air. He coughed reflexively, which didn't help to solve the fact that he was slowly suffocating. He tried to shield his mouth and breathe, but the sand was starting to overwhelm him. He'd survived the jump from the train, only to die from having the wind knocked out of him in a sandstorm.

The hands that wrapped around his arms made him flinch, but there was no energy left for him to determine whether they were friend or foe. They lifted him to his feet and then the wind and sand abated. He could hear himself coughing and gagging on the sand, spitting mouthfuls of it out, but the air was starting to come in. The stars were still in his eyes, but he was no longer feeling like he was going to pass out. Someone was slapping him on his back.

"Jesus, big man! You dive in with your mouth open?" Kevin said in his ear.

"Tripped…train jerked…wasn't ready," Doug coughed.

Doug wiped tears and sand from his eyes. Kevin had thrown his jacket over their heads. They could hear the train still continuing by.

"What the fuck took you guys so long to jump?" Chris said.

"My fault," Doug said, still spitting sand from his mouth. His throat felt like it had been lined with grit.

"No…mine," Kevin said.

"Doesn't matter. Now what?" Chris said.

"We should make our way along the line. If there is a town, maybe we can sneak into it and hide until whoever it is who's stopped the train moves on," Kevin said.

"They know we were on that train. As soon as they see that the door is open, they'll know what's up. They don't just leave doors open anymore," Chris said.

"If this storm keeps up, maybe they won't be able to see that door," Kevin said.

"If we don't move soon, they'll just have to look for the three small dunes by the side of the train tracks," Doug said, spitting one last time.

They heard the last of the train pass with a clack-clack. Chris started walking with the edge of the railroad ties at his feet. Doug and Kevin followed in single file. Doug found it hard going in the sand. The uneven ground and a lack of firm ground to place his cane on was a bad combination. He stumbled several times with Kevin hanging just behind him to give him a hand.

"I'm sorry," Doug shouted over his shoulder after a few minutes of walking.

"I don't blame you," Kevin said.

"It's hard to know what to believe anymore," Doug said.

"We're still alive. That's all I need to believe in."

"I wish that did it for me...oof!"

Doug had walked right into Chris who had stopped dead. He felt Kevin return the favor by walking right into his back.

"What the…" Kevin said

"Shhhh…do you hear that?" Chris said.

They were all silent. Doug could hear nothing over the wind and the sound of sand showering around them. He could just make out Chris in front of him, cupping his hands over his ears. Then he heard it. It was an engine idling.

"It's a car," Doug said.

"There must be a road," Chris said.

"The train…do you think it stopped?"

They all moved forward slowly. The sand gradually sloped upward and Chris brought them to a halt again.

"There," he said and turned, pushing on their shoulders to get them down.

He was pointing just to their right and when the wind shifted, Doug could just make out the shadow of a car amongst the sand. Its headlights were on, just barely denting the darkness of the sand.

"I think I can hear the train too," Doug said.

"Only one car. No town, no nothing. They stopped a train in the middle of nowhere for one car," Kevin said.

"One guess as to who it is," Doug said.

"Let's move around the back of the car. Maybe it's just some guy who got caught at the crossing," Chris said

"There is no crossing! No lights, no guards, nothing!" Doug said.

"Redcoats!" Kevin said.

"Maybe it's only one!" Chris said.

"Still not a fair fight if he's got a gun!" Kevin said.

"Still not a fair fight if he doesn't," Doug said.

Doug ducked down behind Chris, taking a moment's respite from the full blast of the sand. As the adrenaline from the jump had worn off, it was replaced by an increasingly sharp pain that emanated from deep within his surgically repaired hip. He hadn't felt that kind of pain since the accident and the pills he'd used to quell the physical and emotional sting of ruining his life in such a swift fashion. He gritted his teeth, trying to bring himself back to the moment. The pain was winning though and he knew that if it got much worse, he'd be worse than useless.

"Doug? You still with us?" Kevin said.

"Barely...," Doug replied.

"You ok?"

"That jump screwed my hip up pretty bad," Doug said.

"Can you walk?" Chris asked.

"He doesn't have to," Kevin said.

"I can...," Doug began.

"No, Chris and I will take care of these guys," Kevin said.

"You and Chris," Doug said, unable to hold back the chuckle.

"Element of surprise," Chris said.

"You'd better hurry...I think the wind is starting to die down," Doug said.

He watched as the two stood and turned to face the car. Chris moved close to Kevin and said something that Doug couldn't make out, but Kevin's shrug of the shoulder was perfectly clear. Kevin had no idea what he and Chris were going to do and Doug was going to have to sit in the sand and hope it all went down ok. They moved away from him and as much as he wanted to stand up and follow them, the pain in his hip told him no. His eyes watered as he attempted to put weight on the hip. At that moment, there was no amount of effort that was going to lift him to his feet, let alone walk.

He watched through his fingers as the two moved away from him in a direction parallel to the car. Then, they were gone; swallowed by the sand. He lowered his hand and closed his eyes, straining to hear something above the wind and sand that pelted him. He counted off a minute, then two. The gunshot that pierced the blanket of white noise defied the pain in his mind and body and he found himself standing upright, teeth clenched so tight he could taste blood. He staggered toward the car, gripping his cane like a club instead of actually using it for its intended purpose.

Each of the two dozen steps to the car was agonizing and walking in the sand felt like walking backward. There was a sudden dip in the sand and the car materialized before him. An older model sedan, Doug couldn't tell if it was brown or just looked that way in the desert. Chris and Kevin were nowhere to be seen. Doug lowered his cane to the ground and found it sturdy enough to support his weight. He made his way to the driver's side and opened the door. Sliding into the seat and closing the door was a relief to the senses. His skin still tingled as if he was still being pelted by sand. His ears felt like they were filled with cotton from the noise of the sand and wind. He raised his hands and scraped away the caked-on dirt from his eyes and face. He shifted his legs to get more comfortable.

Doug scanned around the entire car. The slam of hands on the passenger side window made him jump. It was Kevin, with Chris just over his shoulder. They were looking frantic. Doug pressed the unlock button and the two jumped into the car, a cloud of sand trailing them.

"What the hell happened?" Doug asked.

"Just go. We'll explain on the way," Kevin said.

Chris coughed and sputtered from the back seat.

"Go where? Can you see?" Doug asked.

"Give it a second…it's letting up…I think. There!," Kevin said, pointing to the glimpse of asphalt that appeared before them.

Doug moved the car forward at a crawl.

"I thought you said you couldn't move!" Chris said finally.

"Amazing what fear will drive a man to do. I'm going to pay for it though…I can feel it," Doug said.

"Awe, he was coming to rescue us," Kevin said.

"It's not funny. What the hell was I supposed to do? I heard a gunshot!" Doug said.

"He missed," Kevin said.

"You're a couple of idiots," Doug said.

"Not me. He's the one who ran up to the window and hollered like some kind of sand banshee. I think he actually scared the shit out of the guy. Took him a minute to react, but once he did, he was on Kevin quick. Took everything I had to overrun him and crack him on the head with a rock," Chris said.

"For cryin' out loud, is he dead?" Doug asked.

"Barely dropped the gun when he hit him. I think he was more pissed that Chris ruined his hat," Kevin said.

"So, he's still out there?"

Kevin nodded and Doug reached over and locked the doors. The sand was starting to clear a little more, which allowed him to increase the pace of the car. There was an unspoken sigh between the three of them.

"I think this is East," Doug said.

"I don't really care," Chris said.

"When we reach civilization, we'll get directions," Kevin said.

"Let's hope civilization is fairly close," Doug said.

"Why's that?" Chris asked.

"We've only got a half-a tank of gas to get there," Doug said.

Chapter 23

"You've been avoiding me," Nicole said.

It was now nearly three o'clock in the afternoon and she hadn't seen Ted since his confrontation with Tollgate almost six hours before. She'd sat alone in the loft of the barn, flipping through a historic picture regional picture book. It was among a handful of dusty books on a small impromptu shelf that was between the two sleeping areas. The books, in general, were classics she had read or attempted to read in the past. But, the book in question had a yellow sticky note attached to one page and that had caught her eye. The page in question had several photos of the farm from across the years. Apparently, the main house had been built in the late 1800s. That wasn't what had been keeping her attention though. It was the fuzzy photograph in the lower right-hand corner of the page. The oldest of the bunch, it was the worst quality of all. There was nothing of interest in the photo except for the farmer behind the plow in the field. A massive, broad-shouldered man, he made the plow and the mule pulling the contraption look small. There was something rather familiar about the way the man stood.

Ted climbed up to the loft, slowly. She held the book up before her and watched as he crested the top step, glancing from the book to him and back. She shook her head.

"Sebastian was showing me something. What's that look for?" he said.

"Nothing, just reading up on some local lore," she said.

"Anything interesting?"

"Nah. What did Sebastian show you?"

"His lab," Ted said.

"Seriously?"

"It's awful."

"He doesn't have…more, does he?," Nicole asked.

"No. He seems to have halted…production, so to say. Now he's just focused on manipulation. He's got a half dozen white coats all working around the clock," he said.

"Guess we didn't make their acquaintance," Nicole chimed.

"According to him, they prefer to work and eat and sleep in the lab," he said.

"I don't get it. What's he offering them to stay?" she asked.

"An open lab where they're free to conduct whatever genetics-based experiments they like. Stuff they couldn't do in a publicly funded lab. He's brought in the best equipment and let the kids play with the toys. The results are running all over this godforsaken farm," he said.

"Tollgate included," she said.

"He's his pride and joy. Like they took a brilliant adult's brain and slapped it in the little bastard," Ted said.

"He's still a little boy, with little boy needs," Nicole said.

"They should all—," but he stopped himself from going any further with the thought.

Nicole closed the book, careful to tuck the yellow sticky back under the page before placing it on the bed next to her.

Ted was staring at the floor, balling and unballing his fists at his sides. He didn't even notice her approach. He spoke to the floor.

"A part of me…," he paused and began again. "Back then, a part of me felt like what I did was stopping this kind of thing. This kind of manipulation. I thought their wrong outweighed my wrong. Then I did it and I changed my mind. Like a fool, I let my feelings get in the way of reason. If I had known then, none of this would be here. We wouldn't be here—"

"James wouldn't be here," Nicole said.

Ted couldn't look her in the eye. She wrapped her arms around him and pressed her face against his chest. He smelled like the cold Canadian air. She felt him stand rigid for a moment before relaxing and accepting her embrace. He pulled her tighter for a moment.

"I'm so sorry," he said.

"Stop apologizing for what you can't undo," she said.

He released himself from her grip and stood back away from her.

"Then I'm sorry for what I could have changed. I'm sorry for knowing more than I ever let on. He told you, didn't he. I can see it in your face. He wasn't lying. I've known about all of this for a very long time. But, they got to me before I could do anything about it…and I was too late anyway, wasn't I? I feel like I've done nothing but make poor decisions in my life, Nicole. And it's worn me down. I can't put up the strong exterior anymore. I just can't put on the show anymore," he said.

He walked to his bed and eased into it, lying flat on his back. Nicole had never seen him look so small. She sat at the edge of the bed. The creak of the ladder made them both turn. Tollgate's head popped up over the lip.

"I'm not disturbing you, am I?" he asked.

"No, it's ok," Nicole said.

"I just thought you should know that James is on his way here. In Uncle's plane," he said.

"What? Did they catch him?" Nicole asked, moving over to the window and gazing out into the dusky sky as if she might see him.

"There was a bit of an accident at Uncle's house. We're not sure," he said.

"An accident," Nicole said, turning back to the boy.

"We think he's ok. He's with Steve," Tollgate said.

"Who's Steve?" Ted said, sitting up in the bed.

"The creep they trained to be like James. To try to fool me," she said.

"What?"

"Nevermind. Not important now. What does that mean, Tollgate? What does Steve being with them mean?"

"It could mean he's bringing them in," he said.

"This Steve can fly a plane?"

"He could if he needed to," Tollgate said.

"And what if he isn't bringing them in?"

"Then they might get shot down," Tollgate said.

Chapter 24

If Ted had been any slower, he would have been picking Nicole and the boy up off the barn floor. He'd caught her by the wrist and wrapped her arms as gently as he could, despite her thrashings.

"You little bastard! Did they take out your heart when they gave you that extra dose of brains? Goddamn you!"

"We have rules to protect us. If we make an exception, we could—"

"You're going to kill him!"

"Not necessarily," Tollgate said.

Tollgate showed no sign of emotion as he watched her writhe in Ted's arms. Nicole wanted to slap him. She wanted to make him hurt; make him feel something other than the elevated sense of superiority that he made apparently clear. He turned and put a foot on the ladder before stopping. He didn't look back, but spoke to the top rung of the ladder.

"For your sake, I hope he comes in just fine," he said. He then continued down the ladder and they heard the barn door brush closed.

Only then did Ted release Nicole. She turned and fell into his arms, her anger turning to tears.

"I don't think I can take much more of this," she said between heavy sobs.

"Hey, listen to me. They won't do that. Sebastian needs him. Don't you give up on me now. You're the strong one, remember? I'm the one that's falling apart," Ted said.

She wiped her face with her jacket sleeve and pushed back away from his chest, nodding and holding back her desire to cry. She was tired of living in what felt like someone else's nightmare.

"You're right. He won't do it. He'll stop them. For me, he'll stop them," she said.

She turned and made her way down the ladder. Ted followed and was at the bottom when she pushed her way through the barn door. There, just a few steps from the doors, was Tollgate, his back to them. His shoulders were shaking. He turned around to face them, tears silently streaming down his cheeks, his lips curled together.

"I can't stop them!" he sobbed, throwing his hands in the air. He pounded on his chest. "I know it's wrong. I know it here. I know I shouldn't understand any of this and I hate myself because I understand it all too well. Most of the others, they're just doing what they're told. They're just little kids! Me? I understand what's asked of me. I know exactly what's going on. And I still do as I'm told. But, I'm just supposed to be a kid and I look down and see a kid's body. But I don't have little boy thoughts anymore. I think I had them once. But, I can't remember. And you came along and…and…and I don't want to make you cry anymore."

With that, he fell running into Nicole's arms. She coddled his head and her own tears flowed. Sobs shook his whole body; they had an age and depth beyond his small frame. She held him until he let go. He looked around as he did so, then make

216

quick work of wiping his tears away and regaining his composure.

"I don't think anyone saw," Nicole said.

"Perhaps not. Best that they don't. I can't stop them now, but there's other ways."

"You'll help us."

"I'll do what I can without making it obvious. That would endanger everyone."

He sniffed and shoved his hands deep into his coat pockets.

"Thank you," Nicole said.

"You can thank me if I manage to help help you," Tollgate said.

"I'm thanking you for having a change of heart," she said.

"It feels right," he said.

He turned and walked away across the compound. Nicole watched him until he disappeared through the doors of the main building. She glanced back up at the sky before turning back to Ted.

"Amazing what a little caring can do," he said.

"Let's hope it's enough," she said.

Chapter 25

"There's no way he didn't see the call sign," James said, glancing back over his shoulder at the airfield they had just climbed away from.

"Who needs a call sign? How many bright yellow water planes are flying today?"

"His lights weren't on and it's not like he was flying down the road. Maybe it was a routine call," New Kevin said.

"To an airport where an old man had just been shot. I'm not buying that," James said.

"It won't matter what he was doing once he finds the old man. We'd better get where we're going in a hurry," Paynter said.

"And just where is that again?" James asked, turning to New Kevin.

"Sudbury. Got a map?"

"Uhhh...map...right. Lemme check."

James looked around his seat and opened the compartment in the dash in front of him. He was immediately brought back to his Uncle. A handful of objects were neatly placed inside, their containers neatly secured to the plane to avoid movement during flight. He pulled out a black-handled flashlight. Inside a small round case was a spare compass. A thin box contained a multipurpose knife. A flat box revealed the plane's important legal paperwork and his Uncle's pilot's license. James grabbed the papers and lifted them, exposing a small surprise.

"Always prepared," he said.

Paynter glanced over at the .38 caliber pistol James pulled from the compartment.

"Might want to keep that where it is. Just in case," he said.

"Seemed like your Uncle Ted was a 'just in case' kind of guy," New Kevin said.

"Yes, it does," James said.

He flipped through the papers and found a small, worn, folded map. Gently, James opened the map to its full two-page width. Apparently, it was a portion of a larger map of the southern portion of central Canada. However, it clearly indicated both where his Uncle had lived and the city of Sudbury they were headed to. There were no edges and the original key was missing. It had been substituted with a brief, crudely written key with two objects of interest; "airports" and "large farms." In pen, his Uncle had indicated a handful of each within a 15-mile radius of the city of Sudbury. Several had been circled in the faintest of red pen with a corresponding X through them. James squinted at the scrawl on the map. There was something not quite right.

"Anything interesting?" New Kevin said from the back.

James made to cover the map, but his hands fumbled it and he heard the paper tear in his hands.

"Shit…yeah. There's a part of a map. It's old though and I almost just tore it in half."

James then did something he hoped he wouldn't regret. His thumb quietly pushed through the spot where the ad lib key was, removing the writing completely. He released the piece and watched as it fell to the floor beside him. He turned in his seat and handed it to New Kevin. He looked into the man's face as he received the piece of paper and he saw everything he'd needed to see.

"What do you think, Kevin?" James said, turning back around in his seat.

"What do you think these marks mean? Strange your uncle didn't write down a key."

"Maybe it was off the edge," James said.

"Maybe, but this was torn out a long time ago. The bottom right, though…that was clearly torn recently."

"Clearly," James said.

"Ok, so the map was torn a couple times. What does it show? Stick it up on the dash." Paynter said.

James took the map from New Kevin without looking at him and placed the map up on the dash to Paynter's right. A small clipboard seemed perfectly placed for just such a task.

"Well, I'll be damned if some of these aren't airports. Strange that he didn't use a newer map that would have shown that kind of stuff," Paynter said.

"Strange," James said.

"Let's try that one. Circled, but without the X."

James glanced over at it. Luckily, Paynter had picked an airport and not a large farm or James might have had a hard time convincing him otherwise. It was the only spot close to them without an X through it.

"If we're here," Paynter continued, "We just need to head a little to the North and East."

They passed the time without speaking. The constant hum of the engine drowned out everything around them and James watched as the quiet country passed below. He envied the occasional driver he saw who was otherwise preoccupied with getting to and from work or home. He wanted to be back there. He wanted the blissful ignorance that his life had been.

"What's the plan?" James said.

"To find your Uncle and Nicole," Paynter said, then adding, "Right?"

"This whole thing is a setup," James said.

"What?"

"Even if we could fly in and rescue them, where would we go? What are we doing? Where is this gonna end? If the US government is behind all of this, where do we run and hide?"

"We're going to stop running once we have all the pieces in place, James. Then we tell the world what happened here," Paynter said.

"And what if the world doesn't want to know? Or worse…that they don't care."

"They'll care," Paynter said.

"You sound so sure. These are the same people who are so desensitized to Big Brother that they'd willingly let him into their lives because it's more comforting to think that *someone* is watching instead of thinking that no one is watching. Is it enough to go through all of this just to hope that someone cares in the end? Whether I die a nobody today or a somebody tomorrow, I'm still dead."

"But you already are somebody, James," New Kevin said.

James quickly reached for the gun in the glove compartment and turned on New Kevin in the back seat.

"But who the hell…are…Jesus—" James said, faltering.

"What the…" Paynter said.

James stared back down the barrel of one of his Uncle's pistols that was aimed at his head. New Kevin had a calm look to him, but one that belied a sense of disappointment.

"Steve. You can call me Steve. Dr. Paynter, I'd appreciate it if you could just stay the course for the moment. The airport you're heading to is close enough to where we're going. I'm strapped in fairly tight, so don't try any acrobatic nonsense."

"You bastard," Paynter said.

"We could have left you there to rot," James said.

"You should have," Steve said.

"But they were counting on that, weren't they," James said.

"Yes. Now put the gun down. They're blanks anyway."

"Replaced when you put the fake map in," James said.

"You noticed."

"My Uncle had unique handwriting. I'd say it's nearly impossible to reproduce. And the map was too old. He'd only had the plane recently. Before that, he was all about nautical charts of the region."

"Keen eye, James. Kudos to you."

223

"Gee, thanks, Steve. Better stop before I get all warm and fuzzy. So, which phase was this one produced in?" James said, turning to Paynter.

"I think this one is off label," Paynter said.

"Looks like they got the mixture wrong somehow. A bit scraggly. Maybe this one was the runt," James said.

"Nice. Shut it and turn around," Steve said.

"What are you going to do, shoot me? Wouldn't that put a damper on your bosses' day," James said.

"I said…what the—"

With a slight tap of his foot against the console, James had confirmed what Paynter had attempted to signal to him with facial expressions. At least, that's what James had hoped he'd been trying to do. Otherwise, the man had an itchy nose and James was about to be shot as he threw himself at Steve. But, Paynter had turned the yoke to the left and though a shot rang out, gravity had pulled the gun and James into different lines of fire. James reached out for the gun and allowed himself to roll with the plane, pulling the firearm with him, with little resistance from the shocked Steve. For his part, Steve flailed out with his other hand, trying to grasp any part of James that he could. Meanwhile, as James felt the plane come back to level, he fought against the moment of weightlessness and found a handful of Steve's wild hair with one hand. He directed the other in a balled fist back to the first, making contact with what felt like Steve's temple.

"Ow!" James said, then repeated the process, aiming slightly lower and hoping for a softer target. For a moment, he was afraid that the resultant crunching sound had been his own fingers. He heard the thud of the gun hitting the floor as the plane leveled back out. James held the gun on his lap, holding it level with Steve's knees. Still strapped into his chair, Steve clutched his face; blood poured from the bridge of his nose in large quantities.

"Not again," Steve muttered.

"You started it," James said.

A sudden flash and bang outside the window shook the entire plane.

"What the hell was that?" James shouted.

"I…I think it was flak," Paynter said.

"Flak? Flak?!"

"Flak! You know, like in the old war movies? They're trying to shoot us down."

James put the gun in his seat and moved into the back, grabbing Steve by the jacket. He shook as hard as he could while Paynter turned the plane into an evasive dive.

"Make them stop!"

"I can't! It's too late. I was supposed to fly in at a certain altitude. We're too low now…we're dead!"

"If I can just get over that bank of trees, I should get out of their line of sight," Paynter said.

"So, you were supposed to capture us before we left the house?" James asked, shaking him again. Steve nodded furiously.

"Knock it off! The idiots used too much explosive!"

James released Steve as Paynter banked ever lower. He could see the treetops out of the corner of his eye, but refused to look away from Steve. He settled back into his seat, picking the gun back up.

"What did he say?" Paynter shouted over another explosion that threw enough debris to shake the plane violently.

"Explosives! Explosives!" Steve shouted.

"So, it wasn't meant to kill us, just knock us out."

"They don't want you dead," Steve said, trying to staunch the blood flow with his sleeve.

"Could've fuckin' fooled me!"

There was a rending explosion and a metallic tearing sound that pulled the air that would have completed James' sentence out of him. They were falling and it occurred to him that he wasn't strapped in as he rose from his seat and felt the ceiling of the cockpit strike his head. The rest was a blur.

Chapter 26

Flanked by two pedestrian alleys on either side, the cathedral offered several opportunities for entrance, but few that were open. They made their way up Pirate Alley with no luck, rounded the back of the building and made their way down Pere Antoine. The first door they encountered was the least ornate. The door led in to a small mud room attached to what appeared to be a large office that had been converted into a maintenance closet. Norris opened the door a crack and looked out before stepping out into the corridor.

"A bit sparse," Taylor said.

"Not a sign in sight," Norris said.

"Guess they don't expect visitors in this section," Taylor said.

To their right, the corridor came to the corner of the building. To the left, a pair of swinging doors opened onto another hallway. Footsteps from that direction made up their minds. Rounding the corner, they came to the entrance of a stairwell. At the top of the second flight of stairs Norris had to stop. He clutched the burning pain that had developed in his chest. That was a new one. Normally, the pain came only with the coughing. He rubbed the spot, hoping it would help. It didn't. He waved off Taylor's look of concern.

At the top of the third flight, there was a small sitting area just outside another set of swinging doors. A small sign identified the entrance to the choir lofts. A stoic-looking chair and coffee table stood against one side of a sitting area. A well-read collection of magazines were scattered across the top of the table; a lidded coffee cup was sitting at the edge. Norris reached down, grasped the cup, sniffed the contents, and put it back.

"Still warm," Norris said.

"His?"

"Think anyone else would be hanging out in the wings of a church drinking a cup of hot chocolate and reading a two-year-old copy of Catholic Digest?"

Norris gazed through the windows of the double doors before pushing one side open and walking out into the loft. The lofts of the cathedral were the largest Norris had ever seen, which wasn't saying much. Cathedrals weren't high on his list of building visits. They ran the length of the building and were twenty-five feet wide. Where they stood now, they were nearest the altar and on the opposite side from where Peter had been.

"Nice and easy, Doc. We don't want to spook him," Norris whispered.

Taylor nodded and the two men made their way toward the railing wall at the edge of the loft. They were both focused on where Peter had been. When they reached the railing, Norris glanced down below and stopped short, holding a hand out to stop Taylor from completely crashing into him. Taylor followed Norris' gaze down below to find Father Daniel staring icily back up at them; his mouth so taught, it had no definition. Standing just over his shoulder was Peter, his cheeks flushed. He had either run all the way to Father Daniel, or he was embarrassed by what was transpiring, or perhaps, Norris thought, both. Norris stood gazing down upon them, only able to shake his head in disbelief. The front doors of the cathedral swung open with a thud, drawing his attention. The hair stood up on the back of his neck.

There was only one of them. His red coat had a halo around it as the light from outside bathed him before the doors swung back closed. Taller than the others he had seen, this redcoat wore thick-rimmed glasses and had a pronounced limp as he sauntered into the building and Norris could see that his left pant leg was bloodied. The redcoat spotted Peter immediately and, even at that distance, Norris thought he smiled a bit as he drew the gun out of his coat pocket.

"Peter! Run!" Norris shouted, which drew the exact response he had expected.

Norris shoved Taylor to the ground and followed him as the bullet ricocheted against the wall above them. Screams followed from the crowd below and the sounds of scrambling and footsteps soon echoed throughout the space. Norris drew his own gun, crawled along the railing, and popped up above it several feet from where they had been. The redcoat had already begun moving toward Peter, but knowing Norris was there forced him under the loft they were on.

"Doc, move!"

Norris backtracked to the stairwell and raced to the stairs, skipping steps at times. Taylor struggled to keep up. They made their way to a door that entered the worship area behind the altar. A shot rang out, and Norris hesitated near the door. He peered out through the glass window and watched as the redcoat headed into the entryway where Peter had been standing. He stepped out cautiously, eyeing the front door for reinforcements. Seeing nothing, Norris quickly crossed the space, stopping when he saw the body.

Father Daniel was rolled on his side in a pool of his own blood. His left hand clutched a small silver cross at his neck. Norris quickly reached down, pressing the sides of his neck, confirming what he already knew. He closed the man's eyes, taking with it the look of utter surprise.

"Jesus Christ. He killed the priest," Taylor said.

"These guys still surprise you, Doc," Norris said.

"People have always surprised me, Agent Norris. That's why being on my own never bothered me," Taylor said.

They made their way into the doorway and found themselves back out on Pirate Alley. Norris and Taylor watched as the redcoat moved around the back of the building, apparently in hot pursuit of Peter.

"Doc, get the car and bring it around to the West side of the building. I'll wait at the corner of Royal," Norris said, tossing Taylor the keys.

Taylor bobbled the keys, dropping them at his feet. He reached down to get them and looked up at Norris.

"And what if you're not there?" Taylor said.

Norris paused.

"Well, I hadn't thought of it that way, Doc. Jesus. If I'm not there, then I won't have anything to worry about anymore. You, on the other hand, had better get the hell out of Dodge," Norris said.

With that, Norris turned and pursued the redcoat. He reached the corner and peered around. A shot rang out, ricocheting off the ground just beyond his feet. The redcoat had paused in the middle of the square at the back of the building and waited for someone to round the corner. Norris checked the safety on his own gun and peeked back around the corner again. The redcoat had put another twenty feet between them. Norris followed, but kept the statue that adorned the middle of the square within the line of sight between to the two of them for cover.

Norris strained to see some evidence of Peter, but there was none. The redcoat, however, seemed to know exactly where he was heading. When Norris reached the corner of Royal, he was torn as he watched the redcoat continue on. He looked back to the east. Taylor would be another minute at least. He turned back to the West. The redcoat was still moving quickly down Royal. Norris crossed to the other side of the street, slipping his gun into the shoulder holster he wore.

Norris looked around at the traffic on the block. A couple were strolling with their newborn. A bicyclist made his way along the cross street. A few cars passed in both directions. No one paid him any mind. He heard the car before he saw it, turning to see the Barracuda move up the street and slide over to his side. Norris ran in front of the car and opened the door before he realized Taylor was sitting in the back seat. He glanced in to see the man in black behind the wheel, dried blood covering the crooked side of his face, Taylor's gun held limply in his hand and directed toward Norris.

"Motherfucker," Norris said.

"Nice to see you too, Rich. Now get in the car. We've got a kid to get."

Norris obeyed and slipped in to the passenger seat. He put his seat belt on like it was just another ride.

"Awe, see, like a big happy family all back together again," the man said, glancing around the car.

"Shut up and let's get this over with," Norris said.

"No chance to reminisce? No sharing of stories? No one wants to know how many bones I broke in that little debacle around the corner? Figured that would buy you fellas plenty of time to find the kid and make off with him. But, nooo. These fucking freaks found him again. That red-coated bastard should be dead. Instead, he rolled out a moment after you left and acted like he'd just had a fender bender. Something not quite right about that. Me, on the other hand. Well, as you can tell, it's improved my looks some," the man rambled.

"And your faculties. Big improvement," Norris said.

"I could still kill the both of you with one hand," the man said.

Norris screamed, reached over and grabbed the man by the collar. They were nose to nose.

232

"Then why don't you?!"

The metal click of the hammer being drawn back was the only sound.

"Because that's not how it's supposed to end, now is it, Rich?"

"Well, I'm getting tired of waiting for the ending. Nothing worse than having to slog through the bullshit in the middle when you know how it ends. Sort of like watching *Titanic*. The boat still fucking sinks, doesn't it."

Norris reached down for the gun and pulled it closer to him.

"So why don't we write a new ending...right here, right now," Norris breathed.

The scream from outside the car drew the attention of all three men. Had Norris not known the stakes of what he now saw, he might have thought it comical. Peter was running across the street a block ahead of them, the redcoat close to his heels. The kid was red-faced and moving just fast enough to outpace the gimpy old timer. The redcoat was waving what looked to be the bag from Peter's backpack at him before dropping it in the gutter. They disappeared around the corner.

"No time for funny business, Rich," the man said, wrenching his pistol free and slamming on the gas.

The car hurtled up the block and turned left at Toulouse Street. They came to an abrupt halt and the man had to jerk the wheel to the right to avoid a van that was sitting in the middle of the road. Being a typical New Orleans street, there was just

233

enough room for one parked car and one lane of traffic. Being the third car meant going nowhere. Just as the man in black was about to lay on the horn, the van began to creep along.

"Jesus fucking Christ," the man shouted, slamming his fist against the wheel.

He leaned out the window and veered as far right as he could.

"Dammit, they're getting away. Come on jackass! Move!"

They continued to creep the rest of the way along the block.

"Shame Peter's not a sprinter," Norris said.

"Kid's been hittin' up the loaves too often, needs to stick to the fishes. Come on, my dead grandmother moves faster," the man said, shouting the last bit out the window at the van, which paid no mind.

They arrived at Chartres and the man cursed a streak of blue as the van seemed to be purposely placing itself in the spot that took up the most room. It went straight across after stopping and the Barracuda followed without really stopping at the intersection. Norris clutched the door handle as they came to a screeching halt. This time, the man laid on the horn. Norris watch as the back door of the van creaked open. The tip of the barrel was all he needed to see.

"Oh shit."

"Motherfu…," the man's words were cut off by the shotgun blast to the front grill. He slammed the shifter into reverse and peeled back out onto Chartres.

"I was hoping to die with my gun in my hand, not strapped into your goddamn passenger seat," Norris shouted as he ducked behind the passenger-side door. The second shot shattered the glass of his window, sending shards throughout the car. A cry of pain from the back seat told Norris that Taylor had taken a hit.

"Doc?" Norris called out.

"God dammit...just glass...I think," Taylor called back.

The man showed his skill with the car and a third shot barely ticked off the back bumper as they peeled back down Chartres. Halfway up the block, they turned right onto Wilkinson Street, a one way crossover that led back onto Decatur. Looking to the right, they all watched as the tragicomedy continued through the crosswalk. The van was tailing just behind.

"Why the fuck don't they just have someone else chase him?" the man said, pulling out onto Decatur.

"Maybe it's a seniority thing," Taylor said.

Norris and the man glanced at one another, then they both glanced back at Dr. Taylor. Norris looked back at the driver and half whispered.

"I know why *I* didn't kill him, but what the fuck stopped you?"

"He kinda grew on me," the man said.

He downshifted and flew out into traffic, driving into the oncoming lane to get around the traffic at the light and slip in front of the van. The van driver had instinctively swerved away, not realizing who was driving the car. It clipped a car waiting for the red light, then quickly corrected and pursued.

"You're going to run out of road here," Norris shouted.

The road turned quickly and they watched as Peter led the crippled old redcoat toward the Mississippi, which lay only a hundred feet away. Before them, an electronic gate was looming. They had pulled into a public parking lot. The man floored the gas, then came to such an abrupt halt at the gate that Norris and Taylor swore. The man rolled down the window and pressed the button for a ticket. It was his turn to be stared at.

"That's a LiftMaster 5000. Son of a bitch would take the roof off before we got through," the man said.

They just slipped through as the van pulled up. Taylor and Norris turned to watch as the van accelerated toward the gate. The man had been right, but the van had more mass and a lower point of impact. The gate arm took most of the left quarter panel of the van with it before relenting. The car hung a quick left. The man headed toward an opening in the curb that would allow them to circumvent the traffic barriers that had been put in place to prevent just such a move. Norris tightened his seat belt, just before he made his move.

At the last moment, he reached out and jerked the steering wheel quickly to the right. The effect was immediate. Instead of avoiding the barrier, Norris had pulled it into their immediate path. They hit harder than he imagined they would. The strike planted the concrete barrier solidly into the center of the engine block. The windshield shattered and the steam and smoke allowed him to reach over in the confusion and retrieve his gun. The man had slammed his head against the windshield in the crash and renewed blood was pouring down his face. He was cursing and trying to find his gun. Norris wasn't going to wait to see if he found it.

Leaping from the car, Norris quickly turned to face the oncoming van, placing two shots from his pistol into the driver's side window. The van swerved to the left of the Barracuda and rocked the back of it as it came to a halt. Norris turned and watched people scattering and screaming. One man stood nearby, wide-eyed, with what looked like the remnants of a beignet in his hand and powdered sugar at the corners of his mouth. Norris screamed at him as he began to run toward Peter.

"Get the fuck out of here, this ain't no movie!"

He spotted Peter and the old man in the crowds heading down toward the water. A large white and red paddle wheel boat lay docked at the edge of the water. He crossed some railroad lines and felt his chest tighten. He staggered slightly and the scene before him wavered. He clenched his fist and pounded at his own chest. He stopped in his tracks, watching as tourists eyed him warily and moved away, looking from his gun to his face and back. The pain subsided and his vision cleared. He watched as Peter plowed past a security guard and flopped over a short railing on the side of the boat. The redcoat followed and waved his gun at the angered security guard who changed his mind about pursuing the two. The guard was shouting into his cell phone when Norris passed him. Norris flashed his badge at the man who was obviously calling 911.

The first deck of the ship was empty and Norris cautiously entered the door where he'd seen the two go in. He pushed through to a dining hall. Several stunned-looking wait staff pointed up a flight of stairs when Norris waved his badge. He nodded his appreciation, then stopped at the bottom of the stairs. If he had the fit now, he might be too late to save Peter. It was there. He could feel it. If he waited, it might come at the moment he needed to be most alert. He forced it back and pressed on. As he reached the top of the stairs, he could hear Peter's voice.

"Leave me alone," he said.

"Not very smart, boy. Running onto a ship," the redcoat said.

"And Peter got down out of the boat, walked on the water, and came toward Jesus," Peter said in his firmest oratorical voice.

"Think I'd pay money to see that," the redcoat chuffed.

Norris found the two men. Peter was cornered. He'd turned the wrong way and found only a wall and tables between himself and the redcoat. The old man stood with his hands spread out wide, a wooden cane in his left hand.

"Back off," Norris announced.

"Agent Norris, how nice of you to join us. Now, be a good chap and get the hell out of here," the redcoat said.

Norris cocked his pistol.

"I said back off," Norris repeated.

The redcoat slowly lowered his arms, placing the tip of the cane on the ground and shifting his weight to it. He sighed audibly.

"You're a persistent bastard, I'll give you that," the redcoat said, turning to face Norris. "But, your time is up, Agent. You're on the wrong side. In fact, you might just be on your own side. Alone. We've got the others, you know. They just don't know it yet," he said.

Norris raised the pistol and aimed it at the man's head. He glanced at Peter, who was sweating profusely, breathing heavily, and frantically looking for any chance of escape between muttered.

"Empty words meant to delay me long enough to get your backup," Norris said.

"Perhaps, but at least I have backup. What do you have, Agent? A deaf doctor and a sociopathic paid serial killer whose past his prime and much more eager to kill the boy than we are?"

The redcoat reached up and adjusted the cracked, thick-rimmed glasses perched on his face. A face that held something familiar in it. Something Norris just couldn't put his finger on.

Without warning, Peter broke for the nearest door, but the redcoat was ready. His walking stick swung out and struck Peter in the temple, sending him flying into a set of chairs near the doorway. But the blow didn't have the effect that the redcoat had expected. Peter brushed it off and rolled into the doorway before getting up and continuing his flight down a set of stairs. Norris lurched toward the redcoat, bringing the butt of his gun down upon the white straw fedora. The man crumpled to his knees, but cursed colorfully, swinging back at Norris with the walking stick and barely missing his mark. Norris took the firm blow to the inside thigh and hobbled to the doorway, turning his gun on the man.

"I don't want to put a bullet in you, but I will if you follow me down these stairs," Norris said.

The redcoat removed his hat and wiped angry blood from his brow with the sleeve of his coat.

"Run along, little man. I might not catch you, but time will," the redcoat said and placed his hat back atop his head with a strange smile on his lips.

Norris ran down the stairs as fast as he could. It led back out to the outer walkway. To his left, Peter was running back toward the bow. To his right, Norris saw two men swing around the stern end of the ship. Their haste was all he needed to confirm they were the redcoat's backup. Norris ran after Peter. He was nearly on top of him as he ran up one of the gangplanks that graced the front of the paddle steamer. *SS Natchez* was emblazoned across the life preservers. Norris reached out and grabbed the young man's arm.

"Peter, please," Norris said.

Peter whipped around, brushing Norris' hand away with force. For the first time since Norris had seen the boy, his chubby face was contorted with rage.

"Get away from me…all of you!" Peter screamed.

He backed toward the end of the gangplank, gripping the railing. They both jumped when the shot rang out. Norris turned, his gun raised, expecting to see the redcoats behind him. But, it was the man in black, standing on the other side of the ship, his face bloodied and his gun aimed at Peter. Norris pulled the trigger. The *Click!* resounded across the space between them.

"Rich! I expect better of you! No hesitation? Is this the end game? Did I miss my invite?"

"Don't you die?" Norris asked, putting himself between Peter and the man. He could hear Peter praying under his breath.

"Whatever you think will help, kid."

"I'm going to kill the boy, Rich."

"Yea, though I walk through the valley of the shadow of death…," Peter murmured.

The man tried to smile as he spoke, but it seemed to be difficult. The best he could do was smirk.

"You know I can't let you do that, Eric," Norris said.

He saw the man pause at the sound of his own name.

"…I will fear no evil, for thou art with me…," Peter continued.

"Been a long time since you called me that," Eric said.

"That's because I don't know that man anymore," Norris said.

"Touching, Rich. Very touching," Eric said.

"…thy rod and thy staff they comfort me," Peter finished. He then began chanting something in Latin that Norris didn't understand.

Norris watched as the two men rounded the corner and Eric reacted with a shot in their direction. They skidded to a halt and there now began a cross-ship firefight. Norris and Peter had nowhere to hide. Out on the gangplank, they had only one option for escape and that was into the water.

"Can you swim?" Norris asked, interrupting Peter's sermon just long enough for him to shake his head in the negative. Eric quickly clipped one of the men who crawled his way back to a door, making his way back inside the ship. Norris watched as the second man ran out of shells in his shotgun, left himself vulnerable for only a moment, and died for his mistake. Eric put a bullet between his eyes. The man flinched, dropped the gun, and fell face down on the deck. Eric limped forward a step and returned his attention to his prey.

"Peter, you've got to jump," Norris said.

"I'll drown," Peter said.

"You're about to get shot. Pick your poison," Norris said.

"I can't…"

They had backed out onto the gangplank as far as they could go. Peter was so close now that Norris could feel the boy shaking behind him. There were sirens somewhere off in the

242

distance. They would be too late. He watched as the man cocked his gun and lifted it to eye level.

That's when the engine roared and tires screeched just beyond the dock. Norris watched as the Barracuda maneuvered between barriers, came hurtling down a small embankment, and made a bead for the ship and, more importantly, Eric. Norris could just make out Taylor's spectacled face through the shattered glass of the window before the car was airborne from dockside. Eric, having not reacted to any of it, possibly out of fear of distraction, turned just as the car plowed through a portable barrier, off the dock, and onto the ship. The resulting crash sent parts of the ship flying through the air and the car landed in heap of burning rubber, torn metal, and shattered glass. The port side gangplank was sent crashing into the one that Norris and Peter stood on and they gripped the railing to save themselves from being tossed into the muddy waters of the Mississippi below. The entire ship lurched to starboard and, for a brief moment, Norris wondered if he had it in him to rescue a drowning man.

Then it was over and ship sloshed slowly back to rest. They moved off of the gangplank carefully. Through the smoke and steam, they could just make out the car. The railing and floor where Eric had been standing was gone. And so, apparently, was Eric. Norris gazed down into the water. A black newsboy cap was floating atop an oil-slicked patch of still churning water. The car hung precariously on the bow of the ship and opening the passenger door appeared to threaten its stability. Inside, Taylor was leaning against the wheel, his head facing Norris. Blood was pouring out of his mouth, both of his arms were clearly broken, and a large gash had opened up his temple to a point that made Norris want to look away.

"I got him, didn't I," Taylor said, gurgling through the blood in his throat and mouth.

"You did…you saved us," Norris said, glancing over his shoulder at Peter.

For his part, Peter glanced in, turned a shade of pink and crossed himself.

"Get him out of here," Taylor said.

"I will, but…" Norris tried.

"Don't…not going any further than this. Done running," Taylor said.

"Ok," Norris said.

"Agent?"

"Yeah?"

"He… he was…right," Taylor managed.

"Who…about what?"

"The man said…said I'd learn…learn to love this car. Best fucking car…ever."

And with that, Dr. Taylor said no more.

Chapter 27

The nightmare smelled like blood and smoke and pine
trees and there was someone screaming and the only light
flickered in an all too familiar way. James was staring down at
his blood-soaked hands as they pressed into the soft pine-
needle covered forest floor. Someone was shouting his name.
Blinking felt like a lifetime between the darkness and light.
The pain brought him out of it. A searing, needle-like pain was
in the side of his left arm. He turned his head to find Paynter
just a few feet away, the man's jacket charred and smoldering,
eyes wide, shouting James' name. He was struggling to keep
Steve down and, for a moment, James thought the two were
fighting. Then he saw the look in Steve's eye; he was terrified.
Paynter pushed him back flat on the ground, then called out to
James again, pointing to Steve's foot.

The unnatural angle immediately told James that
something was drastically wrong. When he saw what he knew
to be bone protruding from the bottom of Steve's pants, he
turned away, his eyes gravitating back to the flickering light
from the fire burning shell of what remained of the plane. The
flames were moving up through the cockpit, quickly engulfing
the chairs they had been in moments before. They should have
all died, it was really that simple. But the pain in his arm didn't
allow his mind to dwell on what should have happened. He
turned, holding his arm out into the light. A six-inch streak of
silver was protruding from his arm. The instinct to pull it out
overwhelmed the potential pain or damage that doing so might

cause. He reached up, wrenched the object out, and staggered as a wave of nausea and dizziness accompanied the ragged scraping he felt as the metal passed across the bone in his arm. He leaned over, gagging several times, clutching his arm.

"James, give me your belt!"

Paynter's words broke through the chaos, but James was still focused on his arm, looking at the jagged piece of fuselage he had just pulled from his own flesh. He could feel the warmth of the blood as it soaked into his jacket and he struggled to take it off. It was crimson mess, but as he exposed the wound to the light, a part of him was relieved. Instead of the hose-like flood he had half expected, he was greeted by a slow trickle. He pulled his belt off and tossed it to Paynter. He then made a tourniquet out of a strip of his undershirt. The shock and adrenaline was beginning to wear off and cold night air was starting to sink in. He realized just how many points of pain he was starting to feel. When he turned back to Paynter, he was standing over Steve, whose eyes were still wide, but less frantic than they had been. His breathing had slowed.

Paynter had tied off the wound at the bottom of the calf and wrapped the exposed ankle in a spare sweatshirt he'd pulled from the plane. Steve looked between Paynter and James. He was covered in his own blood.

"It's the best I can do given the circumstances," Paynter said.

"Great. Leave him," James said.

"Wha...what? Please don't leave me," Steve whispered.

"You might die if we try and move you," Paynter said.

"I'm as good as dead if you leave me. Believe me, I'll take the chance. Please, you can't leave me," Steve said.

James moved closer and stood over him, pointing his bloodied finger inches from Steve's face and growling just louder than the fire that was crackling through the plane.

"Why the fuck should we save your sorry ass when it's you who got us here?"

Steve struggled to raise his head and the pain and fear were apparent in every word he said.

"Because I failed again and I don't know anyone who's failed twice."

James turned away from both of them, balling his hands into fists. The fingers of his left hand tingled from the loss of blood. He wanted nothing more to scream, but the urge was quelled when he looked out into the forest. Flashlights were piercing the night.

"Fuck. Fuck!" James hissed.

He turned around, marched over to Steve, reached down and lifted him by the collar and stared into the frightened man's face.

"You get this and you get this good. I own you now. Got me? Make me regret saving your sorry ass for even a moment and you'd better kill me cuz I'll end you. Am I clear?"

"You got it, boss."

James struggled to lift him the rest of the way off the ground with his good arm and Paynter stepped in, grabbing his other side. They felt Steve waver in their grasp.

"We're not going to get far," Paynter said.

"I don't plan on going far. We just have to not be such easy targets. Use the darkness to our advantage. Just remember which direction they came from."

"Sure, in the dark. No problem," Paynter said.

"Just try, ok? Just because I have an idea, doesn't mean I know what the fuck I'm doing," James said.

They moved further away from the plane and into the darkness. It was slow going and Steve was barely able to put pressure on his good leg. They were at the furthest edge of any kind of light from the flames when James stopped.

"Here. This'll have to do. Put him down here," James said.

"What? Why?" Steve mumbled.

"Bait," James said as they placed Steve down against the trunk of the fallen tree.

"What?" Paynter and Steve said simultaneously.

"They'll come to help you," James said.

"You think," Steve said.

James reached into his pockets and pulled out both pistols, handing one to Paynter.

"James, I…," Paynter said, looking at the revolver and looking back at James.

"I'm not ready to kill anyone either, Doc. Just aim low. If we're lucky, we won't even need them," James said.

"Luck hasn't exactly been on our side lately," Paynter said.

"We just fell out of the goddamn sky and survived. I'd call that pretty fucking lucky. That tree over there should give you a good angle. The blood trail should lead them right in here," James said.

"What do you want me to do?" Steve said.

"Act like you're in a lot of pain. Shouldn't be too hard. Nothing too obvious though, but loud enough to hear. Oh, and try not to bleed too much," James said.

"Is this what…?" Steve began, but James interrupted.

"Is this what you have to look forward to? Yes! Get used to it. Do what I ask and we might just get out of this. Stranger things have happened."

James and Paynter turned to move away from the fallen tree when Paynter stopped. He stared out into the darkness beyond.

"James?" Paynter said.

"Yeah?"

"You ever been hunting?"

"No. I'm not keen on shooting at anything that hasn't shot at me first. Why do you ask?"

"You might have to shoot them," Paynter said

"I know," James said.

He turned and watched as the lights crested a hill in the forest. They'd reach the wreck in two minutes. They'd be on top of them in four, tops. By his best guess, there were four or five of them. He glanced around at his surroundings, peering into the absolute darkness beyond the fading light of the fire.

"Well, we're not going to keep running. Hopefully this is the last thing they expect. And, honestly, I've got nothing else, Doc. We're alone in the middle of the woods in fucking Canada with a cripple, a couple guns, and no clear way out. Maybe if I had a paperclip, some chewing gum, a tank, and another twenty-four hours I could MacGyver my way out of this happy nonsense," James said.

"You can drive a tank?" Paynter said.

"No, but I bet you could fake it if I asked you to," James said.

"Haha. You overestimate my abilities," Paynter said.

"Oh, I don't know, Doc. I think you've lived up to the hype."

"You two gonna keep up this little love fest till they're on top of us," Steve intervened weakly from the other side of the log.

James slipped in behind the nearest tree and watched as Paynter moved in behind another about twenty feet away. Steve began talking to himself about his leg, raising his voice at times and bemoaning his fate. It wasn't hard to believe that most of it was heartfelt.

The wait was agonizing and the pain in James' arm and the cold night air were starting to sink deep into him. He watched as the lights made their way down the hill, converging on the wreckage. He counted six distinct lights and hoped that there weren't more who were not carrying lights.

One of them heard Steve. Another found the blood trail. It wasn't difficult to follow. Steve increased the volume of his moaning, even calling out to the lights. The gun felt slippery in James' hand. He ran his free hand across it, searching for the safety, but not wanting to move out from the shadow of the tree. He would just have to hope for the best.

There were six men with lights; not a single redcoat among them. All appeared to be carrying rifles. James ducked behind the tree as they came upon Steve, not wanting to risk being seen. He began doubting the validity of his plan. He needed them to drop their guard, but what if they didn't. They would know that Steve couldn't have made it out that far on his own. And what if Steve turned on him. He owed James nothing. What if he used that tidbit of info in a last-ditch effort to save his skin. Would he take that chance? He was about to find out. James listened.

"Oh, Jesus, Steve! What the fuck happened to you? You look awful!"

James' heart sank. There was no empathy in the man's voice at all. They would sooner kill Steve than have to deal with a failure and a broken failure at that. Who were these people? He found himself with his back against the tree, unable to convince himself to move, fearing that he'd be seen and they would all be shot.

"Leg's bad. If exposure doesn't get him, the animals will," came another voice; this one less cold, but bordering on analytical.

"Who bandaged you up, Stevie boy? The good doctor?" the first voice said.

"Bastards left me! I had them, but they dropped the plane on purpose. Then they left me here to die," Steve said. His voice had faded into a whimper.

"Seems like a lot of trouble to go through. Seems like they could have just left you to die in the burning wreckage of the plane. And where exactly are they going? There's nothing around here for miles," the man said.

"I...I don't know...they didn't tell me anything. I...," Steve said, his voice trailing off.

James strained to hear, turning against the trunk of the tree and leaning as close to the group as possible. Either Steve had stopped talking, or he was whispering something. James paranoia shot through his skull. He raised the gun, prepared to step out from behind the tree.

"I think he passed out," said the second man.

James found himself breathing again.

"Leave him. Sebastian will just chew us out for bringing back a body. They couldn't have gotten much farther into the woods," the first man said.

"You sure we just leave him? Sebastian would be more pissed if he somehow crawled out of the woods and ended up on the evening news," a third man chimed in.

"And that, Ronny, is why the big man doesn't take you seriously. You don't think. Look at his scrawny ass. He's just about bled out as it is. He's passed out. He ain't walking out. It's a five mile crawl to any road with traffic. Oh, and between the bears and the mountain lions, yeah…"

"Bloodthirsty bastard," the second man said.

"Just covering my ass," said the third.

"As always, Ronny. As always," said the first.

James watched as the flashlights began moving toward the gap between James' tree and Paynter's tree. He almost couldn't believe it. James inched his way out of their line of sight as the flashlight beams drew nearer. They were going to walk right past them. That was when James' foot landed on the twig that rolled his foot out from under him and he landed awkwardly on his knee.

"Over there!"

James raised the gun at the tree and waited for the first man to round the corner. This was it. He was going to have to kill someone or be killed himself. His finger clutched at the trigger. He'd have one shot before they were on him. Perhaps if Paynter reacted quickly enough it wouldn't be all six. It was over before he even had a moment to consider it. There were six shots in succession. Six cracks of gunfire, six muzzle flashes, and six flashlight beams leapt and fell to the ground, motionless. A man fell against the corner of James' tree, his own flashlight still grasped in his hand, now pointing up into his startled face. He looked at James with his gun, as if, perhaps, he had somehow shot him through the tree. Then he rolled over onto the forest floor, dead.

That was it. James stood a moment longer, still awaiting the onslaught that never came. He felt the acid building up in his arms as he held the gun tightly at eye level. There was nothing. No movement. Not a single sound until Steve's voice called out to him.

"James? Dr. Paynter? You ok?"

James peeked around the corner of the tree. In the light of a flashlight, he could just make out Steve, sitting up and leaning over the fallen tree, a pistol in his hand. The six men lay sprawled out on the ground before them. Each of them silent and motionless.

"Jesus, Steve," James whispered.

Paynter came out from behind the tree, gun raised and aimed at the prone bodies. He moved among them all, piling weapons, and checking pulses. He looked at James and shook his head, then went back and collected the flashlights.

"You killed them. You killed all of them! There were six of them! Jesus Christ!" James said.

James pocketed his handgun and rubbed the cramp that had developed in his right hand.

"They were going to leave me here to die…and the plans they have for you…," Steve's voice trailed off.

"But you passed out," James said.

"Old party trick," Steve said.

James looked back down at the bodies in disbelief.

"They taught me. They turned me into what I am. I'm a killer, James. It's what I've been trained to do my entire life. I make my decision on whether I want to kill someone or not. They should have known better," Steve said.

"And you had that gun on you the whole time?" Paynter asked.

"Always keep a spare somewhere," Steve said.

Pulling his handgun back out, James stared at it for a moment.

"James?" Paynter said.

"I couldn't have done it. I would have been dead. They would have had to pry it from my fingers, but it would have had all the bullets in it. I realized it in that moment. I'll always be a victim because I'll always consider the other guy first. Here's hoping I don't do anything to make you change your mind about me," James said.

"Here's hoping," Steve said.

"Here," James said, handing Steve the gun.

Steve reached for the weapon, then hesitated, glancing at Paynter.

"You sure?" Steve asked.

"Not my call. You apparently could have killed us whenever you wanted to. Not much to stop you from doing so now," Paynter said.

"No good in my hands, that's for sure," James said.

Steve took the weapon from James, pulled out the cartridge, slipped it back in, checked the safety, then slipped both guns into his hoodie. Paynter and James moved in to lift him off the ground.

"The safety was on, by the way," Steve said.

"Great. Good to know. Glad my incompetence is what will be my downfall. By the way. What you did just now? Fucking scary. I'm either sweating profusely, or I might have wet myself a little bit back there, though I'll deny that to the end. But, I'm pretty sure my ownership of you just ended," James said.

"Sure, boss, whatever you say," Steve said.

Chapter 28

Doug sat at the wheel, drumming his fingers against the hot black plastic. They were getting nowhere, and fast. But, now they were slowing down again. He looked in the rearview mirror. Kevin and Chris were done. He could see it in their faces. They couldn't push anymore.

He brought the car to a halt, threw on the emergency brake, and opened the driver's side door. He could hear both of them panting in the heat of the afternoon.

"We're not getting anywhere," Chris said, leaning heavily against the back of the car.

"I can't see shit," Kevin countered looking down the road.

"Take a break. You've been pushing for an hour now," Doug said.

Both fell into the back seat, still breathing heavily. They had driven into the middle of nowhere of West Texas along the only road there was for eight hours. They had no map and not once had they passed a gas station or a sign for a major highway. Kevin had considered the existence of such a road in the United States to be "unfuckingbelievable." He had also voiced his opinion, several hours too late, that perhaps they should have just ditched the car and gotten back on the train. Chris and Doug agreed that they would have simply been caught elsewhere. Now, getting caught was starting to look good.

There had been a single bottle of water in the car that the three of them had rationed out amongst themselves. It was now lying empty on the passenger side floor.

"Now what?" Chris asked.

"I don't think I can push anymore," Kevin said.

"Wish I could help," Doug said.

"Maybe we could fashion a wheel chair out of two tires and one of those bucket seats," Kevin said.

"I'd rather die in the car, thanks," Doug said.

"I knew you'd say that. Stubborn bastard," Kevin said.

"What good would it do? So you two can keel over and die and I'm stuck watching the buzzards pick at your eyes?" Doug said.

"Wow, there's a pleasant thought," Chris said.

"He's a regular ray of sunshine, isn't he?" Kevin said.

"Was that supposed to be funny?" Chris asked.

"Either laugh or cry," Doug said.

"I don't think there's enough moisture left in my body," Kevin said.

Doug glanced in the rearview mirror. The dust was kicking up again. He considered putting his window up, but thought better of it. Perhaps it wasn't another storm. He turned awkwardly in his seat and looked out the back window.

"Crap," he said.

Chris and Kevin jumped and simultaneously turned to watch as the trail of dust rose up into the sky from the road they had just traveled down.

"Dammit, if they're not persistent," Kevin said.

"How did he get a new car?" Chris asked.

Doug coughed a half-hearted laugh.

"They never travel alone. They're like the velociraptors from *Jurassic Park*. If you see one, and he doesn't see you, it's because he's distracting you from the one just under your nose."

Kevin glanced back out the front window nervously and Doug half expected him to shout out a warning. But, it didn't come. There was only one because they were sitting ducks.

"We could run," Chris said.

"You can run. At best, I could amble a few feet out into the desert and fall down. That might confuse them," Doug said.

Doug watched as the source of the dust cloud came closer, the first glint of metal shining in the sun. If it was pursuing them, it sure was taking its sweet time. Doug was the first to leave the car, slowly shifting his legs out and leaning heavily on the cane. The piercing pain was back, but he didn't want to be sitting for this. They could knock him down, but they'd have to try.

"That looks like an old pickup truck," Kevin said, shading his eyes with his hand.

"Great, some poor farmer got waylaid," Doug said.

"Yeah, cuz there's a whole lot of farming going on out here," Kevin said.

The white pickup truck meandered its way toward them. Even when they could be certain the driver had seen them, there was no change in its pace.

"I don't see a redcoat, do you?" Chris said.

"Or a white fuckin' hat," Kevin said.

"We're saved," Doug said.

They began to wave. The truck slowed down and came to a stop a couple car lengths away. Doug was smiling his 4 AM bagel-store smile. Forced, but genuine in heart. Then he felt it fade. The man behind the wheel was the color of the sand. There was no distinguishing between where his old cowboy hat ended and the skin of his forehead began. The whites of his knuckles told Doug he was gripping the steering wheel extraordinarily tight. His lips moved and he glanced down ever so slightly to the passenger seat.

"Crap in a damn hat," Doug breathed.

As if on cue, the redcoat sat up in the passenger seat, gun in hand and smiling a perfect false-teeth smile. He retrieved his hat from the floor and placed it back on the thin white hair. He glanced around at the three young men, taking special care to look at Kevin. The smile left him and his head cocked to the side for a moment before he opened the door.

"Steve?" he said, directly to Kevin.

"Kevin," Kevin said looking startled.

"Don't fuck around with me Steve," the redcoat said.

Doug watched the exchange with renewed interest. This man recognized Kevin. Somehow, there was something about

260

Kevin that this man was recognizing and that fact was tearing a hole in Doug's mind. Kevin looked scared. He had either lied to Doug repeatedly, and set them on this path, or this redcoat was mistaken. Either way, it dawned upon Doug that this was perhaps the only opportunity to get out of the current situation.

"You fucking bastard," Doug said.

Both Chris and Kevin turned as if Doug had reached out and slapped them and he tried to hold back his revulsion of the words that had left his lips. What would his mother say? She would say that he did it because the situation called for it. Yes, that was what he had to tell himself. He let fly again.

"You lying bag of crap," he said.

It didn't carry as much venom, but he felt better about saying it.

"Doug, I…" Kevin blurted out, glancing between the redcoat and Doug, but Doug shouted over him before he could continue.

"You…you lied to me! You lied to us! You're a…a gosh-darned traitor!"

"Doug…Jesus," but Kevin couldn't get anything out before he had to dodge Doug's cane.

And then Doug was lunging at him. There was shouting and, despite the rending pain, Doug had barreled into Kevin with his full weight before anyone could stop him. The two went to the ground in a cloud of sand. Doug leaned on his good leg and Kevin to prop himself back up, before lifting Kevin to his feet. The look on Kevin's face was one of absolute terror and Doug begged forgiveness in his mind before rearing back and cracking him in the eye. The result told him exactly what he needed to know. Kevin cried out like a kicked dog. This was no traitor. This was just a kid from Jersey who was getting a beating from someone he'd trusted moments before. He reared back to strike again, preparing to glance the next blow when he felt Chris's arms wrap around his waist. He shifted his weight to try and shrug him off. Where was the redcoat? He'd have to intervene. Doug could hear him telling them to knock it off. He missed with his next swing, purposely smacking Kevin's upheld hand. The redcoat fired into the air, startling all of them, but Doug wouldn't relent. Then, the redcoat's hand was on his other arm, the surprisingly strong grip coming from long thin fingers. With one move, Doug tossed Kevin and threw an elbow into redcoat's face, connecting with the stunned man's nose. Doug watched as the gun came up and he grabbed the scrawny wrist and pushed it over his head.

The redcoat screamed with rage and Doug felt a surge of strength come from the man. His free hand caught Doug at the base of his neck and it took all of his energy to not let go of the gun hand. He turned into the man and pulled the redcoat's arm over his shoulder. He could toss him, but that would bring the gun around into his path. He shook the hand wildly, the gun wavering in Chris and Kevin's direction and they scattered to each side as Doug slowly turned. No amount of shaking appeared to be loosening the man's grip. Doug saw the redcoat's hand fly out of the corner of his eye. He raised his arm to ward off the blow and leaned with all of his weight, taking him and the man to the ground; the pistol lodging into the sand. Doug half-expected to feel the weight of the man on his back slam onto him, but it was as if a small child had asked for a piggy-back ride. He immediately rolled over onto the man, and watched as the revolver came out of his hand. But, the redcoat was now wrapping both hands around Doug's neck. He could almost feel the bones in the man's hand trying to pierce his flesh.

"The gun...get the gun!" Doug gasped.

He had put himself in a position of weakness, laid out on his back, unable to reach around and release the redcoat's grip. He threw his elbow into the man's midsection, but despite groans of pain, it was having no effect. It only made the fingers grasp his throat tighter and stars began to pop in his eyes.

He waved his arms frantically and tried to roll over again, but the pain in his hip, the energy he'd exerted in the fight, and his increasing lack of oxygen was starting to take its toll. He couldn't even see Chris or Kevin. The shotgun blast made him jump and it startled the redcoat just enough for Doug to roll away from his grip. He breathed heavy into the sand before looking up.

"The next one ain't gonna be in the air, mister."

The old man who'd been driving the truck was standing alone near the bumper, the double-barreled shotgun resting haphazardly on his left forearm, still aimed at Doug and the redcoat. To Doug's right, he could see Chris and Kevin standing beside one another. Chris had the redcoat's pistol in his hand, but hidden behind Kevin's back.

"Ain't seen nothin' so crook'd as this barrel o' snakes right here," the old man said, his eyes flitting between the four men.

"Sir, I'm a…," the redcoat began, reaching into his coat.

The shotgun jerked up in line with the redcoat.

"Not my first rodeo, fella. That there coat'd cover up the blood nicely, least until the buzzards snuffed ya out," the old man said.

"Big words for a cowboy," the redcoat said, now pausing to brush the dirt from his coat.

"If you done it, it ain't braggin'," the old man said cooly.

Doug sensed just a bit of crazy in the old man. He was as weather beaten as the cowboy boots he wore. The shirt Doug had believed to be brown might have been white at one point in its life, but that had been long ago. His dusty jeans hung loosely around his legs, only really hanging on by the black leather belt around his waist and the only pristine object on the man's body; a shining oversized silver belt buckle that might have been new out of the box.

Doug moved into a sitting position and glanced around for his cane. It was resting several feet away. He looked up at the old man and back at the cane.

"You a cripple, boy?"

"More now than ever," Doug said, half wincing from the pain in his leg, half from the honesty.

264

"You, the one hidin' the pea shooter. Put that thing on the ground and get him his cane," the old man said.

Chris stared at him, confused. He pulled the gun out from behind his back, looked at it, and back up at the old man.

"Is he deaf?" The old man asked of no one in particular.

"Chris," Doug said.

Chris gave one glance to the redcoat and let the pistol fall to the ground. He picked up Doug's cane and helped his brother to his feet. They could hear the old man muttering to himself.

"Engine's runnin', but no one's drivin'," he said.

"I'm a U.S. Marshall," the redcoat said, catching them all off guard.

Kevin laughed a short nervous bark.

"Son, if you're a U.S. Marshall, I'm a gol'durn horny toad," the old man said.

"I have my badge," the redcoat said.

"And I had a big red bridge out 'Frisco way once. Yew kin show that piece o' metal to someone who gives a rat's behind," retorted the old man.

He took a moment to glance around at the boys, then back at the redcoat.

"Funny thing when one of the dogs yelp and t'others keep quiet, ain't it?"

"We stole his car," Kevin said.

"Whut?" the old man said.

"Jeez," Doug said.

"But, he's been trying to kill us," said Chris.

"That's a lie. If I wanted you dead, you'd have never made it out of Ohio," the redcoat spat.

That's when Doug heard it. It was the velociraptor waiting in the bushes. They'd spent the last twenty minutes staring at one when the other was maneuvering in for the kill. He turned and glanced up into the sky, the faint *dub-dub-dub* barely audible over the sound of the wind. There, in the distance, a red and white helicopter was closing fast.

"I hate to interrupt this little party, but if we don't get in your truck and down that road in about ten seconds, we're going to have more than one of him to worry about," Doug said, pointing first to the horizon and then at the redcoat.

"Whut?" the old man said, turning to look where Doug had pointed.

The redcoat had been waiting for this and ran straight at the old man. But Chris had kept his senses and threw himself in between the two, taking the redcoat and himself to the ground. Doug struggled toward the truck and Kevin ran over to help Chris who was trying to repel the rapid punches of the now infuriated redcoat. The old man seemed to sense whose side he should take and proceeded to crack the redcoat across the back of the head with the butt end of his gun. The redcoat's eyes rolled back and he collapsed on the ground. His white straw fedora rolled off his head and into the sand.

Doug managed to pull himself into the passenger's seat. Chris and Kevin heaved themselves over the sides of the truck bed and the old man moved sprightly into the driver's seat. He tossed the shotgun out the back window into the truck bed and followed it with a box of shells.

"No time for shakin', but names Clem."

The boys shouted out their names and thanked Clem for saving them.

"Savin' means bein' outta danger. We ain't there yet. Ever used a scattergun, boy?"

Chris picked up the gun, broke the chambers open and slipped a new shell into the empty barrel.

"Enough to get by," Chris said.

"Don't wait for 'em to shoot first," Clem said.

He shifted gears and took off at a pace that made Doug proud. Clem was a driver after his own heart. He looked back out the window between Kevin and Chris and watched as the helicopter pulled in to land where they had been. A man jumped out of the chopper, pressing his hat against his head. He first ran to grab his fallen comrade's hat, then went over and appeared to lift him off the ground. The truck was too far away for them to see what happened next, but it mattered little as the helicopter lifted back off from the ground and pursued its prey.

"Damn if there isn't always someone helping those bastards," Kevin shouted.

They watched as the helicopter quickly devoured the distance between them. Chris cocked the gun and lifted the barrel to the sky.

"Aim high, boy, and don't pussy foot around with 'em. Give 'em both barrels. Got plenty of shells," Clem shouted.

"Where are we headed?" Doug shouted.

"Town's just a spell yonder. 'Bout two mile."

"Two miles? For cryin' out loud," Doug said.

He heard, before he saw, the shotgun blast and he turned quickly around. The shot had shattered the co-pilot's window, and the coptor peeled off to their left. It kept pace, but hung back to deter Chris from taking another shot.

"Reload! That'll make 'em think, but it won't stop 'em," Clem shouted.

"Can this thing go any faster?" Kevin yelled.

"Pedal's on the floor, boy. Truck's stud days are long gone, but he's still got the legs," Clem said.

The chopper moved up to a point that was parallel with the truck.

"That can't be good," Doug said.

He watched as the side door slid open. The high-powered rifle was not hard to see.

"Brakes, Clem! Brakes!"

Clem hit the brakes so hard, Doug was afraid that the back end would come up over the front. Or worse, that Kevin and Chris would go flying over the roof onto the road. Neither happened and they watched as the helicopter flew past them at a high rate.

"Get that gun faced front, boy!" Clem shouted, putting the truck in gear again.

Chris knelt up and leaned over the roof of the truck. The chopper peeled off once more and maneuvered into position.

"Only 'nother mile before we're home free. Gotta have balls 'o brass to go into a town and start shootin' it up," Clem said.

"I wouldn't underestimate the size or consistency of their balls," Kevin said.

"Yeah, but they ain't from Texas," Clem said.

The truck lurched forward and they were back at top speed. Doug could see the town coming up in the distance. But, the chopper was moving back into position, this time at an angle off of their back left. The side door opened again. Doug watched as Chris aimed up and to the left of the chopper. It was too far to be effective, but the shot might still rattle the cage a bit. He let fly and the barrels roared again. This time, they could actually hear the shot as it hit the cabin and blades. The copter shuddered for a moment and the movement threw off the shooter and the door closed. A thin smoke trail started to come from the engine and Chris threw a fist in the air and whooped a cheer as if he'd won a prize at the carnival.

"Reload, boy!" Clem shouted.

But, it was too late. The chopper saw the opportunity and swept in right over the back of the truck. Doug heard Chris and Kevin swear as they were forced to the bottom of the truck bed.

"Whatever you do, Clem, don't stop! They'll kill us all!"

Doug turned and watched as the pilot used the chopper's landing pads to push the bed of the truck. Clem struggled with the wheel as the truck was shoved off its path. The chopper backed off as the truck slowed down, but then came in again. Doug watched helplessly as Chris struggled with the shotgun. It had fallen into the bed and now the shells were scattered about the bed, bouncing with every bump in the road. He turned to look back out the front window. They only had a half mile of road left until the town, but it wasn't coming quickly enough.

The next bump nearly took them off the road altogether.

"Gol' durn it! What'd you do ta stir up this nest o' bees?" Clem shouted.

"Pull over!" Came a voice on a bullhorn.

"Over my dead body!" Clem said.

Doug turned back again just in time to see Chris raise the barrel of the gun to the chopper again. It was too close to miss. And this time, it would do more than shatter the glass. Chris fired and Doug watched in horror. They'd been too close. Chris's shot had been too good. And Doug didn't know if he could pray that quickly.

The shot ripped into the cabin and the chopper tipped forward in the air, the blades leaning down toward the bed of the truck. Kevin and Chris screamed and pulled their legs toward themselves and then the blades made contact and the truck was thrown off of the road with a quarter of its bed shorn off and then they were rolling and there was an explosion and Doug wasn't sure which way was up and which was down. And then the blackness came over him.

Chapter 29

The climb to where the search party had left their vehicles was longer than James had expected. Steve had expended a lot of energy doing what he did and the steepness of the slope up the hill had only increased the closer they got to the top of the hill. The hill crested before sloping back down to the road. They found a rather large tree to rest behind and survey the situation. They had moved through the darkness, back past the smoldering embers of what was left of the plane and gradually up the hill. They had stopped several times on the way to allow Steve to rest and James didn't have to see Paynter's face to understand the shared sense of concern for the man. He was getting weaker with every step. He nearly fell to the forest floor as they lowered him.

"I don't know how much longer he can last. We've got to get him help," Paynter said.

"Well, help might be in the form of those cars," James said.

From there, they could see the road and two black Dodge Chargers with the engines still kicking out plumes of thick exhaust into the cold night air. With the windows blacked out, it was impossible to see whether anyone was still in the vehicles.

"Do you really think they left them alone?" James said, sitting down behind a tree several yards above the roadway.

"Not likely," Paynter said.

Steve coughed and spoke slowly.

"No, and not per protocol either. There's a man in each car. Not a redcoat. Just civvies, paid by Sebastian. But, I imagine they're getting nervous now. Their comrades have been gone a while. They might have even tried to call them on the radio. Didn't think to check for that."

"Sebastian? Sebastian Walters?" Paynter asked.

"I don't know his last name. Not many do. He is Sebastian, eldest brother. I never heard anyone call him by another name. One of the other boys called him Seb, once. He was punished. Sebastian runs the show, but he's a teacher too. He taught me everything the others couldn't. He raised me, for what it's worth," Steve said.

James now noticed that there was no emotion in anything that Steve said. Everything that he spoke about was flat and without form. He was an unapologetic killer. What he had done to the men in the woods was merely a reflex. All he had known was death and killing in a world where that was all that mattered. And while this Sebastian held much respect, there was a distinct sense of fear behind the praise.

"You think you know him?" James asked, looking at Paynter.

"Do you remember when I told you about your past?" Paynter said.

"It's a bit of a blur now, but yeah...I think I remember," James said.

"Well, when they chose a specimen for the cloning, it was a young soldier by the name of Walters. But, they locked him

272

up afterward. Leaked him the information of what they were doing and, when he tried to tell, they threw him in an asylum for the criminally insane," Paynter said.

"What better way to get back at the system, than to use its own creations against it?" James said.

"Makes sense to me," Steve said.

"Makes perfect sense. But, it doesn't explain how he's making it all work. No one civilian has the kind of control that he's shown. Even if he had every clone behind him, he'd still need a way back into the system," Paynter said.

"Sebastian says there's a hole in every wall…and sometimes its greatest weakness is its strongest point," Steve added.

"Well, let's wax poetic later. We've got to get out of here…Jesus," James said.

Steve passed out, his eyes going back to the whites. James and Paynter knelt back down beside him as he blinked back to consciousness.

"There's nothing I can do for him out here and the cold is slowly killing him," Paynter stage whispered to James.

"I'm not leaving him here. Not after what he did for us," James said.

"He's lost a lot of blood, James," Paynter said.

James was starting to feel frantic. Perhaps it was the adrenaline finally wearing off after the crash. His entire body was beginning to hurt. The cold was starting to creep over him.

His vision seemed to be blurry at the edges. And the more he thought of each of these symptoms, the more frantic he felt.

"God dammit," he said.

He leaned in to Steve as if to check on him, and slipped the gun out of his hand. Standing, he looked at Paynter.

"What are you going to do with that?" Paynter asked.

"I don't know. I'm hoping to think of something between here and the first car," James said.

"Don't," Steve mumbled, raising a weak hand in protest.

"I don't know what else to do, and waiting here for something to happen... well, we're just waiting for you to die or something. And I can't let that happen. Not now. Not after all this," James said.

Without another word, James turned and walked out from behind the tree at a brisk pace toward the first car. He held the gun just behind his right hip and only raised it when the driver's side door cracked open on the second car. He pulled the trigger and sent a shot into the bottom of the door, which produced the exact result he was looking for; it closed again. He then pointed it at the darkened driver's side window of the car closest to him.

"Open it and come out or I'll blow your goddamn head off," James announced, the pit of his stomach roiling as he said it.

He hoped that whoever was in the car couldn't see how badly his hand was shaking. Between the fear, the cold, and the pain James had a hard time believing he'd hit the car at all.

"Open up the goddamn door!" James shouted.

There was still no response from the car before him. He glanced over at the second car, barely able to see the shadow moving behind the windshield. James reached for the door handle, gun wavering badly in his hand. He pulled. There was no one in the driver's seat, but he could feel the warmth of the heated air escaping, tempting him into the cabin. He turned again to the rear car and began walking toward it, gun aimed at the driver's side.

"Open up," James announced.

Instead, the engine revved and the car flew into reverse, skidding on the snow covered road. James bolted for the opposite side of the first car. The other car spun its wheels for a moment, then tore past James. Its red lights disappeared up and over the crest in the road and the silence of the forest and gentle idling of the car in front of him were the only sounds.

Clap!

James turned and looked at the source of the single clap. Paynter and Steve were leaning against the other side of the tree where he had left them. Paynter clapped his hands together again. Steve raised his hand weakly.

"Steve says 'nice job…you lucky son of a bitch'," Paynter said.

They carried Steve over to the car and lay him in the back seat. James sat behind the wheel and looked over the controls. In the dash, a GPS navigation system glowed in shades of grey.

A CB speaker hung loosely above the shifter. He tapped what appeared to be a garage door opener clipped to the sun visor.

"Now what?" James asked.

Paynter pushed a button on the GPS, bringing up a menu with several destination choices. He highlighted each one in succession and watched as a small map popped up after each.

"Well, the nearest town is here…about 30 minutes if I'm reading this thing properly," Paynter said.

"Think they'll have somewhere we can drop him off without raising suspicion?"

"If you're hoping for a large hospital, I think we're out of luck. Might have to knock on a door or two," Paynter said.

"We don't have time for that," James said.

"I don't think we have much choice," Paynter said.

"What about a police station?" James said.

"You want to risk that?" Paynter asked.

"If it's the difference between him living and dying? Yes…I'll risk that," James said.

"Ok, then let's go… follow the bouncing ball," Paytner said.

James looked at the GPS as a digitized voice told him to continue on his current route with a right hand turn in 2.4 miles. He slipped the car into drive and left the trees, the death, the cold, and the last pieces of his uncle's burning plane behind them.

Chapter 30

"It's awfully empty looking for a police station," James said.

On the outskirts of Sault St. Marie, they had found the small building that passed for a police station. To James, it looked like what might have passed for a landscaping service back in New Jersey. A couple of pickup trucks, but no marked car. Only a simple wooden sign above the door identified this as an Ontario Provincial Police building. A light in the doorway was the only indication that the building was occupied.

"Let's get this over with," Paynter said.

James watched as Paynter crossed the small parking lot and pulled at the locked front door before knocking. Paynter pulled his collar up against the night air. James could see the man's breath and realized that Paynter had quite a bit of blood on his coat. They had not thought this through.

"Steve, you still with me?" James asked, looking into the back seat.

Steve blinked at him and sighed.

"I hear ya. We're trying to get help," James said, not sounding as convincing as he wanted.

A rather large man in uniform came to the door of the station. He pulled a paper napkin away from his collar and leaned out the door, casting a wary glance at Paynter's clothing. James couldn't hear what Paynter was saying, but whatever it was got the officer's attention. He nodded at

Paynter and disappeared before returning with a cap and large winter coat. They moved toward the car and James got out, looking expectantly at Paynter.

"This is Officer O'Brien," Paynter said.

James nodded at the officer and opened the back door. O'Brien peeked in at Steve.

"Skiing, eh?" he said.

Paynter nodded. O'Brien turned to James who felt his temperature rise.

"You took the time to take his ski boots off and put his sneakers on?" O'Brien asked.

"The man needs help. Please," James said.

"You want to tell me the truth?" O'Brien asked.

"You wouldn't believe me," James said.

O'Brien puffed out a large breath cloud.

"Try me," he said.

"This boy needs help and quick. Your delaying could kill him," Paynter said.

O'Brien looked back at Paynter.

"If he's that injured, why not take him directly to the hospital yourself?" he asked.

"He's an assassin that was sent to capture us, but we didn't know and he got injured and we were flying into Canada to find my kidnapped uncle and girlfriend when he turned on us, then someone was shooting at us and we crash-landed in the woods and he was injured in the crash and the people that have my uncle and girlfriend sent people to find us and... we escaped and the GPS led us here and if you don't take him and help him and let us go, we won't be able to find my girlfriend and uncle and he's gonna die," James spat out, breathless.

O'Brien stared at James for a moment before speaking.

"The skiing story was better," he said.

"I warned you," James said.

"Get him out of the car and into the office. I'll call for an ambulance. You two should really be looked at as well," O'Brien said.

"I don't have that kind of time," James said.

He and Paynter lifted Steve out of the car and walked him into the small building that passed as a police station. There was a small counter inside and three desks behind a wall that stretched two-thirds of the way across the room. O'Brien pointed to a bench chair in the small lobby and they placed Steve there. He was barely clinging to consciousness. Paynter elevated his leg the best he could. James watched as O'Brien shrugged off his overcoat and hung it next to his hat. A tallish round man, James couldn't tell if his head was balding or the hair was simply cut close. A thin brown mustache crested his upper lip and ended at the bottom of his chin on both sides. O'Brien walked to the desk that was furthest from the front, picked up the receiver, pressed a button and spoke briefly.

"Two minutes," he said, returning to them.

"Can we leave him in your custody?" James asked.

"I think it'd be best if you waited for the ambulance," O'Brien said.

"We've really got to be on our way," James said.

"You didn't really expect me to let you two walk out of here, did you? I'm no back woods Mountie, ya know." O'Brien said, resting his hand on the sidearm on his hip.

"My uncle and girlfriend are in danger," James said.

"Then why haven't you called the police?"

"Because they…are…the police," James said, his voice trailing off.

"What was that?" O'Brien asked.

"Sonofabitch. How could I have been so stupid," James said.

He took a step back toward the door. O'Brien unsnapped the release on his holster.

"Don't do it, boy," O'Brien said, glancing back and forth between Paynter and James.

"I'm a fucking idiot. After all this goddamn time, I walked right into it. You even told me. And we did it anyway. What the hell were we thinking?" James said, looking at Paynter.

"I'm sorry," Paynter said.

"You need to relax, son. We're just going to go downtown and have a nice chat about all this. Just as soon as the ambulance gets here," O'Brien said.

"You've already called them. You didn't call the hospital. We're not going anywhere. You called them. You heard my story and called them instead," James said.

"I don't know what you're talking about, son, but you're making me nervous. And I don't like to be nervous," O'Brien said, slipping the silver revolver out of his holster and grasping it with both hands.

"Don't lie to me! I can see it in your face. You didn't call for an ambulance. You called *them*!"

"Son, I think you need to sit down. You've been through a lot and you're obviously in some sort of shock. The ambulance will be here shortly, please relax and lower your voice," O'Brien said.

"Relax? I've heard that before. It doesn't seem to be something you can do when people are always waving guns around and shooting people and kidnapping your loved ones. I don't think I understand this whole relax concept. And I don't think I'm going to sit around waiting for an ambulance that isn't coming. You'll just have to shoot me," James said.

"Then what's that?" O'Brien said, tipping his chin to the window behind James.

Streaks of ruby- and cobalt-colored lights filled the room. James turned to look out the window, unbelieving. He heard the rattle of a stretcher and the scratching of the wheels on the ground. Turning back to O'Brien, he was greeted with a fearful look that contained no lie. He had been legitimately afraid of James. Then his face changed. James turned around. A man dressed in white was backing the stretcher into the door. An older man with a white straw fedora, boat shoes, and thick black glasses. James leaped, but the disguised redcoat was ready. He swept James out of the way with one arm and raised a pistol with the other. The gun erupted in the small room and

O'Brien and James hit the ground at the same time. James found himself staring across the room at the surprised, dead officer's face; a single line of blood trickled down from the entry hole in the middle of the man's forehead.

James screamed, a guttural cry, raised himself from the floor, and threw himself back at the man, caring little for the pistol in his hand. They struggled for a moment, the gun waving in the air over their heads.

"I'll fucking kill you! I'll fucking kill yuuungh…," James said before an unseen hand landed the blow to the back of his head and the room swam. His knees buckled and he was aware of the floor making rough contact with his hands. He jerked his head back reflexively and just avoided striking his chin upon the floor. It was like he had fallen into a pocket of time; everything around him moved as normal, but he felt like time was mud-like in his little pocket. He shook his head and tried to focus on a spot on the floor. It refused to come into focus. The time pocket refused to burst. He shook his head again and raised a foot up so that he was on one knee. Something happened that he couldn't see and there was a sound of hurried movement all around, then a screamed oath, and a gun erupted again. James turned away from it, his hands rising to the sides of his head as if they could stop the pulse of sound that had been so close to him. He found himself standing, hands on the side of his head. He turned, and saw Steve, pale and deathlike, sitting up and holding the pistol outstretched in his hand. The first redcoat was crouched on the ground, clutching his arm.

Paynter hovered between Steve and the redcoat who stood next to James.

In that moment, their focus had each turned to Steve, James recognized his opportunity. The redcoat saw the move coming, but it was too late; James made solid contact with the side of his head, knocking the thick black-rimmed glasses off of the man's face. James slipped in behind the man and managed to wrap up the arm with the gun in it. This redcoat, who was larger than the others with regard to thickness, was still surprisingly light in stature. It didn't take much for James to lift him off the ground in the struggle. And with that, he realized his next move.

James raised his knee into the man's back and used that moment of weakness to lift him in a sort of half-nelson and rush across the room onto the other redcoat who stared at them like a deer watching the oncoming car. The three men slammed to the floor and there was a muffled sound of a gun discharging before falling to the floor. Startled, James released his grip and stood up. The redcoat, at whose back he'd been, immediately spun off his fallen brother.

The man on the bottom looked stunned. His hands found the source of the blood that was flowing from his chest. He coughed once, a trickle of blood appearing at corner of his mouth.

"Barnes?" the larger redcoat said, unbelieving.

"You've killed me, Auric," he said.

"You…," Auric replied.

"I don't think…," he said before taking a deep ragged breath, "I don't think he's…right. I'm so…afraid." And he spoke no more.

That was when Paynter threw himself across the room and picked up the gun the redcoat named Auric had dropped. James didn't think it mattered much. Auric sat on the floor staring at his dead brother.

"That ambulance," Paynter said, raising the gun to Auric's head. "That's our ticket out of here."

"Are those sirens?" James asked.

"Probably the real deal this time," Paynter said.

"Gunfire will do that," Steve said.

They lifted Steve from the couch and walked gingerly around the redcoats. Auric had removed his hat and closed his brother's eyes. He hadn't moved. He paid them no mind as they left.

Paynter and James hoisted the gurney into the back of the truck.

"You drive. It looks like this thing's actually stocked. I'm going to hook Steve up to some fluids," Paynter said.

"I'm done running," James said.

"We're done running," Paynter said.

"Oh?" James said.

"We're taking it to them," Paynter said.

"I'm not sure how that can help," James said.

"Well, this is our ticket into the castle where they're keeping the princess. We're not going to get another chance," Paynter said.

"Enough said. Let's go," James said.

Chapter 31

Nicole had lost track of how long she'd been standing at the table in the barn, her hands pressed against its surface as if she was holding it down. Long enough to start feeling stiff. Long enough that Ted had stopped trying to calm her down. But not long enough to unhear the cracks of gunfire that signaled the clones had shot at James' plane. It had been too dark to see the results, but it didn't matter to Nicole. As far as she was concerned, the strange men who had piled into the black sedans and sped off into the night were simply going out to retrieve a corpse. She couldn't find the tears to cry. She just couldn't comprehend how they had gotten to this point in time. And that James had come all this way, having been baited into it by her abduction, only to have them shoot him out of the sky. None of it made any sense. She had been contemplating how far she could get before they sent someone out after her when Tollgate's voice interrupted.

"He survived. I don't know how, but he survived. They all did, though Steve got the worst of it from what I've heard," he said.

She turned and looked at him. His cold demeanor had returned, but he cocked his head in a gesture that showed her he was making an effort for her.

"He's really quite resourceful," he said.

"Where is he now?"

"On his way here," Tollgate said.

"What?"

"They've commandeered our ambulance and are headed here. They'll be able to get through the gate with the opener in the ambulance. They're coming for you. Elder Auric called in and I acknowledged his call, but I took it myself and haven't passed along the information. Please don't overreact. They'll know something is wrong. But, be ready."

"I could kiss you," Nicole said.

"I'd like that, but save it for when we're all in a better place," Tollgate said, a smirk escaping the corner of his mouth.

"Deal," she said.

"Why don't you come with us?" Ted asked from the loft.

Tollgate barely hesitated.

"My family is still here. Dysfunctional as it is, I've got to do my best by them," Tollgate said.

"But they'll punish you," Nicole said.

"Sebastian will punish me. That's a certainty. But, what I'm doing is only giving you a window of opportunity. Don't doubt that he'll come after James. And this time? He'll probably do it himself."

Chapter 32

"I can't believe you pulled that gun. I didn't even think you were conscious!" James called into the back of the ambulance.

They had made their way back the way they had come and, with some direction from Steve, had found the road on which the farm could be found. The darkness of the countryside oppressed everything.

"The elders would have killed me anyway," Steve said.

"They've bred monsters and turned them loose," James said.

"One of those monsters saved us. When it came down to it, he proved that they could only train him to be a monster, they couldn't make him believe he is one. Get some rest, Steve. The opportunity might not last long," Paytner said.

"Not like the others," James said.

"Like most monsters, they live in fear. You were right, you know. They won't kill you, even if they want to. They're afraid to. You've got to use that to your advantage," Paynter said.

"I feel like I'm losing my mind. I don't know if I can do this anymore," James said.

"You don't have a choice. I won't let you curl up and fade away," Paynter said.

"You might have to carry me," James said.

"If I have to, I will," Paynter said.

Paynter reached into his coat pocket and produced a cell phone. He flipped it open, held it up on the steering wheel and began typing numbers in haphazardly with one eye on the road. He then passed the phone to James.

"Where did you get this?" James asked.

"It's Steve's. Press send. When you hear someone pick up, tell them your name and that you're ready to come in," Paynter said.

"What?"

"Do you trust me?"

"Do you really want me to answer that?"

"No. Just make the call."

James stared down at the phone. The small blue screen was filled with numbers he couldn't seem to focus on.

"If I call, all hell breaks loose, doesn't it," James said.

"It might," Paynter said.

"And how do we make it turn out the way we want?" James asked.

"If I knew that, we'd have done it by now," Paynter said.

James stared at the phone. A few days earlier he had been afraid of calling his brother. That now seemed like a year ago. How he wished that this call was that simple. How he wished a lot of things right now.

"Wishing won't change anything," James said.

"What?" Paynter asked.

"Nothing," James said.

He pushed the send button and pressed the phone to his ear. He grew impatient at four rings.

"No one is answering," James said.

"What?" Paynter asked from the rear of the ambulance.

"No one is picking up! What does that mean?"

"It means we might be on our own. Just leave it. Don't even hang up. Just stick it in the console," Paynter said.

"Just like that," James said.

"I guess," Paynter said.

"You guess?"

"I've never exactly done this before."

"Who told you to do it that way?" James asked.

"An old friend," Paynter said.

"Now what?" James enquired.

"Let's crash this little farm party."

"I sure hope you know what you're doing," James said.

"Yeah, me too," Paynter said.

James shot him a look over his shoulder and saw the half-smile on Paynter's face. He couldn't help but laugh. It was a nervous reaction and, at that point, the emotion felt so unnatural to James now. There had just been so little to laugh about lately. He wondered where it was all heading and only one answer seemed logical. Things like this didn't just have a magical and happy ending. He wiped his forehead with his sleeve and, in the darkness of the cabin, could smell the dried blood on his sleeve. Or was it from his own face? There'd been so much blood. He fought off the sinking feeling in his stomach and tried to steel himself against the coming storm.

"Let's get this over with then," James said.

"Steve said it was another two miles or so up on the right," Paynter said.

"What are you expecting?" James asked.

"I expect it'll look like any other farm around. Probably tucked back off the road. Something inconspicuous. Nothing out in the open, but every bell and whistle just beneath the surface," Paynter said.

It wasn't long before they were back in the middle of nowhere. The headlights showed them clear fields on either side, but only a half mile up, the fields gave way to forest that encroached upon the roadway.

"There," Paynter said, pointing to a line of hedges that formed a border along the tree line.

A metal gate, the kind one might use to keep livestock in a field, hung across the opening to the lane. But, James knew this was no ordinary farm gate. Sturdy steel hinges were embedded into a stone pillar; the pillar had been designed in such a way that it was hard to distinguish from the tree.

James slowed the truck to a crawl as they approached.

"So much for surprising anyone," Paynter said.

"Think this thing could get through it?" James asked.

"Only one way to find out," Paynter said.

"Wait," James said.

He turned on the cabin light and looked around. There, stuck to the sun visor, was what he was looking for. He reached up and pressed the first button on the generic-looking garage door opener; the same kind he'd seen in the Charger. The gate swung open out into the road.

"Viola!" James said.

"Smarter than the average bear, I guess," Paynter said.

James eased the truck back into gear and slipped through the gate and along the narrow lane. The large pines to their left and the thick hedge to their right created a tunnel-like darkness around them. James glanced back at the gate and watched as it closed behind them.

"That might not be an option on the way back," he said.

James sat forward, straining to see what lay before them as the headlights seemed to barely cast a pallor across the woods ahead of them. As the road turned into the forest, the hedge gave way to more trees. The path wasn't paved, but the way was free of the ruts found in a typical dirt road. James applied more pressure to the gas and they moved move quickly now. They rounded another bend in the woods and saw an opening ahead of them. The road led out onto an open field with several buildings clustered in the far center. Even from this distance, they could tell that their presence was drawing attention.

"Looks like we might've stirred the hive," Paynter said.

"What the hell do we do now? Drive around until they tell us where they are?" James shouted excitedly.

He slammed his fist against the horn, which let out a blaring half-sick sound.

"Look at the buildings. If you were captive, where would you be?"

James scanned what little he could see. A few lights illuminated a roof, a window, a doorway of the buildings in the cluster. Then, away from the rest, there was a single lonely looking bulb.

"There!" Paynter shouted, pointing to the lone speck of light out in the field ahead of them.

Without hesitation, James turned toward it, leaving the road and plunging the truck over uneven surfaces. He could hear Paynter struggling to stay seated and was glad the doctor had had the foresight of strapping Steve down to the gurney. He watched as the headlights jumped up and down across a furrowed field before them. James swerved and ran along the furrows instead, immediately improving the ride, but taking them parallel to their target. James punched the horn again. James could see two people emerge from a barn door. Lit from within, it revealed the shadowed shapes of a girl and a large man. He wanted to leap out the window and run to them across the field.

"There! There they are! Hurry!" Paynter shouted.

James turned the wheel again and they were perpendicular to the furrows once more, but nearly out of the field. Nicole was waving at them frantically. He was nearly on top of them when he turned the wheel sharply once more and slid the truck in beside them.

Ted wasted no time and threw open the back doors of the ambulance. James was almost out of the truck before he'd made a complete stop. He moved around the back of the truck and was nearly bowled over by Nicole. For a moment, he was lost in her hair and scent and crying embrace. She kissed him and pressed herself against his chest.

"I thought you were gone," she cried.

"I was," he cried.

"You found me."

"I did."

"This is madness."

"I know."

"James, let's go. They won't be caught off guard for long," Ted said.

He was closing up the back of the truck. Nicole ran around to the passenger side and climbed in. Paynter got behind the wheel. The truck had reached the edge of the woods again before Paynter spotted a chase vehicle.

"How come they didn't know we were coming?" James asked over the commotion of reunion.

"I made a friend," Nicole said.

Uncle Ted stuck reached out his hand and patted James on the shoulder.

"You look like hell, boyo," Ted said.

"Good to see you too. We have to talk," James said.

"You're right," Ted replied. James had never heard such nervousness in his uncle's voice.

"We might not have much time," James said.

"I'm not a carpenter," Ted said.

"I know that...now. Hold on!" James shouted.

They were approaching the gate again and no amount of button pressing was going to get it open. When the truck hit, it was like they had replaced the gate with a small concrete wall. They lost a headlight and, judging by the number of parts that flew off the front of the truck, he half expected them to come to screeching halt. But Paynter managed to turn back onto the road without too much momentum lost and the breached gate fell off to the side as they made their getaway. Nicole gave a little victory cry from inside the cabin.

"It won't be that simple," James said.

"I agree. It's almost like they wanted us to take you," Paynter shouted back.

"Sebastian's not as well prepared as he would want us to think," Ted said.

"I don't like it," James said before turning his attention back to Ted, expectantly.

"Where were you?"

"I was a Navy SEAL," Ted said.

"I know that too. Try harder!" James said.

"Tell me what you want to know, James!"

"What was your involvement in all this? How much did you know?"

"I knew…everything," Ted said, his voice failing on the last word.

"Sorry? What was that last bit," James said, the cynicism rising in his chest.

"Everything! I knew everything. Not at first! They didn't tell me everything right away. My team was called in to clean up their mess. They didn't want anything left behind. But, we didn't know that they'd already started other projects and had no plan of getting rid of them. Just the broken models. Your only fault…was being normal. They didn't want normal. They wanted soldiers. They made monsters instead. Those red-coated freaks of nature were made in Sebastian's likeness as well. Their genes were messed with though. They hoped to create heroes. Instead, they got age-accelerated sociopaths. They didn't stop there, though, James. They got better as they went along."

"We know. Have you met Steve?" James said.

"Yes," Nicole said and James was suddenly distracted.

"Oh yeah?" James offered.

"We'll talk later," Nicole said.

Ted continued. "Sebastian was never supposed to see the light of day. It was going to give them the best cover possible. How could a non-existent man be blamed for anything? But, their little test rabbit was a lot smarter than they had realized. He made contacts and got out and rounded up everyone involved. By then, the testing had fallen through the government cracks. As far as they were concerned, it had ended when we disposed of your group and the others."

James cut him off.

"What others? The redcoats?"

Ted shook his head.

"They came later. There was another group of boys. We…dealt with them before we…before I…had a change of heart. That's when I found out Robert was involved. He and I and Dr. Taylor worked together to try and fix it," Ted said.

"You killed children. Babies. You killed babies," James said.

"I was a soldier, given a directive. I convinced myself that it was the right thing. That it was something that should just go away, for everyone's sake. James, there's a lot of things you don't know about our government. Hell, any government for that matter. There are things they do inside and out of this country that would make you sick. They didn't tell me there were babies in that building. They told me there were targets in that building that needed to be eliminated without raising suspicion. We did our job," he said.

"You murdered them," James said.

"Is that what you want me to say? Is that what you need to hear from me? Fine. I murdered them. I'm a murderer! If you think there's a night that goes by that I'm not cursed with the sounds of their cries in my head, you are gravely mistaken. That decision made my life a living hell, James. My own personal hell, right here on Earth. And I could have willingly gone further down that path. Instead, I tried to save myself…by saving you. The deed was already done. I couldn't unmake the demons, but I could prevent making more."

James realized that he'd been clutching the gurney rail as hard as if they were going through the gate again. He relaxed his grip.

"So, you gave me to your brother," James said.

"And he raised you into a fine young man. He gave my decision credibility. And he did so without ever knowing all of the truth," Ted said.

"He'd never have spoken to you again," James said.

"Which is why I never told him. It would have broken his heart. He had too much respect for me. Misguided, apparently," Ted said.

"Not misguided. Just poorly informed," James said.

James stared into the darkness behind, watching the road slip by. There was something hypnotic about the flashing of the dashed yellow lines.

"I'm sorry," Ted said.

"For what? You saved my life. If you hadn't killed them, you might have never had that moment of regret," James said.

"It's not that simple, James."

"You're right, it isn't. But nothing's simple, is it? And the fact is that knowing this only changes the future if I let it. It can't change what is," James said.

"Very insightful," Ted said.

"What's he doing now? Sebastian."

"He's refined his skills. He's learned a lot," Ted said.

At this point, Nicole stuck her head into the back window.

"He's made more of himself…and they look just like you…only they're younger. Much younger, but they don't look it. And some of them don't act it. His lab rats have figured out how to accelerate their mental and physical maturity," Nicole said.

"That's not all. He's also learned how to change how they look. If he has the DNA, he can make them look like anyone," Ted said.

"I don't get it—," James began, but the sudden appearance of headlights behind them caught his attention. "They've caught up!"

"We're almost back into town. Ted, where am I going?" Paynter asked.

"Second Line to Carmen's Way!" Ted shouted back.

"Here, Navy SEAL!" Paynter said, handing Ted the pistol over his shoulder.

Ted moved to the back door, opened it, and squeezed off two rounds before closing the door and sitting back down. A single headlight from the nearest car had disappeared in the process.

"Better not do that again," James said.

"I won't. Just giving us some distance. I think they got the message," Ted said.

"Hold on," Paynter announced.

James and Ted held on as the truck shifted into a right hand turn through a yellow traffic light. A block later and they were turning left. Sirens started to wail in the distance. James

300

looked back up the block and could see police headed in their direction.

"How far is that bridge?" James said.

"Another half mile," Ted said.

James watched as lights came closer. Then, Sebastian's pursuit cars were behind them again and the police lights faded into the distance. James looked at Ted in the rearview.

"I thought you said he wasn't that well organized," James said.

"He isn't, but he obviously has more power here. James, listen to me. You can't let them catch you on this side," Ted said.

"They're not going to catch us," James said.

"James, we're approaching an international border crossing. They're going to catch us," Ted said.

Ted was right, of course. James had been a fool to think that they would just cross back over into the US like it was nothing. In an ambulance, no less, that had been at the scene of two murders. His heart sank as he thought of Nicole going back into captivity. This was supposed to be her rescue. He was failing her, again, and he couldn't stand it.

The truck came to a stop in the line of traffic that waited at the farthest edge of the bridge. James looked into the single line of cars and trucks ahead of them.

"Who the fuck builds a single lane highway as an international crossing? Seriously?" he ranted.

Turning, he watched as Sebastian's cars pulled into line three cars behind them. He watched to see if a door opened. Nothing happened. He looked through the cabin of the truck. He could just make out two uniformed figures moving down the walkway at the side of the bridge toward them.

"Give me the gun," James said.

"What the hell are you going to do?" Ted asked, holding the gun away from James' outstretched hand.

"I'm going to get rid of the problem," James said.

"The hell you are," Ted said.

"I'll do it with or without the gun," James said.

"You're doing exactly what he wants," Ted said, but he moved the gun toward James.

"James, what are you doing?" Nicole asked.

He leaned through the opening in the ambulance and kissed her quickly, but deeply. "I'm sorry. I love you," he said. He then took the gun and jumped out the back door.

"James!" Nicole cried out after him.

He wasn't hearing it anymore. The blood from his heart was pumping right into his ear and the pounding of his feet against the asphalt as he sprinted at the three pursuit cars was all he could hear. Horns began to blare as soon as he raised the gun. He aimed for the engine of the first car and let three rounds fly. When a door opened on the second car, he turned his attention to the tires of that car and pulled the trigger again. A second pull proved fruitless. The clip was empty. He hurled the gun at the window of the nearest car. Turning, he put a leg up over the guardrail, gauged the distance to the bottom and decided to jump despite a sudden sense that it was probably too far to fall safely.

It was, and there was a distinct snapping sound from his knee when he landed. He stifled a cry and limped along beneath the highway that ran above.

Despite having reached the edge of the bridge, there was still plenty of distance to the water. This had to work. He would be the distraction the others needed to make it across. And he would swim across. He laughed as the truth of the idea came into his mind. That was the part of the idea that he'd ignored to this point. His only way of not getting caught in this country was to somehow get into the water and make it to the other side. On one side, Sebastian and the Canadian police, who were apparently on Sebastian's side, or at least in his pocket. On the other, the US police who would take him in for questioning regarding several murders, including that of a US Senator. It was a win-win situation. And, now, he would have to swim with a busted knee in the dark and in freezing unfamiliar waters, if he could even find them.

"This was fucking brilliant," James muttered to himself.

There were shouts behind him. He moved into the darkest spot under the elevated roadway. He pressed his pace, despite the shooting pain that was emanating from his knee. He moved to the right and his foot caught on something solid just off the ground. He half caught himself, but still fell to one knee. He reached out in the dark and found a train rail. He propped himself back up and felt around with his foot. It wasn't just a forgotten derelict. It was actually a track. A track that ran parallel to the highway. A track that must run across to the other side, James thought.

He quickened his pace now as best he could. The voices behind him were getting closer. The sound of water was getting closer and he made sure he was positioned between the rails as he continued. The tracks were moving out from beside the road and out of the safety of the utter darkness. He was feeling more exposed when a shot rang out. He was certain he'd heard the cut of the wind as the bullet zipped by.

"Stop, James," called a voice.

"No thanks," James shouted over his shoulder as he continued.

He flinched when the next shot came.

"The next one won't miss, James!"

"Then I guess you'll have to kill me!" James cried out again over his shoulder.

He realized that he had moved out over water. Gingerly, he was sure to plant his feet squarely on each tie as he walked. The next shot ricocheted off of the railroad tie at his feet. It was so close, he could feel the reverberations from the struck steel. He refused to allow himself to stop.

He was across to other side, but he was nowhere near even the middle of the bridge. Apparently, this was an island in the river. Hobbling along as best as he could now that he was back on solid ground, he followed the tracks again to the sound of water. The pain in his knee sent knives up his thigh with each step. He stiffened as he came to where the tracks should have gone across. He was staring at a large train trestle that was turned perpendicular to the tracks he had followed. It was on a turntable and because there was no train, there was no reason for them to be turned out across the water. He turned frantically, seeing shadowy figures coming across the tracks behind him. A road went off to his left, back under the bridge and further up the island. It wasn't the right direction, but that mattered little at this point. He turned and cried out at the pain. His teeth were beginning to hurt from the amount he was grinding them.

He tottered along the road that led up the island. He was heading toward lights and he could see that the activity on the bridge was increasing. They were pointing at him as he slipped into the brief darkness beneath the roadway. Sebastian's men were coming up behind him. James felt that any man running at a decent pace would be on top of him in moments. He came out of the safety of the shadow and continued along the little road. The concrete formations grew closer and he recognized what must have been a sort of lock for a canal. A small walkway crossed the span. He reached the railing and turned, half expecting to confront someone right on his heels. There was no one. Beyond the darkness, beneath the bridge, he could see someone running, as if they had just crossed. Had he been faster than he thought? He turned, confused, and decided to carry on. It would do no good to stand around waiting for them to answer his questions for him.

A voice cried out behind him.

"Hey, you! You're not supposed to be here!"

James didn't turn to see. There were bushes on the other side and that meant some cover. He used the small trees and brush and moved from darkness to darkness. He also managed to lose the path, and fell out from some dense foliage into a small pond on the island. Splashing frantically for a moment, he lifted himself out of the waist deep water and onto the other side. The only benefit to being soaked and freezing was that he was now having a hard time feeling his knee. However, not being able to feel much was becoming a problem. His legs were beginning to fail him. He staggered from tree to tree more out of an inability to stay upright without them, than for cover. He found another path and followed it until it turned. He continued straight into the trees and found himself wading in knee-deep river water. Spotlights honed in on him from the bridge. There was nowhere to hide anymore. No trees to duck behind. Only another concrete wall ahead.

He slogged his way to the wall and pulled himself up. Someone was saying something on a bullhorn from the bridge that he couldn't distinguish. He thought he could hear the distant sound of a helicopter. His teeth were chattering and he realized that he could no longer control the shaking of his upper body. He stood on the concrete embankment and looked up at the bridge. He'd done it. Somehow, he had managed to cross the border. He'd passed the middle of the bridge as he'd waded over. But, now, he was trapped. There was no way to the other side and a deep channel of rapidly moving water spanning thirty feet was between him and the next island. He had only one option and that was to walk back to the bridge.

The sound of the motor wasn't as startling as it should have been. Perhaps the cold was beginning to affect all of his senses. He turned and saw it making its way toward him out of the darkness of the river. It was not a police boat from either side. There was a lone figure at the wheel and, judging by his familiarity, it could only be one man. Sebastian called out to him as he approached.

"Bravo, James. Bravo," he called.

James looked around on the ground around him and found the largest stone he could see. His frozen hand struggled to grasp it, but he managed to fling it against the hull of the small speedboat.

"Get the f-f-fuck away from me," James seethed, unable to control the shivering that seemed to go from the top of his head to his feet which he could no longer feel. "Why can't you j-j-just leave well enough al-l-lone?"

James struggled to find another rock. Sebastian maneuvered the boat as closely as he could while keeping it as still as possible in the river's fast-moving current.

"Well enough? Were you well enough in New Jersey, James? Sitting at your little desk, rotting away? Now look at you! You're a man! You're magnificent!" Sebastian said.

James flung the next rock, less successfully this time, and it splashed harmlessly into the water.

"What would you kn-n-now? What would you kn-n-now about anything?" James cried.

"You were built for greatness, James! They just didn't know what they had! I know what you can be and I want to share that greatness with you. I want to harness that potential!" Sebastian said, even managing to smile in the process.

James stared at this older version of himself. He was the epitome of confidence; hair blowing in the breeze, hands firmly in control of the boat, a look on his face that told James he always got what he wanted.

"You're a l-l-lunatic! You've k-k-killed innocent people—" James began, but Sebastian cut him off.

"Not innocent, James. There's no such thing. Just ignorant. And sometimes the ignorant die because of their inability to see the truth," Sebastian said. There was no smile now.

"And you're going to t-t-tell me the t-t-truth? I've heard that b-b-before. It's only l-l-led to more l-l-lies," James shouted.

"Look at where you're running to, James. Do you think they'll welcome you with open arms? Do you think the truth lies over there? Think they'll just forget about the murders?"

"M-m-murders you orchestrated!" James screamed, the frustration starting to break through his will.

"Nonetheless, James, you're a man without a country. Come with me. Hear me out," Sebastian said.

"And what if I d-d-don't like what I h-h-hear? You'll just l-l-let me walk?" James said, incredulously.

"You know I can't promise you that," Sebastian said.

"Then we're at an imp-p-passe," James said.

Sebastian adjusted the boat due to a shift in the current all while keeping an eye on James. Even now, it seemed like second nature to him. James couldn't understand how calm this man could be. This was all just part of the plan.

"It would be a lot easier for both of us if you just came with me now. No one else has to be hurt, James," Sebastian said.

James raged out from the edge of the concrete wall.

"N-n-no one sh-sh-should have ever been hurt, you f-f-fucker! You're out of your g-g-goddamn mind if you th-th-think I'd willingly g-g-go with you! You've r-r-ruined m-m-my life!"

"No, James! They ruined your life the day they chose to throw you away! I'm here to show you how you can take it all back. How you can take back what they took and live the rest of your life in the kind of freedom you'll never find over there. You know they're wrong, James. You know it in your heart. You've seen it in their indifference. The revolution is coming. In fact, it's already begun. With the least amount of bloodshed! They just don't know it yet," Sebastian said.

Sebastian turned the boat and moved it as close to the concrete wall as he could. He reached out a hand. James stared at it before turning to look downriver. There was another boat coming up. Red and blue lights pierced the darkness. He turned back to Sebastian who looked as if the entire U.S. Army would not have fazed him; his arm still extended.

"You're n-n-never going to s-s-stop, are you?" James said.

"James, I'm the only one who's been on your side all along," Sebastian said.

"You m-m-must think I'm p-p-pretty stupid," James said.

"No, but I do think you're tired of running. There's still a chance. Come with me. You'll be a free man," Sebastian said.

For a moment, it seemed like a good idea. It was hard to look at this older version of himself without some strange sense of comfort. And yet, he hated that feeling. He just wanted it to end. Anything had to be better than running. Then he thought of Nicole, and Steve, and Mr. Isaacson, and that Senator, and Kevin and Doug, and the other brothers, and the countless other people he didn't know who'd been affected by this man. He wanted to stretch out his hand and drag him into the river. But, there was no fight left in him. Even pressed into a corner, James had no resistance to give.

"F-f-free is all relative," James muttered.

"What?" Sebastian asked over the dull roar of the diesel.

"G-g-goodbye, Sebastian. I hope y-y-you find what you're r-r-really looking f-f-for," James said. He then took three quick steps along the wall, past the end of the boat, and threw himself into the water.

Chapter 33

Cold wet darkness. The sense of cold passed quickly and the water and darkness pressed in around him. Soon, all sense was gone but for one. He was being pulled. Then there was cold and water again and coughing and vomiting of river water and air and voices and blankets and his clothes being cut from his body and warmth and light and James found himself staring up into the face of a paramedic in the back of an ambulance.

"Nice try, pal," the man said.

James went to lift his hand, but found that it had been secured to the gurney he was on. He breathed in through an oxygen mask and realized he was still shivering violently. The paramedic tucked the edges of the blanket back under James as tight as he could.

The engine of the ambulance rumbled to life and the back door opened. James could just make out a heavily armed police officer enter and sit opposite the paramedic. He wore what James assumed was riot gear; black from head to toe with a white- and blue-visored helmet. The CB hung at his right shoulder, but the place where a name tag would have gone was empty. The M-16–looking rifle was held loosely across his lap, the tip of the barrel pointed in James' relative direction. James eyed them both with distrust.

"Not so tough now, huh," the officer said.

James wasn't sure his throat would cooperate, so he said nothing. He could feel the van shift and accelerate to what he supposed was highway speed.

"But, I guess I've seen it all then, haven't I? Fifteen years on duty, I guess I was bound to come across a wolf or two in sheep's clothing," the officer continued.

James glanced back at the paramedic who was busy looking busy. He fiddled with the IV line that was apparently in James' arm.

"Cat got your—"

"Sh-sh-shut up," James managed, pulling a ragged breath from the oxygen tank.

The officer's face contorted in rage and he leaned forward.

"If it had been up to me, you'd still be floating down that goddamn river," he snarled.

"If it had b-b-been up to m-m-m-me, you'd have g-g-gotten your wish," James said.

"What's that supposed to mean?" the officer said.

"F-f-for your s-s-sake, I hope he l-l-leaves me al-l-lone," James said.

"That water must've rinsed your brains, kid. Well, now that you're in custody, folks should be able to sleep easy," the Mountie said.

"You k-k-keep dreaming that d-d-dream. See how f-f-far it g-g-gets you," James said.

"Are you threatening me son?"

James couldn't stifle the laugh. He had neither the words, nor the energy with which to speak them.

"I could t-t-tell you that I'm innocent, but that w-w-won't change your m-m-mind. You've already c-c-convicted me in your m-m-mind," James said.

"You haven't said anything to convince me otherwise," the officer said.

"That's b-b-because you haven't been l-l-listening," James said.

James closed his eyes and listened to the droning of the wheels. He realized that he was so exhausted, sleep would come quickly if he let it. The first waves of unconsciousness were just coming over him when the van lurched.

"What the hell?" the officer said and grabbed for the CB at his shoulder.

His hand slipped off of it as the van lurched again, sending the paramedic sprawling over James' legs. He looked over at James, his eyes wide.

"This is your doing," he said.

"N-n-no," James said, looking toward the back door and shouted again, "N-n-no!"

An explosive ball of fire rocked the van from behind, sending the two unsecured men flying once more. They heard the tires squeal and the ambulance swerved again, but managed to stay its course.

"Report!" the officer screamed into his CB.

Confused and frightened voices came back. Someone was attacking the convoy, there were officers down, and someone

313

was screaming his last breath. The officer looked at James and raised his gun, sliding the bolt back.

"You stop this," he said.

"I t-t-tried, but you d-d-decided to save m-m-me instead," James said.

In that moment, he thought he saw something that resembled moment of understanding in the man's eyes. There was another explosion, this time to one side of the van. It sent the officer flying and knocked out the paramedic. The van lurched right, then left, then quickly back to the right. He heard and felt the van leave the smooth surface of the road and hit the gravel on the shoulder, then the quiet of grass. Then they were tipping and James' instinct was to put his hands out, but the restraints held him down and the officer screamed aloud as the van rolled; two, three, and almost a fourth time before finally coming to rest.

A single light in the back of the ambulance survived the wreck. James' head swam. The paramedic lay in a heap in the corner and might have been dead for his lack of movement. James could hear the officer groaning in the darkness. Every point of his body that had been restrained was badly bruised and painful now. He made to lift his arms, but the manacles and leather straps had held. The officer's CB was a constant buzz of shouts and confusion. He pressed the button and spoke weakly.

"This is Henderson. Convoy compromised. Dog sled is down."

He released the button and they listened for a response. There was none. In fact, there was no sound whatsoever. James listened as the officer retried his requests, dialed different stations, and became more and more frustrated with the lack of response.

There was metallic thud against the back door. James imagined the worst and turned his head away. He'd been right to do so.

"Holy hell!" the officer roared as the back door was blown off its hinges.

James looked back around. Out of the smoke and the headlights that were now illuminating the rear of the van stood a tall and all too familiar figure. Sebastian put one booted foot up on the gaping hole and leaned on his knee casually. A smile teased at the corner of his mouth.

"Come James, we've still got a third act yet to play."

About the Author

Raised in the "wilds" of northwestern NJ, Andy admittedly led a bit of a sheltered life. Books and a vivid imagination were a large part of his childhood. After an ill-fated and thankfully brief college career as a Chemistry student, he discovered a love of writing. He studied Literature and Creative Writing at The Richard Stockton College of NJ, where he first got the idea for *Multiples of Six*.

He now lives in the not-so-wilds of NJ, with his wife, son, three cats, two chinchillas, a salamander named Fred, and an ever-diminishing number of fish that may...just may...have cannibalistic tendencies. He looks forward to telling stories that people like to read.

If you liked this book, Andy hopes you'll take the time to let him know on Amazon! If you didn't like it, he hopes you use kind words to tell him so. He can be found all over the internet in various forms:

http://www.samulraney.com

http://facebook.com/AndyRaneAuthor

Twitter: @andyraneauthor

www.ingramcontent.com/pod-product-compliance
Lightning Source LLC
Chambersburg PA
CBHW071242170626
46809CB00001B/48